I0572078

First published by YaY Books 2025

First edition

ISBN: 978-0-6454627-5-3

yaybooks.com,au

LAST SATURDAY IN INVERMAY

Zane Pinner

For Dad, Brad, and everyone bad.

Jake

"Shut the fuck *up,*" whispered Milky.

He eased the screen door open just enough for his skinny body to squeeze through, holding out a splayed hand to stop Jake from following. In his other hand was a lump of scone dough, dotted with sultanas, an offcut of the batch that was now cooking in the bakehouse's enormous oven.

"You've got exactly zero chance," Jake scoffed, but he let the door close in his face. Milky would quit mucking around and get back to work if Jake annoyed him too much.

The back lights were all off, but Jake could see the eyes gleaming amongst the weeds in the backyard that the bakehouse shared with his mum's place.

"How many are there?" Milky asked, peering into the gloom. His white singlet seemed to glow and his thin, pale shoulders were hunched beneath a blonde-tipped mullet.

"Four," Jake replied. "Under the clothesline, two near Mum's shed, and the tom over near the side gate."

"Where's the tom?"

"Look." He pointed. "Just left of the gate, on the ground."

"Oh yeah. I can barely bloody see. How do you know it's him?"

Jake shrugged. "It's where he hangs out."

"I won't get him. I can't *see* him."

"You won't get any of them."

"Watch this then, smartarse."

Milky took a slow step away from the door. The dough rolled between his fingers. The skinny baker fancied himself a cricketer. He was holding the ball of scone dough lightly, testing its weight, checking his grip.

The cats paid no attention.

"Zero chance," Jake reminded him.

Milky didn't reply. He stretched his arm back with a surprisingly graceful poise, then lunged into a hard throw, twisting his fingers at the very last moment.

The cats scattered as scone dough sailed through the night air in a wobbling arc. By the time it splattered onto the concrete they were long gone.

Jake cackled, no longer quiet. "Gotta be quicker than that, Boonie."

"Fuck off," Milky sulked, wrenching the screen door open and storming back into the bakehouse.

The door swung closed with a squeal of complaint but Jake caught it before it could bang against the frame.

My grandfather made this door you twerp.

The bakehouse's whitewashed walls and polished tin floor were bright and clean and the air was heavy with sugared pastry and mince pies and woodsmoke. There were two massive ovens built into the back end of the bakehouse, fired by an enormous furnace that had been broiling away for the better part of a century. Only one of the ovens was still in use; the other had remained empty and dark for decades, its brickwork irreparably cracked in the sixties.

Milky went straight over to the long bench against the far wall and started feeding pastry dough into the roller machine, pointedly ignoring Jake.

John, the head baker, was brushing a tray of party pies with a paint brush dipped in buttery milk. After a few swipes, he threw the brush into a bucket under the table where it made a hollow clatter. His usual cheerful grin was absent. He didn't raise an eye towards Jake. Standing on his toes to reach the rack that was suspended from the ceiling high above, he lifted down a long wooden paddle over three metres long. He slid the flat end underneath the tray of pies, then walked over and unbolted the oven's black iron door.

Despite its size and weight, the oven door swung open easily. Jake tried not to flinch at the blast of heat that wrapped around his body.

The cavernous oven seemed alive. Its breath shimmered, buffeting him even from a few metres away. Radiating heat made the air wobble, but through it he could see steel trays pushed against the oven's brick walls; Shepard's pies, sausage rolls and loaves of bread.

Next to the oven, the furnace's huge iron door glowed a dull orange. Fire roared and crackled behind that door, the beast's burning gut. So much heat, almost within arm's reach, was mesmerising. Even though the furnace was only burning at half its capacity, leaning against that door would sear flesh down to the bone.

A throat cleared. Jake turned to see John looking at him with narrowed eyes, his mouth twisted into a scowl, his hands gripping the paddle's long wooden handle, waiting.

"Sorry John." Jake sidestepped out of his way. "All yours, mate."

Muttering under his breath, John shoved the tray of pies into the oven as though jousting at a dragon's belly. Grimacing into the heat, he lifted the paddle out and dropped it heavily back up onto its rack.

Jake watched the long pole wobble and settle into place. *He's shitty because Collingwood lost again.* He decided to keep his mouth shut, but it made no difference - Lynn came bustling over, wiping her floured hands on her apron.

"Do you want a custard tart, Jake?" She asked lightly as she took Jake by the shoulders and pointed him towards the bakehouse door, away from her grumpy husband.

"No thanks, Lynn." He tried not to look sullen. *Kicking me out already.* "Are there any cartons that need folding?"

"I think they've all been folded."

"I could sweep out the shop floor if you like?"

"It's all been done. Thanks. We'll be out of here soon. It might be time to head over home for the night, I think."

"Okay." Jake's mood was turning sour.

This is *my home. You can't kick* me *out.*

But she *could* kick him out. It was *her* place, hers and John's, at least until the lease came up again. His grandparents *owned* the bakehouse, but John and Lynn were leasing it and it was *their* business. Jake's mum had explained it to him many, many times.

"Will your mum knock off soon?" Lynn asked, as if she had heard his thoughts.

Jake shrugged. His mum was working a late shift cooking burgers and chips at the 24-hour takeaway across town. She would be home a bit after 3am.

"I don't know how she does it." It was something Lynn said all the time.

"She doesn't do too many late shifts," Jake lied.

Lynn knew he was lying, but she nodded sympathetically. "Will you be right?"

Jake waved goodnight. Lynn didn't wait at the screen door to see him home, instead bustling back to whatever she had been doing in the pastry room.

Jake didn't mind. The house he shared with his mum, also owned by his grandparents, was right next to the bakehouse, the two identically coloured buildings only separated by a wide concrete driveway. A shared backyard was littered with weeds and framed by a row of sheds that had once been stables. None of the cats had come back since Milky's pot-shot, not even the patchy old tom.

Jake slipped in through the unlocked back door. He lingered in the kitchen long enough to pour himself a glass of coke, then walked to his room and kicked off his shoes. His double bed was crumpled from where he had been reading earlier and he flopped onto it with a sigh.

The driveway was just outside his bedroom window and the bakehouse was noisy as they finished up. His heavy drapes muffled their voices, but he could still make out every third or fourth word amongst the trays clanging, the doors rolling shut and the cars revving.

"…bring it back…"

"…even if we wanted to…"

"…little pain in the arse…"

His breath caught.

Who was that? John? Milky? Who are they talking about?

He didn't want to know. He picked up a book and flicked on his stereo – a cheap CD stacker he had bought with a year's worth of savings. Kurt Cobain's gravelly voice drowned out the clanging from next door, the squealing of the screen door, the muffled laughter.

By the time *Nevermind* finished, the bakers had gone for the night. The driveway was quiet and dark. In a few hours the morning deliveries would start, but he would be well and truly asleep by then.

The CD stacker clicked and whined and the ethereal sounds of *Enigma* drifted over Jake's bed. Lost in the fourth book of *The Wheel of Time,* he barely noticed. His coke was long gone and he…

A crisp knock rattled his bedroom window and Jake jumped, startled.

After a steadying breath, he marked his place in the book, climbed off the bed and turned the stereo down with a grimace. *Enigma*'s quiet vocals were sensually French, mixed with Gregorian chanting over soft woodwind strains. For a moment he considered quickly flicking the CD stacker onto the next disc – it would be *Metallica*, most likely – but it was too late. At least he was wearing his *Faith No More* t-shirt, with its snarling black and white dog.

He took another breath, then pulled aside the drapes.

"Evening young fella," came Noah Murphy's deep, gruff voice. The leader of the Marauder Motorcycle Club's meaty, tattooed shoulders were almost as wide as the window.

"Hey, Noah."

"You all right?"

"Yeah. Yes. Thanks. You wanna get in?

"If you don't mind, mate, that'd be good."

"No worries, gimme a sec."

Jake let the drapes fall back into place. He pulled his shoes on, snared his keys from the top of his chest of drawers then went outside. He didn't bother locking the back door.

The bikie boss was waiting for him under the awning of the dark bakehouse. He was wearing a faded blue singlet – a wife-beater, Reese would call it. A fuzzy beard hung halfway down his chest, while his head was closely shaven. Despite the VB stubby in his hand, his blue eyes were as sharp as ever.

"Thanks mate," he said as Jake fumbled with the keyring.

"Not a problem. Got a few over?" Jake's voice sounded deeper than usual, to his own ears at least.

The bakehouse's heavy sliding door had three locks – unlock, unlatch, slide – and the iron bolts clinked under his familiar hands.

"Nah, tomorrow. There'll be a few about. We always have a bit of a session after the fights and my boy's gonna clean up."

Jake nodded but didn't ask any more questions.

The less I know, the better.

He rolled the sliding door open and pushed through the screen door that nestled behind it, flicking on the fluorescent lights as he entered the bakehouse. The big bikie followed him in and went straight to the cool room where the pastries and cakes were stored overnight.

"Need a carton?" Jake asked him.

"Yeah will do, thanks mate."

Jake nodded and went to fetch one from the pastry room. By the time he came back, Noah had a double handful of pies – six steak and kidney, six curried chicken. Jake sat the cardboard box on the floor and Noah carefully stacked them in. Jake picked up six sausage rolls and handed them to him.

"Better give me another dozen, it's gonna be a big one," Noah said.

Jake passed them over, trying not to stare at the tattoos on the bikie's forearms. One was a tiger with a name in its mouth.

Noah took a few custards tarts and lamingtons off another tin rack and stacked them in the box too.

"That should do it. Fuckin Chopper likes those custard tarts."

Jake grinned. "Yeah, me too."

"She's all good tucker mate."

They came back out into the main kitchen and Jake pulled the cool room door closed behind them. Noah sat the carton on one of the long benches and fished out his wallet.

"Cheers, boy. I appreciate you doing this for me."

"I don't mind. Can't have you blokes starving."

Noah chuckled and pulled out a fifty dollar note, laying it on the bench. "Will that cover it?"

It was Jake's turn to laugh. "It's too much. Way too much."

"Is it?" Noah raised an eyebrow.

"*Way* too much. That's barely twenty bucks worth," he said, nodding at the carton. "Just drop in and clear it up with Lynn tomorrow if you haven't got any change."

"Hmph." Noah considered him for a few moments, then reached into his wallet again. He pulled out an orange twenty-dollar bill this time, but instead of swapping it for the fifty he held it out to Jake. "Fifty's fine. And this is for you."

Jake looked at the extra twenty, confused. Noah waved it at him.

"Go on, take it."

"What for?"

"For being honest," Noah said, looking him in the eye. "You're doing me a favour letting me in here. And doing the right thing by Lynn from the sounds of it. Take it."

Jake heard his mother's voice.

Take it, don't be rude. He took the twenty.

"Thanks Noah."

"Thank *you*," the big bikie said, scooping the carton into his big arms. "The fellas'll demolish this, don't worry."

"Good stuff."

They walked out of the quiet bakehouse, Jake switching off the light and gently closing the screen door. The sliding door rumbled into place over the screen door and Jake snapped the bolt into place. *Slide, latch, lock* – just as his mother had taught him. Noah waited until he was done, then nodded amiably.

"Thanks mate, look after yourself."

"Cheers Noah, you too mate."

Jake watched the big figure stroll back up the driveway and turn right along Bryan Street.

Once he was out of sight, Jake let out a heavy sigh of relief and went back inside. He wasn't *too* nervous around Noah Murphy – the leader of the Marauders had been dropping by sporadically for the past year or so hunting a midnight feast for his crew – but he was glad to get through it without embarrassing himself.

Without embarrassing myself too *much,* he thought as the gentle tones of *Enigma* reached his ears again. *So what if he thinks I'm a pussy. At least he won't ask me to join his bloody gang.*

He scoffed at the idea as he laid back down on his bed, picked up the novel and imagined himself channeling fire, savings maidens and wielding a heron-marked sword.

Maynard

Sunrise was at least an hour away. The streets of Invermay were grey with wood smoke that sat heavily on the gutters and hedges, muting the orange streetlights of the main road, silencing the churches and parks, curling softly around the well fenced yards. Here and there a yellow light flicked on behind a curtained window as the suburb woke to its daily routines.

A shadow moved through the smog, a dark patch that swayed along the centre of Taylor Street above the whirring buzz of wet BMX wheels.

A smaller, much noisier shadow scampered after it, a dog-shaped bundle of yipping clatter, its high-pitched bark abhorrent in the pre-dawn stillness.

Silly fuckin dog.

Like every morning, Maynard considered pegging one of his newspapers at it. Like every morning, he settled for rolling his eyes instead. The dog, a fat spaniel, would never catch him.

Run, you furry turd.

Maynard's BMX tyres spun on the damp bitumen. His bike was too heavily weighted towards the front for the back wheel to find any real purchase, but he leaned back calmly, redistributing his weight away from the milk crate full of rolled-up newspapers that was tied to the front of his handlebars.

His peddling was constant, measured, and for the briefest moment his squeaking chain fell into perfect rhythm with the fat spaniel's yapping.

"Back to bed, sausage guts," he muttered as he leaned into the corner, rounding past the entrance to the old takeaway store and onto Herbert Street.

The dog reached the corner, yapped another couple of times, then turned around and trotted back into the smog, its job apparently done.

I should put a note in its owner's bloody mailbox. If they were one of the addresses on his list, he might have.

He barely glanced at the list of addresses that was wrapped around his handlebars like a scroll, pinched in place by the weight of the milk crate. The newspapers arrived with a freshly printed list each day, but the addresses on it rarely changed.

Keeping the pace up, he pulled a newspaper out of the crate, gripping it by the heavier end. Saturday's paper was always chunky, with the racing guide adding ten pages. Its weight felt good in his hand. Only a few houses on his route asked that their paper be carefully placed in the mailbox. The rest he could throw, toss, chuck or hurl. Maynard's favourites were the ones he could put a bit of mustard on.

The big house on the corner of Herbert and Burns had a squat concrete fence, an unkempt lawn and a long wooden veranda. It was perfect for a sweeping backhand toss and Maynard executed it as precisely as an Allan Border run-out, the paper sailing evenly through the air, rotating lazily through the smog, dropping in the last few feet to smack solidly on the wooden boards with a single, rolling thud.

Maynard nodded in satisfaction.

Tommy would have whistled at that one.

The thought of his best mate sparked an unusual heat in his gut. Maynard shuddered and tried not to think of the way the sheets had stuck to his belly when he woke up this morning, well before the 4.45am alarm that usually woke him up for his paper round.

Just a dream. Just a stupid fucking delicious dream.

He pushed the thought away as he threaded his BMX down thin side streets, whipping papers over hedge fences, down weatherboard alleyways, over rose bushes and discarded car motors and murky green fishponds. The crate grew lighter as he went and soon the remaining papers were tumbling about whenever he hopped a gutter or barrelled over a crumbling patch of footpath.

As usual, there was light and activity in the middle of Bryan Street, vans and trucks coming and going from the bakery. He eased off the pedals as he always did, peering down the driveway as he passed.

The milkman's truck was rumbling away under the bakery's awning, its chortling engine almost drowned out by its blaring radio. The milkman, Maurice Bird, looked up from where he was rummaging at the truck's side door and raised a gloved hand. Maynard waved back as he rolled past.

I don't know how Jake sleeps with all that bloody noise. He yawned. *At least I'm almost done.*

And he was – there were only six papers left, to be delivered along Forster Street on his way home.

Six papers?

He groaned and pulled the bike up slowly. There were only five drops on Forster St.

"Goddamn it." He ripped the list off the handlebar and quickly scanned it. There it was – a new customer, a new address.

In bloody Churchill Park Drive? Are you shitting me? He scrunched up the list, unscrunched it, looked at it again, groaned again. Churchill Park Drive ran off the far end of Forster, a ten-minute round trip. His boss, the owner of the newsagency was usually pretty fair when it came to the routes, but this was miles off Maynard's usual streets. *For one goddamned paper. What are you doing, Graeme?*

At least the ride would take him past the end of Little Ray Street where, in a tiny cottage, Tommy would be sleeping in the room he shared with his brother.

For a disgusting enchanting moment, Maynard imagined leaning his bike against the powder blue walls of the old cottage, of lifting the window of Tommy's bedroom, of pulling back the curtain and…

He'd tear my fucking head off.

Tommy's reputation as a fighter was known at school, at the footy club, all through Invermay. Nobody had dared press him on the issue since he had broken the nose of one Andrew O'Hern - an ex-Brooks High tough, albeit four years Tommy's senior – in the Brisbane Street mall.

Just a dream. Forget about it.

He shook himself, then glared at the address again, at the papers rattling in his crate. With an annoyed grunt, he hit the pedals and rolled on.

He cruised down the small hill to Forster Street and glided past Invermay Park and the Railyards. When Forster Street jagged left, it became Churchill Park Drive, a part of Invermay he didn't come to often. The North Esk River gurgled brown behind the flood levy on one side of the road, while on the other a procession of warehouses, greasy workshops and scrap yards blurred past. A row of worker's cottages squatted at the gates to Churchill Park, some neat and watertight cosy, others blatantly wearing their age.

Maynard checked his list, then rolled his bike over to number forty-eight. The neat, freshly painted cottage stood out amongst its industrial grey neighbours. A thin porch came right up to the short tin and timber fence that bordered the footpath. Maynard could have touched the front door with his hand if he reached over the fence. The porch was newly painted in a gentle powder blue with a bright white trim.

Yuppies. Probably from the mainland.

Maynard dropped a paper onto the rubber welcome mat and sighed. At least he would be able to chuck the paper from his bike without stopping next time. He leaned on his handlebars and yawned.

It's too far to come for one paper.

As he straightened up to ride again, he was distracted by a dark shape in the sky. Above and behind the squat cottages loomed an old black silo, a burnt steel cylinder suspended over the rooftops. It must have been there for his entire life, but he was sure that he had never noticed it before.

Curious, he pedalled his bike towards it and when he passed the last house in the row, he pulled up his BMX with a surprised expression.

Bloody hell, that's a mess.

It was a small factory, or maybe a timber mill. Fire had gutted the entire building, maybe last week, maybe ten years ago.

The mill's long warehouse ran most of the way across the block, its old-fashioned saw-tooth roof apparently spared the worst of the fire - the walls looked scorched but solid. A workshop was attached to the near end of the warehouse, three storeys of burnt brick cladded with corrugated iron, all scorched by long licks of black that choked out any other colour.

The silo was fixed to the second floor of the workshop, its black and rusted dome reaching high above the building. A long, rusted chute protruded from near the bottom of the silo, warped and segmented like a rickety proboscis. The hatch at the top of the chute appeared to be sealed shut.

The mill was surrounded by vacant land on three sides and a huge white building - *Webster's Woolstore and Auctioneers* - on the other. There were no fences, or even any driveways or paths. The ground was the same combination of dry weeds, crusted earth and broken glass that could be found in any vacant lot in Invermay.

Maynard wheeled his bike into the alleyway between the mill's workshop and the gleaming white woolstore, marvelling at the size and the stillness of the hulking buildings.

The woolstore, a huge three story warehouse half the size of a city block, had been painted a creamy white not so long ago, a startling contrast to the blackened, hulking mill. There were no doors or windows anywhere along the woolstore wall since the building's frontage was on the other side of the block.

The mill's dirty walls were punctuated by a couple of locked doors and what look liked an open roller-door further down the lane.

The alleyway felt secluded, almost remote. The patchy bluestone crackled beneath his feet, and the sound of it seemed to bounce off the alley walls. Even the whispering rush of the North Esk was muted. It felt like he was the only person in the world.

I should bring Tommy down here for a look.

Carefully wiping dust and ash off one of the windowpanes, he peered in. It was a small room with a cheap plastic table, a few chairs and…

Maynard took a step back from the window, disbelieving, then pressed his face to the pane again, unmindful of the dust.

There was skin, so much tanned and toned and tender skin. Red lips, here parting and pursed, here slack, here kissing. Pert flesh, welcoming and wild.

I wasn't seeing things.

A slow smile spread across his face.

Fucking. Jackpot.

Stephanie

The oven door yawned open and hot breath spilled over her, stinging her eyes and cheeks, folding warmly over her shoulders and down the front of her cotton nightie. Stephanie raised the thin oven mitt to shield her face, but it was pointless; the heat had already kissed her.

"Michael?" Aunt Shirley's cracked voice drifted in from the lounge room. "They don't *want* it, Michael."

Stephanie blew her fringe out of her eyes, annoyed. She needed a haircut.

A cut and colour, maybe even a perm. But she wouldn't be getting a new do anytime soon. Not an expensive one, anyway.

The oven door slammed closed. She put the hot tray on the counter, balancing it so the sausages wouldn't roll off into the sink.

"Michael, what are you laughing at?" Her great aunt's voice was thin, but clear enough to carry to their small galley kitchen.

"I'll be there in a minute, Aunt Shirley," Stephanie called.

"*Stop* it, Michael."

"Come and help me cook, *Michael*," Stephanie muttered, then blushed. *That's mean. She can't help it.*

She divided the sausages amongst three orderly plates already piled with scrambled eggs and baked beans. A final dash of salt, then Stephanie picked up two of the three plates – her father wouldn't be up for an hour yet at least - and carried them into the lounge room.

Great Aunt Shirley was alone in the lounge room, perched on the edge of her pale brown armchair like a neat pink bird. Legs as thin as broomsticks poked out from the bottom of her threadbare pink dressing gown and her ancient pink slippers were planted firmly on the carpet. Aunt Shirley liked pink things.

The Down's Syndrome, along with her seventy-odd years, gave her face an irregular slackness. Sometimes her eyes shone with brightness, especially when she was regarding Michael, whom nobody else could see. Mostly though, her lower eyelids hung slack and low, revealing red raw flesh beneath her drifting gaze.

She smiled as Stephanie put her breakfast on the little coffee table. Aunt Shirley's false teeth were oddly even, a straight line amongst folded curves of skin.

"Thank you girl, you're a good girl," she said.

Stephanie plonked down on the couch. "It's nothing fancy."

ABC News was playing on the TV. Stephanie switched it over to *The Saturday Morning Fun Show*, but when the show's host Howie the Yowie introduced the next show, it was *Astro Boy*. She had been hoping for *Gem*.

"*That's* not a book," Shirley sneered at the TV. "It's not a book, *Michael*."

"How are your sausages, Aunt Shirley?"

"What?" Her aunt's hair swung like dry black straw. "What did you say girl?"

"I said *how are your sausages*?" Stephanie raised her voice a little.

Shirley smiled beatifically. "They're lovely, darlin. You do such a good job."

Stephanie snorted. "It's hard to mess up bangers and beans."

"No, they're beautiful, they're perfect. Aren't they Michael? He says you do such a good job."

"Thanks Aunt Shirley."

When *Astro Boy* finished, Stephanie washed the dishes. She collected the newspaper from the front stoop and put it next to her father's plate, frowning at the strip of the strip of yellow pages that separated the racing guide from the obituaries and comics.

Dad'll be at the Inveresk by eleven.

She hated the Inveresk Hotel, with its stale musky bar and its stale musky regulars and its frosted windows and its hole-in-the-wall Tote that swallowed the pensions of drunken gamblers. She hated the thought of her father sitting there, hour after hour, leaving Shirley at home to her own confused devices.

Shirley was reading her magazine. Always the same magazine, a *TV Week* from 1972 with the stars of *Bonanza* on the cover. She made her Aunt a cup of weak tea and ran herself a shower.

The water was only a few degrees below scalding and it lit up her skin, closing over her shoulders and flaying her back deliciously. Sighing, she melted into the heat, her breath mixing with the steam.

Today would be long and boring, but doing the late shift on top of her usual Saturday was worth it. The extra hours added up, and it was time-and-a-half after 6pm. Julie had been covering all of the late shifts for the past few weeks, so Stephanie would jump on the chance to earn a bit extra. Besides, if she wasn't working she would just sink into the lumpy couch with her blanket and a bag of Maltesers to watch *Robin Hood: Prince of Thieves* on TasTV.

She sighed. A long day, but she would put her head down and get on with it. She turned off the water.

Stephanie's bedroom was small, neat and well organised. Along with her single bed she had a little closet, a bedside table with three drawers, a reading desk with more drawers, and an old timber bookshelf.

On top of the bookshelf, nestled behind a framed photograph of the stranger they said was her mother, was a green plastic money box in the shape of a computer. It had a little slot on the front which showed a printed message reflecting the amount of cash the computer held; JUST KEEP GOING. She took the money box dox down and cracked it open.

One and two-dollar coins rained onto her bed with a pleasing jingle. She ran her hand through them, bemused, then plucked out the roll of banknotes that was wedged into the side of the money box.

She split the notes and coins into piles and counted them, jumbled them up, counted them again. Each time, it added up to exactly nine hundred and forty-seven dollars and fifty cents.

Thanks to tonight's extra shift, the money box would soon hold a thousand dollars, an even grand. The slot would read BANK TODAY! in bright green letters.

She smiled at the thought of it.

A thousand bucks. *Her* thousand bucks. She could spend it as she pleased, on whatever she liked, no questions asked, no pleading with her father, nobody's business but hers.

She rolled up the notes and gathered the coins back into the money box, then carefully put it back behind the photograph, out of sight. Good.

Striding through the little worker's cottage, she pulled on her cardigan and kissed Aunt Shirley on her dry cheek.

"Dad will get up soon."

"All right, darlin."

Stephanie had forgotten to clean her work shoes again. The white toes of her Adidas knock-offs were scuffed and smeared with grey. It didn't matter. Nobody would be looking at her feet. But it still bothered her.

No time to worry about it now. Her shift started in a few minutes. Maybe she could find a rag in the storeroom to give them a polish.

"Bye Aunt Shirley."

"Michael? It doesn't *move*, Michael."

"Okay."

JUST KEEP GOING.

It would take another fifteen months or so to get her savings up to three thousand dollars.

Another fifteen months of stacking shelves and sweeping floors and smiling at customers, another fifteen months to save enough for a small car and five driving lessons. And soon after that she would turn seventeen and she would have her driver's license and her own little car. Maybe a red Volkswagon.

JUST KEEP GOING.

She could drive Aunt Shirley to her appointments, rather than catching the bus with her. She could pick up her dad from the Inveresk Hotel each night and save his knees a thirty-minute walk. She could take them both to the supermarket, to the city, maybe even to the football one Saturday.

But more importantly, from time to time, she could get the fuck away from them both.

Dylan

Sweat dripped down the back of Dylan's neck, curled around his hard shoulder and dripped onto the floor. He pushed and exhaled.

"Thirty-*seven*."

"Bullshit," said Liam around a mouthful of *Rice Bubbles.*

Dylan ignored his little brother, lowering himself into another push-up, dripping more sweat into the thin, gritty carpet.

"Thirty-*eight*."

"Five," said Liam. "Thirteen. Six hundred and ninety-two."

He could hear the little shit grinning. Dylan hated that grin. He would slap that grin if their mother wasn't standing over at the kitchen sink.

He lowered himself again.

"Thirty-*nine*."

"Bullshit," Liam, bored, turned back to *The Saturday Morning Fun Show* where Ren and Stimpy were lost in space. "Piss weak."

Dylan grunted, kneeling on his knees, catching his breath. "Like to see you… do better… fat little *fuck*."

"Matthew." Their mother's voice was dangerous. Her voice was always dangerous. She was the only one who still called him by his first name, and he hated it.

She was leaning on the kitchen counter, smoking a Peter Jackson Super Mild, tapping it into the ashtray that lived on their kitchen bench. The toaster was glowing next to her and every now and then she would pry its tin sides open to see if the toast was done.

Dylan rolled his eyes. "Get a new toaster, mum."

She didn't look at him. "Why?"

"Benny's toaster pops the toast up when it's done."

"Like in the movies?" Liam asked. "Can we get one?"

"It does four slices at once," Dylan told him. "Heaps quicker."

"Right." Their mum sounded offended. Offended and dangerous. "Are you going to buy me one, Matthew?"

No. He laughed. Of course he wasn't.

"That's right, you haven't got a job, have you. Too fuckin lazy to go wood cutting."

His smirk became a pout. "I don't want to cut wood."

"Well don't talk about my toaster."

"Sorry mum."

"You will be, *Dylan.*" She rolled her eyes, arms crossed. "More worried about your pretty boy muscles than putting food on the table."

Liam snickered. "Pretty boy."

"Fuck off," Dylan told him, drawing himself up. "My and Benny are going to the fights today and I'm gonna talk to Ray, see if he'll let me glove up. There's cash prizes."

His mother coughed around a mouthful of smoke.

No, not a cough. A *laugh.*

Dylan's stomach tightened.

"Couldn't fight your way out of a wet paper bag," she sneered. Liam laughed again. "And anyway, you have to *pay* to get in.

He pouted. "You don't pay if you're fighting. Ray said he'd put me in the ring,

"Yeah right," his mother screwed the cigarette into the ashtray and retrieved her lightly burnt toast. "Ray would say anything to keep you boys sniffing around. He was the same with your brother."

"Yeah and look at Luke," Dylan said. "He won five-hundred bucks against Bulldog Johnson. Nobody fucks with him. When he gets out, he'll be a fuckin tank too, all the weightlifting he'd be doing."

His mother's eyes narrowed. "Nobody fucks with Luke. The police *fucked* with him though, didn't they Matthew? Him and your father both." She threw the butterknife on to the table where it clanked against her plate. "You'll be next, I suppose. Keep hanging around those bloody Campbells and that'll do it."

Not this again.

"They're all right mum," Dylan said, rubbing his face.

"They're trouble. And if you can't see that, you're stupider than you look. Even Luke knew they were trouble."

"They're all right."

"They're all right," she mimicked, sticking her tongue out. "You wanna watch out, Judy Campbell will stick a skirt on you and sell that little dick of yours to some pervert."

Liam guffawed and clapped his hands.

"Shut up you *fucktard.*" Dylan's cheeks were burning. "I'll knock that fat head off your shoulders."

"They don't want your little dick," his brother said, that sly light in his eyes again.

"You can talk, shit-for-brains." He leaned towards his brother menacingly, but Liam just smirked and nodded towards their mother. "The doctor thought you were a *girl.*"

"You're all your father's children," their mother sighed. "Nothing to brag about there."

"Don't," Dylan said, standing up. *"Don't* talk shit about Dad."

"Why shouldn't I? He's not here to defend himself now, is he?"

"Lucky for you," he muttered. "He'd shut you up."

"Is that right, Matthew?" Her eyes were wide now, the danger in her voice palpable. She raised a finger and pointed it between his eyes. "You're not man enough to try it so you keep your mouth *shut,* pretty boy. Big prize fighter. Pfft. Just a little piss-ant."

He growled. "Shut *up,* mum!"

She leaned back in her chair, lips tight, eyes gleaming. There were toast crumbs around the corners of her mouth.

"Tell me to shut up again and you'll be out on your ear, boyo."

"I'll just go and stay with the Campbells," he said. "Their place is a million times better than this shithole anyway."

"They don't want your little dick though, remember?" Liam goaded. He had finished his *Rice Bubbles*.

"Fuck *off,* Liam!"

"*Don't* you speak to him like that," his mum leaned forward on the table. "You're no better than your stupid bloody father and your stupid bloody brother."

"Well good," he stood up. "I'll go and live with *them.*"

"Yeah in jail," Liam sneered.

"*Yeah, in jail,*" Dylan mimicked viciously. "Stupid little fat fuck."

"Matthew!"

"Dumb little fat shit can't even count."

Liam smirked. "Mum said you've got a little dick."

Without warning, Dylan lashed a straight jab into the boy's twelve-year-old bicep. He didn't punch his brother as hard as he could have… but it was hard enough, and he connected squarely.

Liam yowled in pain, tears brimming, arm dropping uselessly to his side.

"*Matthew!*" His mother glared, a piece of toast held halfway to her mouth.

"Piss off," he muttered, walking out of the kitchen and into their tiny, musty lounge room. The blinds were drawn as always.

"Don't be a sook," he heard his mother say to Liam. "*Matthew! Get back in here, now!*"

"I'm going." He scooped his lighter off the coffee table. *Benny will have some smokes.* Benny always had smokes. "I'll be back later."

"*Matthew!*"

He pushed the front door of the little cottage open and stepped out into the fresh air. It felt like a different world.

"Stupid fucking bitch," he muttered, pulling the door shut.

I want that fight. His older brother, Luke had been a promising fighter. He was training away in the Pink Palace now and would come out twice the size as when he went in. People respected that. *They ain't seen nothing yet.*

He stuck his hands in his pockets and walked towards Bryan Street.

Brad

He tried to distract himself with a few grinds and front-sides, but it was no use. The skateboard wasn't sticking to his feet the way it usually did. He wasn't feeling it. He couldn't focus.

The Post Office was closed for the weekend and the squat, brutalist cement building had just enough ramps, ledges and rails to make it worth skateboarding over to. Brad hadn't found many decent spots in Invermay so far – most of the car parks were gravel and the footpaths were neglected – but this place seemed okay, even if it was in full sight of Invermay Road. Nobody was coming to collect their mail on a Saturday morning.

He pushed his board down the access ramp and tried to ollie onto its guttered edging, but he couldn't stick it and the skateboard clattered loudly on the cement.

Man I want some weed. He tried not to look at the phone boxes in the Post Office's little courtyard. There were two of them, standing side by side like salt and pepper shakers.

It's too early.

Brad had only met Magnus a fortnight ago, but it was safe to assume the old junkie wasn't an early riser. Unless he was on the hunt.

Like me. Hot shame made his gut sour, but he ignored the feeling. It was easy to ignore.

I'm no junkie. Just a stoner. Just a stoner.

He had met Magnus at the *Toilet Bowl*, a monthly skate session at the Patterson Street carpark where there were wooden ramps, home built grinds and even a clapped-out old *Volkswagen* that was set up as a jump.

A couple of dozen teenagers on skateboards, rollerblades or BMX bikes would cruise around the ramps, sailing through the air and clattering around while *Pennywise* or *Bad Religion* blasted from an old pair of crackling speakers. Most of them left Brad alone, too busy with their own stunts to pay him any attention.

The miasma of weed around Magnus had encouraged Brad to introduce himself. Magnus had sold him a quarter – the only weed he had scored in Launceston since moving here almost three months ago – and given him a phone number.

The quarter had run out last night. The four ounces he had brought with him from Hobart were long gone. If he cleaned out his bong, he might be able to dry out the burnt resin and chunks of ash, but smoking black death was an absolute last resort.

He had started calling Magnus a few days ago when the quarter was running out. There was an unmistakable smugness to the junkie's slurring words, which were always the same – *maybe tomorrow.*

Just a deal. Just a bud, for Christ's sake.

Sorry man. Maybe tomorrow.

Brad scowled at the phone box. It had been tomorrow for the past four days.

It's tomorrow now.

Abruptly he marched over to the phone box, pulling four twenty-cent coins out of his murky pocket, enough for two calls. He put forty cents into the coin slot and dialled the number that was written on the side of a wrinkled Metro bus ticket.

Nobody answered and after a dozen or so rings the phone clunked and his coins rattled into the return slot. He fed them in again, dialled the number again, whispering each number as his finger pressed it.

Magnus wasn't going to answer. Brad imagined the thin blonde junkie smoking an enormous bong, reclining on a mattress made of pound bags stuffed with Northern Lights and Silver Haze and Orange Roughy. He wasn't going to answer.

But the tenth ring was cut in a half by Magnus's rusty voice.

"Who is it?"

"Magnus? It's Brad."

"Who?"

"Brad. From the *Toilet Bowl*, remember."

"Brad's in the toilet bowl," Magnus slurred to somebody in the background and there was laughter. "Nah mate, think I'd remember eating that."

"Funny shit."

"Come on mate, cheer up hey."

"Sorry man, just been on the hunt for a bit, you know. Reckon you'll come across anything today?"

"Don't reckon man. Maybe tomorrow."

Brad managed not to grind his teeth. For a moment he thought he could hear a bong gurgling on Magnus's end, but it could have just been his own blood boiling.

"Come on man, you must know *somebody*."

"Yeah man I know heaps of people. But none of them will be on till… maybe tomorrow."

"Righto."

"Right?"

"Yeah righto."

"Good. And don't call so fuckin early."

The phone line hummed in his ear. Magnus had hung up.

Brad wanted to scream, to smash the handset into the phone box's glass walls. Instead, he hung up and closed his eyes, trying to ignore the rising panic in his gut.

I don't get it. It was so easy to score back home.

Back home.

He picked up the handset again, dropped two coins into the slot, then punched in a different number, this one from muscle memory alone. He knew the number better than he knew his own.

"Yeah hello?" Alex sounded annoyed.

Brad was extraordinarily sensitive to the tones in his dealer's voice, enough that he could make two assumptions with a fair accuracy; that Alex was pissed somebody was calling him so early and that Brad's wasn't the first call he'd taken this morning.

"Alex. It's Brad."

"Bradford?" The dealer's voice brightened a little. "What's shaking man? How's the North treating you?"

"Yeah it's all right hey. Tropical weather, friendly chicks, the finest foods and entertainments."

"Bullshit," Alex was laughing. "I've been to Launceston, man."

"There's some good skating. But… it's as dry as a nun's nasty."

"Ah. That's no good."

The disappointment in Alex's voice made Brad grimace.

I should have chatted for longer. Not a mate. Just a customer. Just a stoner. Oh well.

"Yeah it sucks heaps, man. So look, I was thinking I might do a mission down, you know? Catch the next Redline bus down and then get the last one back."

"Right."

"Yeah so do you reckon we'd be able to catch up this arvo? If I get a taxi over to Lenah Valley and then I can ska…"

"Sorry man, I'm all out."

Brad's words died in his throat. He stared at the phone. There was a stiff blob of green chewing gum stuck to its side.

"Probably for a week or so, maybe longer. Maybe not as long. Sorry dude."

"Shit. Man. Really?"

"Sorry dude."

"Not even, like, a stick?"

"You'd catch a bus from Lonny to Hobart and back for a stick? That's like a five-hour trip."

More like seven. "I just want a few cones, you know?"

"Man I hear you, but nah I'm cleaned out. At least for a week I reckon."

"Righto."

"Try again in a few days if you still haven't found anything. But Bradford."

"Yeah?"

"Not so fuckin early. After lunch all right?"

"I…" *If I don't call in the morning, how will I know whether or not to catch the bus?* "No worries, man. Sorry. Just wanted to get sorted, you know."

"Yeah. Talk soon?"

"All right, catch ya."

He slammed the handset into its cradle, again and again and again.

Stephanie

She hurried down Bryan Street, past houses both neat and decrepit.

A few kids on their BMX bikes were skidding on the gravel outside the old church down on the corner, and a pair of dogs jumped up and down beside her for the entire length of their front fence, but she didn't see anyone else until she reached the Campbell's.

There was always someone around at Judy Campbell's house.

The house was similar in size and vintage to the ones on either side, but it jutted like a rotten tooth, dirty, smelly, crusty around the corners. Two decimated car bodies were propped up on the street in front of it, surrounded by a litter of parts, wires, tools and junk. The rusting chain link fence was hung with ropes and rags and fan belts. Engine parts and toys were spread amongst the weeds of the tiny front yard. A plastic fishpond sat on the hard dirt, its green water thick and unmoving.

Over-dressed young women would come and go, grotty boys schlepped around on the veranda, sunglass-wearing men would pull up in *Datsun 180s* and creep nervously through the weeds.

Trouble.

You could smell it a mile off, could see it in the boys' dirty hair, hear it in the way the adults whispered about Judy Campbell.

Amongst the grease and rust and dirt lurked something like a man. Judy Campbell's husband, Allan, was almost always out on the street, tinkering with the cars, a cigarette jutting from the corner of his silent mouth, his navy coveralls patched and filthy. Often only his legs would be visible, poking out from beneath one of the cars.

But sometimes he would glance over as Stephanie passed by on the opposite footpath. He would never acknowledge her – she was grateful for that – but she had heard him speak often enough to know that he had, by far, the deepest voice she had ever heard.

Today Allan was leaning against his wire fence, polishing something with a grey rag. He didn't look up, but even from across the street she could tell that he knew she was there.

Please don't talk to me. She knew that he wouldn't, and he didn't.

But somebody else did.

"Stephanie!" Ben Campbell was sitting on the peeling veranda, squinting into the morning sun. Even from across the street she could see the gaping holes in his thin white t-shirt, the stiff lines of his cheap track pants. "Stephanie!"

Somebody else was leaning against the veranda next to him. Stephanie groaned.

Dylan. She put her head down and walked faster. *Shit shit shit.*

"Steph! Where you going, Stephanie?" Dylan called, his voice as greasy as his slicked blonde hair. "Come and watch me fight, baby."

"Yeah, come and hang out with us Steph." Ben was leering, but in a cheerful, jokey kind of way.

Allan sat down on the gutter, shaking his head and pulling over his mechanic's trolley.

She knew Ben wouldn't do anything to hurt her – he had a big mouth when the other dickhead was around but was polite enough on his own.

Dylan was a different story.

He was seventeen, two years older than her and much taller. He had been a prick and a bully for as long as she could remember, but in the last year or so his shoulders had widened, his arms had hardened and his stupid eyes had taken on an arrogant fury.

He had never held back from hitting, pushing or tripping her when they were kids sharing a playground. She didn't think he would hold back now.

If he had the chance. Cheeks burning, she checked the distance ahead to

Invermay Road. *Don't run, just walk. Just keep going.*

"Stephanie!" Ben was shouting now, his hands cupped around his mouth. "We need a cheerlea…"

"Come back you little *slut!*" Dylan's voice was much louder than Ben's. "Come back and give us all a fuck!"

Don't run, don't *run.* They were laughing and it didn't sound like they were following her, but she didn't want to look back to check. *Stupid assholes.*

"You know you want it, girl!"

When she reached the old church, she turned and shoved a fist in their direction, lifting her skinny middle finger. The boys hooted and laughed.

"Ooh she's tough," Dylan marvelled.

"Don't be like that, sweetheart," Ben called.

She walked a few more steps down Bryan Street, but when she was out of their eye line she ran. She knew they weren't following her. They knew as well as she did that the back door of Sam's was just around the corner.

But she ran anyway.

Sam's General Store was an old-fashioned mix of grocery, lolly shop and newsagency. It fronted onto Invermay Road and was neighboured by a dusty pawn shop and an untidy vacant lot.

She bustled through the open front door. Half of the shop consisted of magazine racks and stationary shelves, books, gifts and knick-knacks. The other half was lined with fridges and freezers, bread racks, shelves of tinned food and baskets of locally-grown fruit and vegetables.

There were three service counters at the front of the shop. The glass counter was where you could get photos developed or buy watch batteries. The grocery counter was where you paid for your milk and potatoes. But the cigarette and lolly counter was Stephanie's favourite by far.

She dropped her purse and jacket into the storeroom and tied on a neat blue apron, making her way back to the grocery counter where Julie was counting her till.

"There's no cricket today," Julie said without looking up. She was copying the number from a small yellow film cannister onto a matching yellow envelope. "They'll only need one of us for the late shift."

"Oh." Stephanie said. "It's going to be *that* quiet?"

"We won't get busy. Barb's taking the night off too." Julie dropped the film canister inside the envelope and sealed it. On a shelf behind her was a Tupperware tray with a dozen identical envelopes and she dropped the new one in. "Summer holidays, most people are away. I can do it."

"The late shift?"

"Yeah, I don't mind doing it."

Like you did it last week and the week before? I want some of that time-and-a-half too.

"I think I was supposed to…"

"I already told Trent I was doing it." Julie was watching her, gauging.

Trent, Julie's boyfriend, didn't have a job and - as far as Stephanie could tell - spent his vast amounts of free time playing a *Nintendo* in their little flat in Mowbray.

"Is that okay?"

Nine hundred and forty-seven fifty.

"Okay." Stephanie smiled. "Thanks. Robin Hood is on TV."

"God, that movie," Julie giggled. "You're a dag, Steph."

"I like it. It's fun." Stephanie could feel her cheeks tingling. "And Robin Hood is… kind of cute."

"Cute?" Julie was scandalised. "Steph, he would have to be twice your age!"

"Are you talking about me?" boomed David, owner of Sam's General Store. He came striding out of the veggie aisle with an armload of calendars, grinning with good humour. At a glance, David seemed too tall, too gangly, too grey to be running a store like this, but he moved about it knowingly, with the kind of confidence that only comes with familiarity.

"You wish," Julie rolled her eyes and winked at Stephanie.

"Well, if you're looking for a date…" He dropped the calendars on the grocery counter and tapped them suggestively.

Julie and Steph groaned.

They fell into the rhythm of working; David restocked the shelves and chatted to the customers, Julie weighed vegetables and put bread into the slicing machine, Stephanie sold newspapers and cigarettes and iced coffees and mixed lollies.

Stephanie liked getting the lollies out of the tall glass cabinet next to the counter, scooping the sweets out of their plastic buckets with her fingertips, choosing from the bright colours, dropping the little treasures into their white paper bags. A kid with a lazy fifty cents could spend a deeply satisfying minute or two selecting their loot; five choc buds, five raspberries, three strawberries and cream, two sour cokes, two snakes (red please) and a candy bracelet for the walk home. Stephanie's favourites were the black cats and she made sure everybody who asked for a mixed bag got at least a couple.

She was restocking the cigarettes in the case on the back wall when there was an impatient *harrumph* behind her. She didn't know the boy, who had the kinds of self-absorbed seriousness only a twelve-year-old boy can muster, but she recognised the yellow cannister in his hand.

She smiled her shop smile. "You want to get a film developed?"

"I don't know," The boy didn't smile. "I think the guy here sold me the wrong type."

Before she could answer, there was movement at the shop's entrance. Stephanie's stomach sank when she recognised the three girls that walked in.

Lily was tall, tough, and had the face of a *Chiko Roll* model. Her simple black skirt and *Pantera* singlet made her look older than her years - a stylish young woman, wielding all the power that natural beauty could provide. Lily had been one of the more popular girls in Stephanie's grade.

Her offsiders, Anna and Chelsea, dressed in a similar style and walked with a similar strut. Anna was loud and abrasive, a bully who painted her fingernails black and had been caught in the boy's toilets more than once over the course of the grade ten year. Chelsea, the quietest of the three, had spent most of her time at school in the art department. Both girls lacked Lily's height, looks or charisma.

She won't even acknowledge me.

Stephanie and Lily had been best friends for a few months in primary school before they were old enough to know any better. They had awkwardly ignored each other ever since.

"Hello?" The boy was frowning now. "Is he here? The old guy?"

"Oh. Wait, I'll get him." She wiped her hands on her apron and called down the aisles. "David? Are you there?"

There was no reply. Stephanie glanced over at Lily, who was looking at the latest *Cosmo* with Anna. Chelsea had choses a *Fruitopia* from the drinks fridge and had come over to queue behind the boy with the film cannister.

"Julie? Can you come up?"

There were other customers lining up behind Chelsea now; an elderly woman with a carton of milk and a cocky looking man in khaki workwear who had a silver streak in his back goatee. Lily had wandered over to one of the grocery aisles, where the first aid and toothbrushes were stocked.

"David, can you come and do a film?"

Still no reply. She smiled her shop smile again.

"He'll be here in a sec, do you want to just wait over there?"

"I'm in a hurry." The boy pouted and held out the film. "Can you just look at it?"

"Oh… I…" She looked down the aisle again. *Where the hell is he?* She smiled at the people queuing behind the boy. "I won't be a moment."

Silver streak shrugged and nodded, but Chelsea rolled her eyes and made a loud *tsk*. Lily had picked something up off the shelf and was studying it; a pink box of Ansell condoms.

Stephanie turned the little yellow canister over in her hands, as if the information printed on the side might actually mean something to her. The kid was watching, his hands gripping the top of the glass counter.

"Super-Fast ISO," she read aloud.

"But it says in the manual to use Ultra-Fast."

"Oh. I don't think they make Ultra-Fast. Only Super-Fast or Lightspeed."

"Then why does it say Ultra-Fast in the manual?"

Stephanie shrugged and put down the film. "It's probably close enough."

"It's supposed to be *Ultra*." The kid rolled his eyes. "The guy here sold me Super-Fast. What if it doesn't develop properly?"

"We can only try. If it works, it works. If not…"

"Don't bother," the kid sighed. "I'll take it into the city. As if some shop girl is gonna know anything about photography."

She ground her teeth together as he sauntered off. Silver streak had picked up the latest *Trading Post* and was flicking through it lazily as Chelsea stepped up to the counter. Lily was…

Lily was casually shoving the box of condoms into the pocket of her small black skirt.

"Hey!" Stephanie's stomach was sinking. David and Julie were still nowhere to be seen. "You can't…"

"I wouldn't." Chelsea murmured to her across the counter.

"What?" Stephanie was surprised. She couldn't recall ever hearing Chelsea speak. "She can't just *steal* something in fr…"

"*She's* going out with the head of the Marauders now." Chelsea looked her in the eye, with a smug slant to her head. "Save yourself the trouble. Nobody messes with Rohan's girlfriend."

Stephanie stared at Chelsea across the counter.

The other girl looked her up and down, shrugged and handed over a two-dollar coin.

"Keep the change."

Chelsea opened the *Fruitopia* as she walked away. Its lid came off with a hollow *pop*.

Lily didn't even glance at Stephanie as she walked out of the shop, the box of condoms poking out of her skirt pocket. Anna was still holding the *Cosmo* magazine. She flashed Stephanie a wide grin, apparently pleased about shoplifting in front of her old schoolmate.

Stephanie felt shame touch her cheeks. She heard Dylan's mocking voice. *Ooh, she's tough!*

The muttering elderly woman shuffled up to the counter and plonked her carton of milk down, glowering at Stephanie. The three girls were gone. Stephanie sighed, looking at the two-dollar coin in her hand. She *would* keep the change, a whole fifty-cents.

Nine hundred and forty-eight dollars.

Just keep going.

Dylan

"Come on man," Dylan said again. "Just for a bit. A couple of games of *Double Dragon* to fire us up, maybe something to eat and just ..."

"Nah man." Ben Campbell wouldn't look at him. "She already said to stay out here."

"They won't fuckin care. Come on, the fights don't start till after lunch. What are they doing in there anyway, it's not even eleven o'clock in the morning."

Ben shrugged. "I reckon they've been going all night."

"We'll just go straight up to your room." Dylan's belly rumbled loudly.

"She said no already."

"She won't care, man. What else we gonna do?"

"All right." Ben rolled his eyes, then frowned at his father's legs poking out from under the Plymouth. "You've gotta be quiet though. Don't say anything till we get to my room, right?"

"Jesus, righto," Dylan scoffed. "It's like Fort Knox anyway."

"Yep," Ben said, standing up. "Just keep quiet, all ri..."

"She told you to stay out here, boy." Allan Campbell's voice was muffled. His legs didn't move.

Dylan grinned at Ben and shrugged.

"It's all right," Ben called back. "We're just gonna go into my room and play the *Amiga* for a bit."

"She'll kick your arse." The legs still didn't move though.

Dylan recoiled in mock fear and Ben snorted. "We'll be quiet."

There was no response, so Ben waved him over to the front door, a finger to his lips. Looking around to make sure nobody else was watching, Ben ran his hand down the left-hand side of the doorframe, then twisted the round brass doorhandle. The heavy door swung open smoothly.

Fort Knox. Dylan knew there was a thick nail sticking out of the side of the doorframe, more or less out of sight. He knew that if you opened the door without pushing the nail in, chimes would ring loudly throughout the house.

A flush of embarrassment passed through him at the memory of the first – and only – time he had pushed that nail to let himself in the front door. Allan's fury had been terrifying, his forearm harder than steel as it pushed against Dylan's twelve-year-old throat. It had been years ago, but the memory still stung

Fuckin wrench monkey.

They crept in. The heavy door snicked behind them, sealing out the day.

Stepping from the peeling paint of the Campbell's front veranda onto the cool, polished timber floor of their home was like stepping into another world.

The hallway was spotless, richly and stylishly appointed. A short Persian rug sat neatly on the gleaming blackwood floorboards. The walls were painted a flawless forest green, punctuated with more blackwood frames and trimmings. Down the hall was polished railing where a stairwell descended into a basement. Above it all, dangling from the centre focus of the ceiling's ornate plasterwork, was a small two-tier chandelier.

Another fucking world.

Hushed voices were coming from a room on the left side of the hallway. Instead of a door, a diaphanous curtain hung across the doorway, just thick enough to obscure the view within.

His finger pressed to his lips again, Ben Campbell gestured down the hallway. His room was at the other end of it, towards the back of the house. Dylan rolled his eyes and walked in an exaggerated tip-toe. Ben didn't see the funny side of it.

As they passed the stairwell's polished blackwood bannisters, Dylan's neck craned. He had never been downstairs and his curiosity burned.

That's where the girls are.

The timber stairs, the hint of plush carpet at the bottom, the voices coming closer from the...

"Shit!" whispered Ben Campbell. "Come on!"

"Who's that?" A man's voice rang out suddenly though the hall. Before they could move, the front room's curtain was swept aside and a man walked out, frowning.

Who's this fuckin bloke?

In his forties or early fifties, the man was wearing a navy blue suit, expensive and well-fitting, trimmed with a black and red tie. He advanced on the two boys without hesitation, his shining black shoes ringing out on the timber.

"Who the fuck are you?" He demanded, looking back and forth from Dylan to Ben and back again. Dylan saw there was another man following him, wearing a similar suit and a relaxed grin. "What's your name?"

"Who the fuck are *you*?" Dylan sneered. *Big prick.*

"Dude, shut *up*!" Ben hissed.

"Boy." The man stood toe to toe with Dylan. He was half a head taller and almost twice as wide. He didn't blink. "You don't want to know who..."

"That's *my* boy, Sergeant."

Judy Campbell's voice was a whip crack from the other room. She flowed under the curtain into the hallway, a short, round woman with bright copper hair and small, dark eyes.

She frowned at Ben, then scowled when she saw Dylan.

"And his mate. Leave them be."

Sergeant? Dylan's blood ran cold. *Cops. They're bloody cops.*

There was a sudden clacking on the stairs, two pairs of high heels making their way up from the basement. The big guy – the Sergeant - grinned, then raised his hands and backed away. The other bloke elbowed him with a chortle.

"Are you fellas all right up there?" A young woman's voice hailed.

There was a giggle, another woman. "Don't start without us!"

Two filthy pigs, Dylan thought, blood rushing to his head. *Two poor girls.*

He was craning his neck again, trying to see down the stairs when a hand latched around his jaw.

"The *fu...*"

His head was turned to face Judy Campbell. She had his face in an iron grip, her tough little fingers digging into his cheeks. He swallowed, abruptly too frightened to move.

One of the men chuckled.

"Did I invite you into my house, pretty boy?" Her voice was low.

"Mum," Ben complained. She raised a finger and he subsided.

"*Did* I?" she growled.

"No," Dylan said sullenly. "We're just gonna play the *Amiga* for a bit."

He heard a giggle from the stairs.

"Are you just." She didn't let go of his face. If anything, her grip tightened, her nails close to breaking his skin.

"Mum, come on."

"You gentleman head downstairs," Judy said. Her eyes didn't leave Dylan's face. "I'll join you momentarily."

The clacking of heels on timber again and a hushed giggle. As the men followed the girls down, Judy Campbell pulled Dylan's face closer. He blanched at the piercing pain in his cheek.

"Listen to me, pretty boy. When you're in this house, you don't *speak*, you don't *stare*, you don't fuckin *breathe* unless I tell you to. Got it, little Dylan?" She shook his chin and finally let go.

"Dylan?" The one she had called Sergeant paused on the stairs. "As in Luke Dylan?"

Dylan straightened up, rubbing his cheeks. "Yeah. Me brother."

Judy Campbell slapped him. It wasn't hard, but it *stung.*

Before Dylan could react, her finger was in his face, millimetres from his eyes.

"Not. Another. *Word.*"

"It's all right," the man said, leaning on the handrail, amused. "I'd think about changing my name if I were you, champ."

"Fu..." Dylan saw the warning in Judy's eyes and bit the words off, contenting himself with a mutter. "He'd kick *your* ass."

The Sergeant laughed. "I reckon so. All that time in the Pink Palace might harden him up. What did he go in for again?"

"Leave it, Sarge," Judy Campbell was annoyed. "Just go downstairs."

"Murder," Dylan muttered. "He'd fuckin kill you too if he got his hands on you."

"Murder?" The Sergeant barked out a surprised laugh, then descended the stairs, chuckling. "Is that what they told you boy? *Murder?* Fuck me."

His laughter followed him into the depths of the brothel.

Judy pushed Dylan in the chest.

"Out!"

She shoved him again, towards the hallway, towards the front door.

"But mum!" Ben complained. "We'll be quiet!"

"Both of you, *out*." She pointed a finger at her son's nose. "We're getting Chinese from Sun Sing delivered at six-thirty. Got it?"

"All right, mum." Ben huffed and led Dylan back out onto the veranda.

When the heavy front door had closed behind them, Ben swore.

"Sorry man, didn't mean to get you in the shit," Dylan offered. His belly rumbled. He had eaten Sun Sing just once, when his brother had shouted the family take-away after one of his wins. *Best fried rice ever.*

"It's all right."

"I can't believe she slapped me." Dylan rubbed at his jaw. It still tingled, but he didn't think it would bruise.

"Already lost your first fight today," Ben smirked.

"Piss off. Maybe I should have slapped her back." Dylan laughed but it had a shrill edge and he eyed the Plymouth nervously.

Ben shook his head in disbelief. "You've got a goddamned death wish."

Brad

The skateboard clattered beneath Brad's feet as he kicked and pushed along Bryan Street. The asphalt footpath hadn't been resurfaced in generations and there were cracks and lumps where tree roots had broken through. His trucks were tight and his bearings hummed, but the gravelly bitumen crunched and scratched under his hard plastic wheels.

It was tough going, but he managed to get up a good speed even with a bag of hot chips grasped firmly in one hand.

A little red-brick church sat a block back from Invermay Road, with a red-brick community hall right next door. They shared a weedy concrete courtyard that opened on to the street. Brad's chips were soaked in tomato sauce and the paper bag would disintegrate before long, so he stepped off the board, kicked it over into the courtyard and sat on the steps near the church's austere wooden door.

His appetite waned as a wave of restless anxiety flushed through him. He put the perfectly cooked crinkle cuts aside.

There's gotta be somewhere to score.

It was the same thought, over and over. At least his tobacco pouch was mostly full. A cigarette, his millionth for the day, would help with the cravings a bit.

A little bit.

His fingers were quick and the cigarette he rolled was perfect.

Standing up, he kicked the skateboard onto its wheels and stepped onto it easily. With the rollie jutting from between his lips he popped a series of small ollies to get his rhythm, then a few kickflips and pop shove-its, most of which he landed comfortably. His heelflips needed work though.

I need a cone though.

The courtyard was only small. He needed to push himself harder. If he wasn't physically exhausted when he went to bed tonight, he would lay there awake until the early hours, his body craving THC.

He gathered up his pouch, wallet and the bag of chips and moved on. Pebbles gristled beneath the wheels and his kneecaps rattled. The streets were tough, but not unmanageable. He opened up the bag of chips and pinched out a few more, shoving them into his mouth as he rolled along.

The old blue ute driving down Bryan Street wasn't rolling much faster than he was, but with his fingers digging deep in the saucy paper bag, Brad didn't notice the ute until it was about to overtake him. He glanced over at it and swore.

A German Sheppard, a monster of a dog, was standing at full attention in the ute's tray. Its eyes were fixed on him. Its muzzle wriggled; its ears were laid back.

Distracted, Brad didn't notice the spiderweb of cracked asphalt that stretched across the footpath and when his front wheels hit it, they jagged violently.

The board kicked out from beneath him. He landed in a heavy run and managed to keep his feet, but the soggy paper bag dropped out of his hand. Saucy crinkle-cut chips scattered across the crumbling asphalt.

Bloody unco!

There was a commotion as the barking dog scrambled out of the moving ute's tray. It landed on the road in a heap of paws and yips and limbs but recovered quickly, bounding over to the footpath before the ute's brakes had even stopped squealing.

Brad watched in dismay as the dog wolfed down every last sauce-splattered chip.

Give me a goddamned break.

The ute's door creaked open.

"What are you fuckin *doing?*" boomed the big bloke who climbed out. He was maybe in his forties, wearing a flannelette shirt with ripped sleeves over a blue singlet. Black sunglasses covered the space between his full beard and his curled mullet, both streaked with grey. "You trying to kill me fuckin dog?"

"What?" Brad blinked, picking up his skateboard. "No! It jumped off the back."

"No fuckin shit, Sherlock." He was closing the distance between them and Brad took a step back. The dog snuffled around the footpath looking for more chips. "*You* waved fuckin food at her, of course she's gonna jump for it."

"Mate, I dropped my lunch." Brad took another step back, raising his free hand. "I was just skating. I didn't *mean* to drop my fuckin lunch."

The bloke paused, chewing on this, his beard moving from side to side, his sunglasses unreadable.

The dog stopped snuffling around. Brad's blood ran cold as the German Sheppard turned its attention to him. The goddamned thing was taller than his waist and probably weighed as much as he did, if not more. It – *she* - wandered over and sniffed at his hand, pushing her wet nose into his palm.

He stroked her muzzle, purely as a reflex. His family had owned a dog once, a big dog like this one. *Kaji.*

Kaji, his Dad's dog, had died only a year or two before its owner. Brad missed them both. It felt nice to pat a dog again.

"She could have broken all her fuckin legs." The heat was gone from the bloke's voice, but he still raised a finger and pointed it at Brad. "Next time be more *fuckin* careful!"

Without waiting for a response he strutted back to his idling ute. The whole vehicle rocked as he plonked back in to the bucket seat and glared over at the dog who was still nuzzling Brad's hand.

"Get in the fuckin ute, Midget. *Midget!*"

The dog gave Brad a last nudge before she spun and bolted towards the ute. Instead of leaping back up into the tray, she ran a circle around the ute, then a circle back the other way.

"Get *in*, Midget," the bloke snarled.

The dog ran another circle around the ute.

"Midget! Fuck!" He blustered back out of the bucket seat again and she ran over to him, tail up, eyes bright. She was happy to see him. "Stupid fuckin dog."

The bloke wrapped one meaty arm under her chest and the other behind her legs. Glaring at Brad, he picked the dog up and plonked her back into the ute's tray. She grinned at him, her tongue hanging out. The bloke muttered, rubbing the German Sheppard's chest, then he climbed into the bucket seat yet again and slammed the ute's door.

The ute revved a couple of times as he wound down the window.

"Go *fuck* yourself!"

Jesus. Brad shrugged and shook his head. *Fucking Invermay.*

The ute's wheels spun a couple of times and Midget barked gleefully, then they were lurching away down Bryan Street, past the dump with the two skeletal car bodies on the footpath ?:

"{\... and the old bloke who was always there working on them.

Taking a deep breath, Brad continued on his way. He carried his skateboard this time. The old bloke was watching him approach.

Neither of those cars has moved in at least three months. He must be the worst goddamned mechanic in Tasmania.

And here he was, leaning on the hood of the old Plymouth, replete in his blue overalls and oil-stained cheeks. The Plymouth looked like an artefact, a monument to rust, a relic doomed to petrification.

As Brad approached, the mechanic nodded in greeting, expressionless. His hands polished some flashing steel part with a dirty rag.

Brad returned the gesture, considering.

Maybe this bloke knows the score.

Before he could ask the question, a voice called from the filthy house's veranda.

"Did that fuckin dog bite you?"

Two blokes were sitting there, both around his own age, both wearing singlets and dopey grins. It was the bigger one with the slick blonde hair who had spoken. There was a smoke between his fingers.

"Oh. Nah." Brad shrugged, shifting his board under his arm. "Nah I dropped some food. Fuckin dog went after it."

The old mechanic, apparently disinterested, disappeared underneath the Plymouth.

"What did he say?" the blonde asked. "Pasco's a mad bastard, even the other bikies won't fuck with him."

"Sorry?"

"Pasco, the bloke in the ute. Was he pissed off?"

"Yeah," Brad was mystified. "Yeah, it was a bit over the top."

"Pasco, mate. Mad bastard."

"He was worried about his dog."

"Fuck his dog."

"Yeah."

"You live around here?"

"Yeah, just down the street. I'm Brad."

"Brad, eh? I'm Dylan. This fuckin rabbit's Ben."

The other kid, silent until now, ducked his head. "Hey Brad."

"How's it going, Ben."

"Not too shabby."

"Um. Don't suppose you fellas know where to get any bud?"

A muffled voice answered him from beneath the Plymouth. "No drugs around here mate."

Jesus, that's the deepest voice I ever heard. Brad shuffled uncomfortably.

"No worries, just thought I'd ask. I moved up from Hobart a couple of months back and I haven't been able to score since…"

The old bloke had rolled out from under the car and was frowning at him. It was a dark frown, a distant storm behind a heavy brow. Brad could see the man's nostrils flaring.

"Leave him alone dad," said Ben.

The old bloke, scowling, rolled back under the car. Dylan scoffed.

"This your place?" Brad asked Ben.

Ben nodded as Dylan stood up.

"Yep, it's his shit hole," the blonde boy sneered, stretching his shoulders.

"Watch your mouth," came the bass rumble from below the Plymouth.

"Finding many good spots to skate?" Ben asked.

"In the city," Brad shrugged. "Not so much around here. Can't find nothing."

"What about behind the warehouse down there?" Dylan pointed towards South Street. "In the car park. Flat cement. Close to your house."

"Really?" Brad brightened a bit. "I haven't seen it. Somewhere flat would be fuckin rad."

"Come on, I'll show you." Dylan flicked his cigarette butt into the green pond.

"Wicked, cheers man."

"You coming Benny?"

"Might as well…"

"Ben." The old blokes voice was flat. "Grab a wrench."

"We're only going for a walk, dad."

"*You're* not. Grab a fuckin wrench."

Ben shrugged and walked back to the balcony, rummaging in a huge toolbox.

Dylan made a disgusted sound. "You still gonna come to the fights?"

Ben nodded, cutting his eyes to the Plymouth. "Catch ya a bit later."

"See you man," Brad raised two fingers to his forehead in a short salute.

"How long you lived here?" Dylan asked as they marched.

"Couple of months. Moved up just before Christmas."

"Where'd you live before that?"

Man that smells good. They were rounding the corner into South Street and the air around the bakery was warm and buttery. *I wish I was stoned.*

"Rosny." Seeing Dylan's blank face, he added "In Hobart."

"Oh yep." Dylan nodded. "Yep. Hobart, eh."

"Yeah. Never had any trouble scoring weed down there."

"Did you say you had some?" Dylan sniffed.

"Nah man," Brad chuckled. "I'm looking for some."

"Oh. Right. Got none?"

"Only death," Brad laughed. Dylan just nodded and Brad eyed him sideways.

He's not fazed by the death. Maybe he'll have a crack with me. It had been months since he'd had a session with anybody else.

"Do you chuff?"

"Yeah man, when I can get a bit yeah."

"Wanna come and smoke some stinky death then man? About the best I can do. Then you can show me this spot."

"Sounds all right man. How the fuck do you skate when you're stoned?"

"That's the best time to do it man. It helps me focus."

"Really?" Dylan looked thoughtful. "Reckon it would help you fight?"

"Huh?"

"If you had a smoke before you had a fight?" Smirking at Brad's expression, he added. "Like boxing, you know, martial arts."

"Dunno man. Maybe. Don't think I've ever had a fight stoned," Brad hadn't been in a fight since primary school, though he had seen a few at the old skate bowl in Hobart. "Are you a boxer?"

"Yeah man. Got a fight this arvo."

"No shit?"

"Yeah man."

"Can people come and watch?"

Dylan laughed. "Nah man. They don't let just anybody in. You've gotta know the blokes running it."

"Right," Brad said. "Spun out. This is my place, just here."

My first visitor in Invermay, he thought as he led Dylan down the laneway to his backyard. *Maybe things are looking up.*

Maynard

Maynard hunched over to catch his breath on the corner of Little Ray Street.

He had covered the distance from his house to Tommy's pretty quickly, but he still regretted leaving his bike at home. He sighed. When he was hanging out with Tommy, it was on foot.

I could just buy him a cheap BMX off the Trading Post. I wonder if he would take it.

His breath returned as he walked up the shaded street. Lined by tall fences on either side, Little Ray was barely wide enough for a single car to fit down, more like a laneway than a street. The only house on Little Ray – a cottage really, a remnant of the time when Invermay was a labourer's slum – was where Tommy, Boofhead and their creepy mother Lorraine lived.

As he pulled up outside the cottage, Maynard saw Tommy in the backyard, trying to juggle a soccer ball with his feet.

A flashing thought of dream-tight sheets tights wrapped around his ankle and something *urgent* and the touch of skin, *of skin so smooth and rough...*

Stop it!

"Oi dickhead," Maynard called in his deepest voice.

The soccer ball ricocheted into Lorraine's tomato plants.

"Nice touch, Maradona."

"Tosser," Tommy shot Maynard a dark look as he retrieved the ball from the garden. He held up a sliver of branch that had been knocked onto the dirt. "I'm gonna blame you for that."

"As if she'll notice."

"As if she won't."

"I'll give her a bottle of mum's sauce. What are you doing?"

"Fuck all."

"Wanna come for a mission?"

"Where to?"

"Does it matter? You're doing fuck all."

"I'm a busy man." Tommy bounced the ball off his foot again.

Maynard looked around the yard. "Where's Boof?"

"Inside, wanking."

Maynard snorted, then lowered his voice. "I found this sick spot."

"Oh yeah?"

"Down past the Railyards. It's an old factory or something."

"Right. Can you get in?"

"I reckon." He lowered his voice. "It's all burnt out, but… I'm pretty keen to go back and check it out. There might still be some good stuff in there."

"What kind of good stuff?"

Skin and lips and sweat and sheets…

"Don't know. I didn't go in yet."

"Right. Because you need me to come and hold your hand."

Tommy's grin was cheeky, infectious, even as Maynard swung a punch at his arm. The bigger boy stepped away easily, dodging Maynard's fist with a chuckle, skipping with a lightness that belied his size.

Before Maynard could swing again, something distracted him. He dropped his fist and nodded towards the woman coming down Little Ray towards them.

Here comes Creepy.

She was striding along, hands clasped behind her back, her deep brown eyes piercing even at a distance.

"Argh fuck. Here we go." Tommy rolled his eyes and turned to face his mother.

Lorraine could have been forty, or fifty, or sixty years old. Her hair was mostly black, streaked with artless strands of white, and her cheap grey track pants matched the cracked grey concrete gutters.

"Tommy-bomb!" She barked from halfway up the street, as loud as a fire alarm. "Where's your brother?"

"How the fuck should I know?" He called back.

"Don't you speak to me like that, tough guy." Her eyes narrowed as she came and stood toe to toe with him, but there was the shadow of an affectionate smile playing across those mean lips. "You'll see how bloody tough you are with a foot in your arse. Where's your brother?"

"I don't *know!"*

*"Bull*shit." She bellowed the word, really leaned into it. "Of course you fuckin do."

Keep your voice down, you goddamned dragon. Maynard couldn't help but look at her faint, black moustache.

"I'm not his babysitter."

"Well how could you be, Tom Thumb? You're both as stupid as each other." *Don't talk to him like that.* It was too much for Maynard.

"We were just going." He took a couple of steps backward and pointed his thumb down Little Ray. "Should we get going?"

She turned on Maynard with those dark eyes that didn't seem to blink as much as they should. For a moment he thought she could somehow see the soiled patch on his belly, see the mess he had made. He shook the thought away. He had showered twice already, once when he had woken up and again after his paper round.

"And where are you boys off to in such a hurry, young Maynard?"

"Just down the park," Tommy lied easily. He took a couple of steps towards Maynard. "Going for a kick."

"Going for a kick, are you, Tom?"

"Yep," said Maynard. "See you a bit later, Lorra..."

"You'll probably want a ball then, won't you?" Her voice was sharp, smug. "You'll need something to kick if you're gonna have a kick."

"We've got one," Maynard chuckled, backing away. "My mate's down there, he's got one."

"I've just come that way, didn't see anyone down the park."

"I'd hide too if I saw a fuckin old dragon creeping around the park."

"Don't you speak to your mother like that," she boomed, clearly trying not to laugh, but they were already running.

"Stay out of trouble!"

"Righto."

"Bye *Maynard*," she crooned, cackling as they ran.

Why does she have to be so goddamned loud!

They legged it down to Forster Street, sprinted straight past the park with the big cricket oval, then jumped the squat wooden fence into the Railyards.

An industrial wasteland, the Railyards was a vast, sharp-edged playground for bored teenagers and a town-sized headache for a few unlucky council workers. It squatted between Invermay and the first inner suburbs of Launceston, it's disused warehouses and trolley carts and loading bays hidden behind the gum trees of Invermay Park. Along the Railyard's boundaries were some ancient, collapsing timber and tin stables that served as accommodation for the less particular drunks and junkies of Invermay, but they were quiet today.

Tommy and Maynard made their way over broken glass, bent weeds and a spiderweb of ancient train tracks until they came to the flood levy that bordered the Railyard's eastern side. The levy doubled as a bike track that followed the curve of the stinking North Esk River until it joined onto Churchill Park Drive.

They were almost at the end of the track when Maynard pointed over the cottage roofs to the rusted silo. It loomed over the burned-out mill, its thin arms holding the decaying building in a death grip.

"See that thing? The big rusty silo?"

"Robot man?"

"Yeah," Maynard chuckled. It *did* look like a robot. "That's the place.".

They walked beyond the last row of houses to the vacant lot and then to the long alleyway that ran between the mill and the woolstore.

"The mill's all burned out. Spooky, eh?"

"Bloody hell," Tommy whistled appreciatively. "Wonder if we can get on the roof."

"Probably," Maynard said doubtfully. "I suppose."

He took a step back, trying to look at the mill's roof, and something soft squished beneath his foot.

"Oh. Oh *shit!*"

Tommy spun… then tilted his head back and laughed to the sky, a full-throated, unselfconscious laugh that boomed up and down the corridor between the two buildings.

"Fuck," said Maynard, chuckling now that he had his balance back. His spine tingled with excitement.

There was a scattering of used condoms, maybe a dozen or more, littered around the alley.

Used.

Used for fucking.

The boy's eyes met for a moment and they both looked away and laughed. Maynard felt the high colour in his cheeks, but he couldn't help glancing back at the little sodden tubes sinking into the gravel.

He couldn't move his hands to cover the hardness in his pants, not without Tommy noticing.

"Look out, someone's coming," Tommy said. He was looking into the distance, his head cocked to one side listening.

Maynard heard it too; the rumble of a motorbike, of a few motorbikes. "Just the Marauders out and about. They're not gonna come here."

"Bloody hope not. Sounds like a few of them."

The motors thrummed in an unholy chorus until, one by one, their voices were silenced.

"They must be at Pasco's. That's their clubhouse, isn't it?"

"His place is further up, on the next block."

"Righto. Does he get the paper?"

Maynard snorted. "Nope. I know it's his place because of that big bloody dog he's got. Come on."

They followed the wall until they reached a loading bay door more than a metre above the ground. It's sliding timber doors had somehow survived the fire but were wide open. Tommy climbed into the loading bay first with Maynard close behind him.

They were standing in a large open room, a workshop with a high roof and a rough concrete floor. A few workbenches were scattered through the room, some still holding tools or stacks of timber. Chains were hanging from the ceiling in a few places, heavy with rust. Although there was some obvious smoke damage around the walls and ceiling, it seemed like this room had escaped the worst of the blaze.

"Spun out," Maynard didn't mention the door in the far corner, didn't even glance at it. *Not yet.* "It's like they walked off the job and just never came back."

"Probably cause the fuckin place was on fire."

"Yeah. But the fire must have been ages ago, why haven't they cleaned it up?"

"Dunno," Tommy strode across the workshop and opened a door on the far side. "Yeah shit. What a mess."

Maynard followed him over. Tommy had stepped gingerly into the small room, coals and ash crunching beneath his feet. The walls and ceiling in here were crumbling, the steel roof beams exposed.

Tommy was standing next to a monstrous cast-iron tank with a furnace on either side of it. The scorch marks seemed to emanate out from it, a dead star robbed of its fiery power. A fire hulk, menacingly still.

"That's a bloody big oven," Maynard nodded. *We could probably both fit inside it.* His spine tingled.

"Not an oven," said Tommy. "A *kiln.*"

"What's a kiln?"

"Like a big oven."

"So it's a fuckin big oven," Maynard rolled his eyes. "Why didn't you just say so? What would they have cooked in it?"

"Timber, I reckon. Like, expensive timber. The sort they make into furniture."

"Listen to you, Mr. Wood," Maynard grinned. That tingle in his spine again.

"I liked MDT. It was the only fuckin class I went to."

They both laughed. Everyone laughed when Tommy laughed.

The came back out into the main workshop and checked some of the other doors. They revealed tiny storage closets or one-desk offices, but Tommy exclaimed when he opened the only set of double-doors.

"What is it?" asked Maynard.

"Come and have a look."

The warehouse was an empty, blackened shell. The cement floor was rough and uneven, stretched between rudimentary whitewashed brick walls. The oddly shaped ceiling dipped and climbed out of sight. The warehouse's only feature was a high balcony with a steel railing that circled the entire room.

"Big empty room."

"Look," Tommy pointed at the balcony. "We should see if we can get up there."

"Why? It's just a different view of the big empty room."

"Should still have a look. If we can get up there, we might be able to get on the roof."

"True," Maynard shrugged. "But why?"

"Why not?"

"Come and have a look in here first," Maynard gestured back into the workshop.

Tommy blinked in surprise but followed him readily enough. Maynard led him to the door in the far corner of the workshop.

Sweat was beading along his hairline, down his back.

Don't be weird about it! Just a goddamned dream.

"In here." He pushed the door open and moved aside. Tommy stepped past him. Maynard couldn't help but grin when he heard the older boy's gasp of delight. He followed him into the room and let smoke-damaged door swing closed behind them.

Tommy was standing in the centre of the room with an expression of wonder, eyes half-lidded, mouth hanging open.

Dozens upon dozens of semi-naked women smiled down on them.

Their smiles were wide, their teeth yellowed with age and smoke, their naked skin tanned and faded and spotted with mildew. Many sported high fringes and heavy makeup, some were splayed over cars or motorbikes, some were ripped or wrinkled or charred. A bare few had faded away to ghostly shapes on brittle, decaying paper.

A thin wooden shelf divided the posters on the back wall. Sitting on it were a couple of empty whisky bottles and several cheap, white candles. There were more condoms on the floor. Maynard tried not to look at them.

"Check it out, it's your mum." Tommy pointed to one of the posters. There was colour in his cheeks.

"She looks all right."

"They *all* look all right." He shook his head, grinning. "How the fuck did you find this place?"

Maynard shrugged and looked at one of the less-faded posters on the outer wall. Two women with breasts larger than their heads appeared to be grappling a petrol hose.

"But they're all from *People* magazine, or *Truckin Life* or whatever bullshit they were into. *Post* even." Tommy sounded a bit disappointed.

"So?"

"So it's just tits."

Maynard wiped his sweaty hands on his pants. "Yeah I guess. *People*. Not *Playboy*."

"So it's not really porn, is it."

"Isn't it? I mean…" he gestured around them.

"But there's no pussy," Tommy complained, his head swivelling like a satellite dish. "Not one."

"It was a work site," Maynard pointed out. "Must have been the rule."

"Still all right though." Tommy started to pick away at the corner of one of the bigger posters.

"You'll never get that off."

"I'll get her off, mate. Every time." He wasn't having much luck though. "Come on baby…"

Paper ripped away in an ugly shred and dust motes floated around the room, the last gasp of a dried mummy.

"Shit. Never mind." He puts his fist on his hips, gazing at the walls.

Maynard's watched his friend turn. His wide shoulders were round and perfectly proportioned, his stomach flat, his…

His pants bulging with an insistent, unmistakable shape.

Oh Christ.

Maynard's spine didn't tingle; it *surged.* His head filled with helium and his tongue felt like sandpaper in his mouth.

Just a dream. Just a dream.

"We've gotta get some chicks down here," Tommy mused.

Maynard snorted. His lips were numb, as though he'd taken a hit from a bong. He forced a smile. "You reckon Stacey Macintosh would be into tits and trucks?"

Tommy grinned at the thought, his hand unconsciously straying towards that bulge. "Glass of whisky, light a few candles and she'd be too busy to notice them."

"Christ. I could go a whisky."

"I could go a blowjob," Tommy laughed, finally adjusting that bulge.

There was a moment of silence and Maynard realised that Tommy was watching him, waiting for a reply.

Say something. Say something!

"Yeah, fuck yeah," he laughed weakly. "Wouldn't mind that at all. Has Stacey got a sister?"

They both laughed but Maynard's was high-pitched and there was colour in Tommy's cheeks.

"Let's get the fuck out of here," Tommy suggested,

They exited the room, a little more quickly than they needed to.

Jake

Jake's cheap chrome BMX was sluggish and heavy, its vinyl seat cracked, and its red handlebar grips almost worn through… but he liked it. It was tough, familiar, and when he yanked it off the stack of firewood next to the back door, it felt like he could go just about anywhere and do just about anything.

He cruised up the driveway past the bakehouse. Slowing down to look through the open roller door, he smiled at Lynn, nodded to John and gave Milky the finger before pedalling out of sight. He paused at the end of the driveway, checking Bryan Street in both directions, then stood on his pedals and rolled out.

As soon as he turned into South Street he spotted Reese and Boof near the phone box at the end of Monash Reserve. When they saw him coming, they lifted their bikes over the ankle-high cement wall and rode into the reserve, a near-featureless rectangle of grass the size of a city block.

"Bout fuckin' time," Boof muttered as Jake caught up to them.

"What's the go?" Jake asked.

Reese, riding with unusual urgency over the uneven ground, wiggled his eyebrows.

"Titty mission."

"What?"

"Tell him, Boof."

Boof cheesed it, grinning widely at Jake, and almost steered his bike into the bushes at the end of the park. Reese bunny-hopped onto the thin concrete path that weaved between two houses and they followed in single file.

"Tell me what?" Jake demanded.

Boof pointedly ignored him, calling to Reese. "I didn't say I'd do it."

"How else will you get twenty bucks?" Reese called back.

"Maybe cupcake here will lend it to me."

"Twenty bucks? What for?" Jake already knew the answer.

"I want to get a stick," Boof bunny-hopped his bike, excited. "I've already got five bucks, just need another twenty. Have you got any cash?"

"Sorry man, I'm broke hey." It was a lie. The twenty Noah had given him last night was snug in his Rip Curl wallet. He nodded at Reese, who was looking ahead to Invermay Road and pretending not to listen. "What's his deal?"

"He wants me to flog a porno from Sam's."

Jake sighed. "Again?"

"He's too chickenshit to do it himself."

"Bullshit," Reese finally touched his brakes and drew even with the others. "I'll do it!"

"As if you will," Boof laughed.

"I will if you will."

"Yeah, see. You just want *me* to do it again."

"Well you're *good* at it."

"You *are* pretty good at it Boof," Jake agreed.

"C'mon Boof," Reese grinned. "Twenty bucks for two magazines. Easy money."

Boof's squinted into the distance, calculating. Reese laughed but Jake shook his head.

"Lorraine'll fuckin skin you if she finds out."

Boof ignored him, rubbing his chin and eyeing Reese. "Twenty bucks, hey?"

Reese shrugged, his hands open. "Yep. Then we can go get a stick off Magnus."

Boof looked to Jake, who shrugged, then back at Reese. "All right. Come on then."

Reese chuckled and gave Boof the thumbs up, then turned to Jake with a sly grin. "Go you halves? Ten bucks each?"

Jake couldn't help but laugh. "Jesus, Reese you're a shark."

Boof rolled his BMX, standing on the pedals with his chest puffed out. "Giddy-up then!"

They glided down Elm Street, riding parallel to the tall green hedge that kept them out of Burwood Estate. Invermay Road was half a block away, busy with noon traffic.

Next to Sam's General Store was a vacant block where old cement foundations were littered with broken glass and long grass. Towards the back of the block was a decrepit timber shed, perhaps an old stable. Long abandoned, it slumped with age, its cheap old wood ripe with graffiti and piss stains. They lay their bikes down in the lot, just far enough back from the footpath to be out of sight from the shop's front windows.

"Right." Boof punched his fist into his palm. "If we have to bolt, meet at Invermay Park?" He met both their eyes in turn before nodding sharply.

If only you took anything else this seriously. "Right. Should we go in together?"

"Me and Boof first," Reese said. "You come in a bit, Jake."

"Righto."

Jake watched them go, butterflies tickling his stomach.

I don't want to steal a fucking magazine. He sighed. *Yet here I am.*

Over at the BP service station there were three cars pulled up at the pumps. Warren, the cheerfully balding manager of the station, was pumping petrol into an old HK Ute. Thankfully he didn't turn around; Jake and his mum and been using the service station for Jake's entire life. Jake liked Warren, so he followed Reese and Boof around the corner before the ruddy little mechanic could spot him.

They had already gone into Sam's. Jake walked to the entrance of the cool, dim shop… and came to an abrupt halt.

Reese was waiting for him, wide eyed. One hand was held up in a subtle *stop* gesture.

The other held something wrapped in clear plastic – a magazine.

A cocky grin was blooming across his features.

That was quick.

Usually they would loiter for a few minutes, scoping the situation, and when it was all clear one of them would stuff the loot down the front of their…

Without warning, Reese *threw* the magazine.

It was just a flick of the wrist, but the mag came spinning toward him at a startling speed.

Cursing, Jake snatched the porno out of the air just before it smacked into his face.

He glared at Reese, who was marching towards the door, clearly struggling to contain a belly laugh. He winked at Jake as he sped by, his face lit with excitement.

"Nice catch, Snakey."

Reese was strutting, and it *had* been a pretty smooth move… but Jake was looking past him with a worried expression.

Oh shit.

Boof hadn't followed Reese out of the shop. Never to be outdone, he had stopped at the same section of the magazine rack with a serious expression.

Jake tried to catch his eye, but it was no good.

Boof peered around the shop, his lips pursed in concentration, then picked up one of the magazines; *Naughty Nurses 11*. This one wasn't wrapped in plastic, and he held it up to his face as though reading it, his eyes darting around, the tip of his tongue poking out, a masterclass in bad acting.

Jake shook his head and took a step backwards.

No! Don't do it!

Boof flung the porno with a grunt.

A squall of paper burst into the air.

Leaflets and posters sprayed from between the magazine's pages before it flew wildly off course and smacked into the lolly cabinet with a loud *crack!*

The three boys froze, their mouths hanging open. Flyers for Melbourne strip clubs fluttered through the air.

"The *fuck* are you doing, Boofhead?" Reese's voice was faint.

"What was that?" A man's concerned voice boomed from deeper in the store.

They scattered.

Reese was already running.

Jake turned to follow him… and jumped, startled. His hands fumbled and almost dropped the porno, but he caught it at the last moment and clutched it against his chest.

There was a face peering out of the store's front window, only a couple of feet away from his own.

Stephanie.

Stephanie, who had gone to his school, who lived around the corner, who *knew* him, knew his mum, knew where he *lived*.

She blinked at him. Looked down at the magazine. Blinked at the magazine.

It wasn't me, he wanted to say.

Running past, Boof punched his shoulder. *"C'mon fuckhead!"*

"Shit!"

Jake took off after him, rounding the corner into the vacant lot. His cheeks were burning, his head was spinning. He couldn't feel his legs, but they still ran well enough.

Reese was on his bike already, pedalling across the weeds for all he was worth. Boof was still hauling his old McBain BMX upright when Jake took off, pushing his bike at a run then swinging onto the seat. The ground in the lot was bumpy and the bike's seat smacked dangerously close to his nuts, but when his back wheel hit the gravel road it only spun once and then he was moving properly.

Reese was already hammering up Elm Street so Jake darted through the white gate into Burwood Estate. Once he was cruising between the hedges, he looked back over his shoulder to see Boof splitting away down the dirt lane that ran parallel to Invermay Road.

She can't follow all three of us. He didn't wait to see who she had chosen.

She doesn't need *to chase us. She saw the porno, looked me full in the face.*

The green hedges of Burwood's leafy driveway folded closed behind him. Despite its careful grooming – or perhaps because of it - the other-worldly colonial garden felt empty, neglected, like the expensive dinner set his mother kept on display but would never dream of serving up. He and Reece and Boof would often dare each other to ride down the driveway that split the old property in two – it was smooth bitumen littered with acorns, beautiful for riding on. It usually took about 12 seconds to race from Burwood's understated service entry on Ray Street to its decorative front gate facing Invermay Road.

But today he pedalled up the driveway, against the natural order of things. With adrenaline in his blood and panic buzzing his thoughts, he noticed details about Burwood that he never usually noticed; the enormous stained-glass windows above the front door of the main lodge, the freshly painted white bannisters on the concrete stairs, the picnic tables waiting on the crisp, manicured lawn.

Even though he had never seen a living soul on the property, he was sure somebody was about to step into the laneway, somebody in an officer's uniform, somebody who would seize him and his bike and his stolen porno.

She won't say anything. Not Steph. Not my old mate good old Steph.

Of course she would. It was her job. And although he didn't really know her, he knew her well enough; Stephanie was as square as they came, quiet, proper, almost nerdy.

I'm caught. Shoplifter. Thief.

His mother would cry, of course, and his grandparents would scold him with morbid disappointment. They were honest people who didn't tolerate thieves or miscreants or disgrace. And what had he stolen?

A goddamned porno. He couldn't even bring himself to look at it, not yet.

I'm so, so screwed.

Stephanie

Stephanie stared out the window at the spot where Jake had been standing.

Two thieves in one day, both from my school.

She didn't know Jake very well – not at all, really – but she hadn't taken him for the type of guy who would steal… one of *those* books.

Reese maybe, and Boof for sure, but stuck-up Cupcake?

She shook her head. All of their parents were regular customers here, all on a first name basis with Barb and David.

Idiots. Do they seriously think they can get away with it?

She remembered Anna's smug smile and Lily's casual disregard.

Ooh she's tough.

As she walked out from behind the lolly counter, a group of motorbikes cruised past on Invermay Road, their engines a deep-throated chorus that vibrated the windows, shook the ground and channelled her mood. Black leather and bright silver gleamed past, dark sunglasses perched on serious faces, long beards splayed by the wind. At the rear of the pack was a younger rider not much older than herself, with tattoos climbing up his muscular, outstretched arms.

They were gone in moments, the howling of their engines receding like a dream.

Naughty Nurses 11 was crumpled against the door frame, a few of its crinkled pages flapping gently against the breeze. Stephanie picked it up with the tips of her fingers.

The woman on the cover pouted out into space, her smile not quite reaching her eyes, her nakedness barely covered by a ridiculous nurse's costume. The cover was slightly scuffed, but she didn't think anybody would notice.

They'd risk getting arrested for this? Guys are so dumb.

She collected up the scattered flyers. Half-price entry to *Goldfingers*. A free lap dance at *Bar20*. A subscription card for *Penthouse*. She shoved them roughly back between the pages.

So dumb.

"What was all that?" David's approaching voice startled her.

"Some magazines fell off the shelf. I'll fix it."

"Were they damaged?" David sat a box of chocolate frogs down on the lolly counter and came over to her.

"Oh. One of *those*."

"Yeah," she said, her cheeks warming. She waved the magazine at him, avoiding his eyes. "It's not too damaged."

"It wouldn't matter." He shrugged and plucked it out of her hand. "If they want them, they'll buy them."

Or steal them, she thought.

David was flicking through the magazine.

Stephanie saw skin on the pages, bright white smiles and flushed cheeks, an awkward wrist, the curve of a breast and a damp inner thigh.

Her back stiffened. She was suddenly aware of how close he was. She cast her eyes into the distance, out the door to Invermay Road, unsure whether it would be rude to walk away.

"Look at this," David said softly.

He angled the magazine towards her and her stomach sank.

The full-page photo showed a woman – a *young* woman – and a much older man.

They were naked.

The woman – the *girl* – was sprawled awkwardly across a blanket of fake fur, while the man crouched just above her shoulders. His freckled, calloused hand was wrapped around the girl's throat.

His *thing* waved near the girl's wide-open mouth...

"Oh, lovely." David sounded breathless, almost like he was talking to himself. "What a good girl."

Abruptly Stephanie realised that her shoulder was touching his arm, leaning *into* him, and she almost stumbled in her haste to step away.

Her cheeks burned. Her mouth was dry. Her pulse thumped in her ears.

He didn't look up from the magazine.

How could he show me that?

"Disgusting." It came out as a whisper.

She cleared her throat to try again, but a woman's voice rang out from the grocery aisle, loud and intrusive.

"How long have those lemons been sitting out back?"

It was Barb. David's wife. Stephanie's other boss.

"Since Thursday." David calmly closed the magazine and dropped it on the rack. He didn't look at Stephanie as he put his hands on his hips. "We'll bring them out in the morning."

"Right." Barb bustled into view and plonked a few bags down on the lolly counter. "They've decided to put on a barbeque over at the Bowl's club tonight. Hi, Stephanie."

Stephanie's mouth hung open. She wanted to march over to Barb and thrust *Naughty Nurses 11* into her face.

See this, Barb? Have a good look! David really liked this one, what do you think?

Instead, standing stiffly at the far end of the magazine rack, she tried and failed to summon a smile.

The older woman barely glanced at her anyway. "If I take three kilos of sausages will there be enough left?"

"They probably won't get through all of that." David clicked his tongue and strode away. "Did Marjorie call, or was it Alfred?"

He disappeared up the grocery aisle, out of sight, and Barb followed him with a long-suffering pout on her lips.

Stephanie exhaled abruptly. She hadn't realised that she was holding her breath, or that her hands were balled into tight fists, or that tears were trying to push into the corners of her eyes.

Guys are so fucking dumb. Even him.

Even her boss, this vaguely kind, mostly distant grey-haired man who was probably older than her father.

A hot tear spilled over. She pushed it away with her wrist. Taking a deep breath, she turned to the stationary shelf and started turning the bottles of Tippex so that their labels were facing frontward.

They were all so fucking dumb.

Brad

The window rattled stubbornly against its wooden frame and gave a reluctant squeal as Brad shoved it open. Wispy lace curtains brushed his shoulders.

Will the smell stick to these curtains? It probably would.

Because the kitchen stank.

Really stank.

He sidestepped the tall cabinet where his mother kept her finer china and pulled the back door open. Warm, fresh air from the back garden drifted in.

But it still stank.

"She's gonna kill you man," Dylan was watching him, propped up at the timber breakfast bar, his threadbare blue singlet and his scabbed and tattooed biceps out of place in the neat, well-stocked timber kitchen.

"She won't notice the smell," Brad lied, waving a tea towel at the window. "She'd be more pissed about someone being here, anyway."

"What, does she think I'm gonna rob you?"

"Probably," Brad laughed. "Nah, I'm just not meant to have anywhere here during the day."

"Man, she must be stuck up."

Brad turned away, smile fading. His mum might be a pain in the arse, but she was still his mum.

Dylan was relentless. "Like she must think she's way better than everyone else, having a fuckin place like this, not letting her boy have any mates over. What's her problem?"

Brad shrugged. It was dawning on him that *he* didn't really want Dylan here either.

"I just knew some dodgy fuckers back in Hobart, I suppose."

He bent down to look through the oven's glass door again. The sooner they smoked up the sticky black mess, the sooner they could go and check out the skating spot Dylan had promised to show him.

Wrapping a clean white tea-towel around his hand, he pulled open the oven door, copping a hot blast of foul, ripe stink. It smelled like somebody had put out a tyre fire with wet hair.

The oven tray held a ceramic ashtray, the kind they used in pubs or TABs. In the middle of the ashtray was a tiny pile of burnt, oozing tar, dotted with a few sparse flecks of brown tobacco and green marijuana. The tar, scraped from the pipe and chamber of Brad's bong not fifteen minutes ago, was still visibly damp.

Brad put the ashtray onto the polished wooden bench, careful not to touch it with his bare hand.

"Is it ready?" Dylan was craning his neck.

"Nah, just gonna chop it up a bit so it dries quicker."

"So you've done this a few times then," Dylan sneered. He seemed to sneer at everything.

"Haven't you?"

"Maybe once or twice."

"Right." Brad put the scissors down and dropped the ashtray back into the oven. Some of the death was stuck to his fingers so he washed them under the tap before it could get on anything else. "I've smoked this shit a thousand times."

"Can't you get anything else?"

"I met this dude in town, Magnus, but he's never holding. I always heard the weed in Launceston was pretty good. And cheap. C'mon man, you must know somebody."

"Nah, I just get shouted most of the time. Whoever's got some, you know."

"Nobody that you could buy a bit from?"

"Don't reckon. If me brother was here, he could sort you out."

"Where's your brother?"

"Down south, mate. Doing hard time."

"Right. Shit. Is he a smoker?"

"Don't reckon."

Brad stifled a frustrated growl. "Hey, what about those bikies that are always about? They'd be selling."

"You should ask 'em."

"Do they sell stuff or not?"

"I don't know. None of my business."

"What," Brad cocked his head, taking in Dylan's blue singlet, his half-flexed muscles. "Are you scared of the bikies, Dylan?"

It was meant to be a joke, but a bit of sting slipped into his voce.

"Fuck off man, *you* go and talk to em. They're not selling *two-fives*, the Marauders don't muck around. Even Judy's careful not to piss them off. They're not gonna sell weed to *you*."

"Bull*shiiiiit*," Brad needled him. He wrapped his hand in the tea towel and opened the oven again. "A bikie's a bikie, they'll sell fuckin Panadol if someone's buying."

"Yeah well good luck with that. How's that death going?"

"Shithouse. But… it *is* ready."

And it was.

The black tar was dry enough to crumble when Brad poked it with the blade of his little scissors. Any moisture had cooked away, leaving a lumpy pile of chunky resin and ash. He mixed in a pinch of tobacco and quickly cut it all into a consistent mull.

Dylan followed him out through the back door and into the stretching, leafy backyard. The yard had obviously been well-cared for before Brad and his mother took over and had grown out stylishly since. The wild weeds and stretching leaves looked bohemian, rather than trashy, at least to Brad.

Half-way down the narrow yard was the small timber woodshed where he kept his glass two-chamber bong.

The bong was remarkably clean, its chambers and pipe having been stripped of black death not half an hour earlier. The water in both chambers was mostly clear, rather than the customary dank green.

"I dunno why you bother coming out here. The house already reeks."

Brad shrugged. "Drying it out's bad, but smoking it's way worse. I'd rather smoke outside anyway."

It was true. Tucked away from the old bitumen footpaths and hidden amongst the cracking federation house and the big, anonymous Colourbond warehouses over the back fence, the garden felt like a secret. His secret.

A secret he would regret revealing to this new-ish mate, this teenage stoner with a chip on his shoulder, this blonde gutter-Fonzie.

"Come on then, pack one up for me."

"Let me just try it first," Brad scoffed.

He pinched some of the black, ashy powder from the ashtray and packed it into the bong's steel cone-piece.

"Nah it's fine, bro, rack me up."

"Dunno though. Let me check it, I just want to make sure the death I scraped from my stem and cooked in my fuckin kitchen is going to smoke up all right through my bong in my backyard."

"Yeah yeah righto," Dylan pouted. "Just fuckin hurry up man, I wanna get one into me, see if it gets me ready to rumble." He punched the air a few times, short sharp jabs.

"Jesus, dude." Brad shook his head in disbelief. He flicked his lighter until a flame popped up, then pushed the bong's mouthpiece against his lips.

The black death crackled and sparked a little, reluctant to burn. He held the flame against it, pulling his breath in slowly, evenly. A normal cone of weed and tobacco would be well and truly lit by now, burning down against the pull of his breath, but the death was stubborn.

"It's still wet," Dylan sneered.

Without raising his eyes or taking his lips from the bong, Brad shook his head. A moment later he dropped the lighter away – the death was glowing in the cone-piece like coal in an ancient brazier.

He pulled until the last bit of glowing tar fell through the cone piece, into the stem from whence it had come, then sat back with his mouth twisted in disgust, eyes closed, a bitter taste on his lips, dirty, biting smoke scratching at his lungs.

"And he pulls it one. You fuckin animal." Dylan was impressed.

Brad shook his head slowly from side to side, then gradually eased the twice-burnt smoke from his lungs. It drifted out of him, thick and white, acrid, its last tendrils dragging on his throat and making him cough.

Holding an elbow over his face as the cough shook his body, he waved the bong at Dylan.

The older boy bit his lip.

"Will you pack it for me man? I don't want that shit on my fingers."

Brad rolled his eyes as his cough trailed away, finally under control. He packed another cone with the stank black powder and waved it at Dylan.

"Fuckin pussy." His voice was a croak.

Dylan pouted. "Well there's no point both of us touching it, is there? Thanks."

He took the bong and lit the cone, sucking through it for all he was worth. After a moment he lowered it again.

"Nothing's coming through. It's blocked."

"Nah man, you've just gotta burn it a bit first before you pull it."

"Like this?" Dylan held the flame over the cone and Brad nodded. A second later, Dylan pulled the bong again, slower this time.

He got halfway through it, then whipped it away from his face and coughed violently. A thick plume drifted from the bong's mouthpiece, mixing with his rattling coughs.

After the fourth or fifth hack, his chiselled face was decidedly flushed. He looked at the bong with watering eyes, holding it at a distance momentarily, before putting it back to his mouth and breathing in deeply.

The last bit of death rattled down and he lowered the bong, holding his breath this time… but only for a few moments. When the smoke came out, it was via a fit of coughing.

Brad nodded, the smirk fading from his face. It was a pretty good effort, especially going back for the second toke after the first one had obviously tickled so bad.

"Fuck man, that's rancid," Dylan passed the bong back to him, its two glass chambers roiling with lazy grey smoke.

"Yep. There's gotta be somewhere we can score." Brad shook his head as his thumb pushed another pinch of death into the cone-piece.

He had a nice buzz on, but there was a trick with death: the proper high took a while to creep up on you but would plateau abruptly, so it was good to punch quick and hard at the start. That way, the buzz was stronger and lasted longer. After another cone, he should be pretty nicely baked in about ten minutes.

"Looks like you're gonna run out of that stuff pretty quick," Dylan noted.

Brad shrugged as he pulled the bong, more slowly this time. The second cone was easier, but the taste didn't get any better..

He waved the bong at Dylan.

"Want another one?" He said around a mouthful of slow smoke. No coughing this time.

"Fuck no. No thanks."

Brad nodded. "Should we go for a skate then?"

Dylan laughed his snarky laugh. "Do I look like a bloody skatie?"

"Fair enough man. Should we go for a walk then? Still wanna show me this spot?"

"Yeah, I suppose. It's just up the road a bit. Then I gotta go get ready for the fights man." He stretched, flexing his back and shoulders.

"Righto then."

Brad's skateboard was propped against the wall next to the house's back door. His rollies were still sitting on the kitchen bench, but he didn't want Dylan to come back in the house, so he pulled the heavy back door closed and locked the deadbolt.

Dylan led him back up South Street, to a driveway across from Monash Reserve. The driveway, its white cement smooth and new compared to the crumbling black bitumen of the footpath, led to a small carpark. Even though there was enough space for two dozen cars, it was completely empty. On the other side of the carpark, another short driveway led to Little Green Street.

As soon as he reached the smooth white cement, Brad dropped his deck and stepped on to it, cruising confidently up the drive. The carpark was flat and even, quiet and private. The cement was only a few years old at most. He didn't have to worry about being hit by a car or moved on by police or neighbours.

Not bad, he thought. *Not bad at all.*

"Oi!" Dylan called. He hadn't followed Brad up the driveway.

Brad twisted his hips and the board u-turned in a smooth arc. He gave Dylan the thumbs up.

"This is a sick spot man, thanks heaps for the inside knowledge."

Dylan nodded, then pointed up South Street. "I'm gonna keep going, start warming up."

"Knock em dead, man," Brad nodded, trying not to look too relieved. "Peace out."

"Yeah catch ya man."

Brad watched him go. Dylan walked with his chest puffed out, shoulders rolling, chin high, eyes squinting into the daylight. He walked like the whole world was watching.

"Wanker," Brad muttered, turning away.

There must be other people in this place. Other skaters. Other stoners.

He sighed, suddenly tired. Dylan was the first person he had hung with in weeks.

He pushed his deck around the carpark, his wheels grabbing at the cement with perfect friction.

Kick, push, kick, push.

His rhythm was solid, his legs strong, his balance fluid. He could ollie about a foot into the air from a standing start and about half that again when he was rolling. He landed about half of his kick flips and a third of his shuttles.

Kick, push.

There were a few long, smooth blocks of cement that lined the end of some of the parking space, ostensibly to stop people driving into the wooden fence behind them. If he came in at the same angle as a long jumper, he could ollie onto one of the blocks grind along it for almost a metre, then ollie off again. He hadn't quite landed the dismount – the skateboard would flick out at odd angles off the block, making it hard to land on and keep rolling – but he would get there.

Kick, push.

Why did we have to move here, mum? He breathed deeply, closed his eyes.

He knew why. It hurt to think about why. They had deserted their family home, the only home he'd ever known, and moved to a smaller city at the other end of the state for a why that he didn't want to think about at all.

Home was dad. Dad was gone.

He steadied himself with a deep breath. Then another. And another.

Then he took another deep, deep breath, filling his nostrils, and all thoughts of moving and mum and Kaji and Dylan and his safe, cosy bedroom back in Rosny disappeared.

His skateboard clattered. He stepped onto it without thinking.

A sweet, sickly smell was tickling the back of his throat.

A smell he knew very well.

Kick, push.

Weed. Lots of weed.

I'm imagining it.

He wasn't imagining it. The air was thick with the reek of sticky bud.

He ollied onto the block, feeling his skateboard's trucks grind perfectly along the cement, then popped the board up again, guiding it with the soles of his shoes. The board landed perfectly, rolling along the smooth cement with Brad perched solidly on top.

He had landed the trick, but he wasn't paying the slightest bit of attention.

The smell of weed was washing over him. It lingered in the carpark, fresh and tart, warm and boisterous, infusing the late summer afternoon.

Somebody was growing marijuana around here.

A lot of marijuana.

Brad grinned to himself.

Things are looking up.

Dylan

"You're back," Allan Campbell's voice was deep and flat, a rock dropped from a cliff. He stared at Dylan, his bushy eyebrows knitted together.

"Yeah," Dylan replied, nonchalant. "Is the big dog around?"

Allan's guttural, bottomless chuckle sounded like a helicopter warming up. His grin was a line of white in an oil and grease smeared face.

"We're all big dogs around here, mate." That easy grin flipped into a scowl. "Except *you. You're* a fuckin dandy."

Dylan tasted bile in the back of his throat and his hands were curling into fists, his jaw clenching.

Your turn will come, old man.

The thought was cottony, with no real strength behind it.

Allan grinned again, a genuine grin, complemented by a twinkle in his eye. There was a wrench in his hand, solid steel almost a foot long.

"Is he here or not?"

Before Allan Campbell could answer, the front door swung open and Ben Campbell came sauntering out. He peered at Dylan.

"You're stoned."

"No, I'm not."

"I know what you look like when you're stoned, and you're stoned."

"I'm *not.* I'm focused man. Fuckin ready to crack some skulls."

"Where's your boyfriend?" Ben asked.

"Who gives a shit."

Ben threw back his head and laughed. "Did he break up with you already?"

"Yeah *ha ha* dickhead. We smoked some death and he's gone for a skate."

"He actually shouted…"

"If you're gonna talk about drugs fuck off somewhere else and do it," Allan grated, rolling back under the deep-blue Plymouth. "Maybe go to *your* house and fuck things up there."

Ben snorted, but Dylan scowled at the old man's legs.

Your turn will come.

"Time to go anyway," he muttered. "They start straight after lunch."

"Righto," Ben poked a cigarette into the corner of his mouth. "Back soon, Dad."

"Not too soon," came the reply.

"What a prick," Dylan muttered when they were far enough away. "Must drive you up the fuckin wall."

"Nah, he's all right," Ben smirked. "He just likes to look tough."

"Should bring him down to the gym, then we'll see how tough he is."

Ben whistled through his teeth, shaking his head. "Reckon they'll let you fight?"

"Course they will." Dylan rolled his shoulders as he picked up the pace. "If we get there on time, come *on* man."

"That smells wicked," Ben was ignoring him.

The savoury scent of mince pies made Dylan's belly rumble, but he clenched his jaw and kept walking.

After I clean up at the fights, I'm going to the Inveresk for a counter meal and Benny can watch me eat the whole goddamned thing.

He shook his head. He couldn't think about food right now.

They walked. Houses and cottages were replaced by warehouses and workshops. They arrived at an open industrial block where a joinery, an auto-electrician, a gymnasium and a mechanic shared a small parking lot.

The lot was busy. Two rows of Harley Davidsons lined opposite side of the car park and more bikes and cars were pulling in as Dylan and Ben Campbell walked over.

The gym took up the entire top floor above the mechanic's workshops. It only had one entrance, a door at the back of the building.

Today, there were two men standing next to that door. Ray looked the same as he always did; scuffed tan leather jacket, neat brown slacks, combed *Brylcreem*, a yellow shirt that might have been white before it was subjected to Ray's pack-a-day smoking habit.

Ray was talking to a bikie twice his size. The bikie wore all black except for the bright red and white patches on his leather vest. The tattoos that covered his arms and neck were a monochrome gunmetal grey, making the patches stand out even more.

They two men broke off their conversation as Dylan and Ben Campbell approached. Ray was already shaking his head.

"The fuck do you two want?" The bikie grunted.

Dylan ignored him. "How you going Ray?"

"Yeah all right, Dylan, all right." The old man pulled a packet of Winfield Blues out of his leather jacket. "Can't let you in today though."

"What?" Dylan's stomach sank. "Why the fuck not?"

"Two hundred bucks entry," the bikie sneered. "You got two hundred bucks, pretty boy?"

"Bullshit," Dylan pouted. "I'm here to fight, mate. I don't fucking need to pay to…"

The bikie laughed, long and loud, twisting Dylan's gut. He clenched his fists and took a step towards the bikie.

Think I'm funny, you fat...

Abruptly Ray had seized Dylan by the arm and was pulling him away from the door. The smirking bikie crossed his arms over his chest while Ben Campbell shifted awkwardly.

"Don't be a fuckin half-wit," Ray said in his ear. "You gonna fight all the Marauders?"

"Why's he even here?" Dylan kept his voice low as well and let himself be led away. "It's *your* bloody gym, just let us in."

"Not today. It's the big one, Romeo Rohan versus Stick Mansell from the Henchmen. Fuckin bikies everywhere." He spat on the ground.

"You said I could get a fight."

"I said you *might* get a fight, one weekend, if you actually trained. *You* don't wanna fight these blokes." He took a deep drag on his smoke. "Anyway, he wasn't lying. It's two hundred bucks to get in."

"No way. What's the purse?"

"Ten grand." Ray chuckled when Dylan's jaw dropped. "They don't muck around mate. This is the real deal. Look."

He nodded towards the car park, where more bikies were arriving. Dylan recognised Pasco's old Rodeo ute, which looked rustier than ever next to the gleaming black Ford Mustang that pulled in beside it.

A lone Harley Davidson motorcycle followed them in.

A tall, tattooed mountain of a man, Rohan Murphy pulled the bike up next to the cars and killed the motor. After stomping down the kickstand, he climbed off the huge bike easily, his movements lithe and dangerous. If he was nervous about his upcoming fight, he showed no sign of it.

"Beautiful vehicles," Ray sighed wistfully. "*Jeez* they must have some coin."

"Listen, Ray," Dylan hunched down so he was closer to the old man's height. "Just let me in, so I can watch. Say I'm your helper or something."

Ray scowled at him. "I told you. Not today. Now piss off, I've got enough to deal with." He turned and walked back towards the door.

"Wait, Ray!" Dylan hissed.

The old man ignored him.

Ten grand. I'd fight bloody Tyson for ten grand.

The Mustang's door opened and Noah Murphy, leader of the Marauder Motorcycle Club, climbed out. Built like an ox and with the posture of a General, he scanned the car park and the entrance of the gym before slamming his door shut. He nodded as Rohan came over to join him and Dylan was struck by how much the younger Murphy resembled his father.

More bikies gathered around them. Pasco climbed out of his ute and quickly walked around to the passenger side of the Mustang, opening the bdoor.

Ben came over to Dylan, hands in his pockets.

"No go?"

Dylan spat. "Fuckin pussy won't let us in."

"Oh well. Maybe we should just head… oh yeah man, check it out."

A young woman was climbing out of the Mustang, her black skirt riding up to reveal a long pair of bare legs.

Pasco offered his hand and the girl took it, giving an easy laugh as he guided her to her feet. She cat-walked over to Rohan and he grinned, the expression out of place on his mean-looking head.

"Lily!" Dylan called, standing on his toes to wave at her.

Lily, Rohan, Noah, all the bikies, all turned to look at Dylan.

Rohan was frowning. Ray muttered something inaudible and turned away. Ben Campbell had his head down.

Dylan was oblivious.

"How's it going Lily?"

She rolled her eyes and looked away.

"Haven't seen you since school," Dylan continued. He took a few steps towards her, stopping at an awkward distance when a couple of the bikies glared. "What you been up to, Lily?"

She rolled her eyes again. "Growing up. Try it, little boy."

Dylan felt the blood rush to his face as the bikies guffawed around her. One of them handed her a bottle of champagne and she forgot about Dylan altogether.

"You said to wait until we got here and we're here, aren't we?" She laughed and waved the bottle at Rohan. "So can I open it?"

Rohan shrugged. "Knock yourself out."

"You're gonna knock *him* out baby," Lily purred as he slipped an arm around her waist. She was tall, but he was enormous. "Can you crack this for me?"

Rohan took the bottle from her and passed it to another bikie without looking at it. He was scanning the car park and the gym entrance, the gathering Henchmen. The other bikie peeled the foil from the champagne and got to work on the cork. When it was open, he handed the bottle back to Lily and the three of them walked over to the gym door, where Noah and Pasco were talking to Ray.

Ray was smoking his cigarette and nodding. Noah asked Pasco a question and the other senior bikie nodded, patting the bulging backpack that was slung over his shoulder.

Lily took a swig from the champagne bottle, offered it around to the men, then took another swig when they all declined.

More motorbikes were pulling in. All of the riders were wearing patches on their backs or sleeves – the confederate flag of the Marauders or the templar cross of the Henchmen.

"Jesus," Ben Campbell whispered. "It's the fuckin village fair. Let's get out of here."

"Not yet," Dylan frowned, then stood on his toes again. "Lily!"

"What are you doing?" Ben whispered.

"Lily!"

She ignored him, but Rohan and the other bikies looked over again. Ray looked as though he'd been goosed and refused to meet Dylan's eye.

Ben put a hand on his shoulder. "You're gonna get our arses kicked."

"Fuckin righto," Dylan muttered. "Was just gonna ask her to sneak us in."

Ben shook his head in disbelief. "Keep calling out to Rohan's girlfriend and you'll be the main event."

"I'm not scared of big fuckin Romeo Rohan."

"Then you're dumber than you look. Let's sit down, at least. I'm gonna roll a smoke."

They settled in.

Jake

"I don't want it." Boof threw the porno onto the grass between their feet.

"Nobody was giving it to you anyway," Reese clicked his tongue and swooped to pick the magazine up. He flicked a bit of dirt off the bottom corner. The dirt was moist and black and stuck to his fingers. "*I* flogged it. *You* fuckin got us caught."

They were standing on the side of Invermay Park, a sprawling, grassy sports ground with a roughly marked cricket oval. In the distance, the Railyard warehouses peeked over the trees. There were a couple of blokes in the cricket nets on the far side of the oval, but otherwise they had the park to themselves.

"We're not caught. Steph won't say anything. Are you still gonna give me the money?"

Reese groaned and slapped his head.

"Why wouldn't she dob us in?" Jake said.

"Steph's all right."

"She's narky as to me," Reese muttered.

"Yeah, but you're a knob." Boof appealed to Jake. "Give us ten bucks and you can take it, Cupcake."

"I own more of it than you do, Boof. I caught the goddamned thing. She saw *me* holding it."

"This is bullshit," Boof pouted. "I just wanna get a stick. Just give us ten bucks, Reese."

"I can't keep it now," Reese said, flicking through the pages again and shuffling from foot to foot. "I've got nowhere to hide it. You know what my olds are like, they'll sniff it out."

"Why did you want to bloody flog it then?"

"For love." Reese turned the magazine around, giving them a good eyeful of a double-page spread.

"Hide it in Elisha's room," Boof said.

"They go through her stuff more often than mine." Reese scoffed. He held out the magazine to Jake. "My room's tiny. You've got that big bedroom and all those sheds out the back."

"Seriously man, I don't want it."

"You do have heaps more space, baker boy." Boof said.

"Well, why don't *you* bloody take it?" Jake asked, nodding at Boof, already knowing the answer.

"Where would I put it? And Mum'd fuckin *whip* me if she found it. She hates stealing. Your mum might go off her face, but mine…" he shrugged.

Reese held the magazine out to Jake. "Yeah man, take it or Boof's mum will fuck him in the arse."

"Piss off Reese," Boof said. "I don't want it anyway. It's crap. All this…" he flapped a hand at the magazine. "…*smut*."

Jake and Reese looked at each other. They spoke almost as one.

"*Bullshit*."

"Nah don't get me wrong, I don't mind the Playboy chicks and whatever, you know, the *classy* stuff, but *this*… nup."

"As if." Reese was flicking through the magazine again. He chose a page, then turned it around to show them. "You reckon she's no good, Boofhead."

Boof chortled. "Well yeah, she's gorgeous. Like… yeah. But still, I…"

"*Boofhead!*"

Three of them spun as one. Tommy and Maynard were standing on the footpath opposite Invermay Park, at the foot of Ray Street's gentle hill. Tommy was tapping his foot, hands on hips.

"What?" Boof shouted back.

"Time to take your face off, the monkey wants its arse back!"

"*You're* a fuckin monkey."

Jake had gone very still. "Do you reckon Lorraine sent em to get us?"

Reece put a hand to his mouth. Boof's head sank.

"Steph wouldn't have said anything," Reese was shaking his head. "Lorraine couldn't know yet,"

Boof shot him a withering a look. "Of course she knows. She always knows. I'm fuckin dead."

"*Oi!*" Tommy yelled again.

"Yeah, righto!" Boof picked up his bike and started pushing it towards the fence.

Jake picked up his bike as well, then turned to look at Reese.

"Coming?"

"No." Reese looked at him blankly. "I'm not going there."

"Come on man. If she knows, she knows. We might as well own it." Jake looked pointedly at Boof, who was pushing his bike across the grass, dejected. "He'll fucking cop it way worse than us."

"Exactly. No thanks."

Jake scowled. "She'll tell your parents. You *know* she will. Probably already has."

"I'll take it from them. I don't want an earful from fuckin Lorraine as well. You'll get off the lightest, you go with him."

"I will… but I didn't offer him money to flog a fuckin porno, did I." Jake turned away, following Boof's tracks across the oval grass.

"You said you'd go halves," Reese mumbled, hauling his bike onto its wheels.

They mounted their bikes once they were through the park's iron gate and clear of the soft grass, cruising across Forster Street's wide lanes.

Suddenly Reese brightened.

"Check this out, fellas!" He wheeled his bike over to Boof's brother, holding out the magazine.

"Oh bullshit!" Tommy took the glossy porno, his face lighting up. Maynard tried to snatch it out of his hands, but Tommy turned away, fending him off. "Where'd you get this?"

"We got it," said Boof, a note of pride in his voice.

"*I* got it," said Reese, scowling at Boof.

"Is this what you knocked off from Sam's?" grinned Tommy, a glint in his eye.

Jake groaned and leaned on his bike's handlebars.

Reese shook his head. "*Fucking* Stephanie. She told your mum, didn't' she."

"It wasn't her," Tommy laughed as he flicked through the porno. "The bloke at the servo saw you all do a runner. Bloody hell, look at *this.*"

"Warren. Goddamn it." Jake's eyes rolled. *He'll tell mum too. And anybody else who'll listen.* "Did Lorraine go to Sam's?"

"She went in and bought some milk, but they didn't say anything to her."

"That prick who works there would have called the police if he thought we flogged something," Boof rubbed his stubbly chin.

"Stephanie *saw* me, for fuck's sake!"

"They didn't say nothing to mum," Tommy shrugged. "She just knows that you three bolted out of there."

Maynard snatched the porno out of his hands and started flicking through it.

"She doesn't know why?" Reese asked.

Tommy looked over Maynard's shoulder, only half-listening. "Nah. Just that you probably pinched something. How did you get this without them seeing?"

"Do you want it?" Reese asked.

Tommy and Maynard looked at Reese as though he might be crazy.

"Yeah, take it," Jake agreed. "Just ma…"

"Twenty bucks and you can have it," Boof interjected.

"Twenty bucks?" Tommy was outraged. "I could go and buy it for twelve."

"You don't have twelve bucks."

"But Maynard does," said Reese. "Don't you, paperboy?"

"You were just about to give it to us," Maynard pointed out. "Why should I buy it?"

"He wants to get a stick," Reese cocked a thumb at Boof.

"I've got five bucks already," Boof bragged. "I just need another twenty and I can go score."

"Yeah, I wouldn't mind a chuff actually," Tommy said thoughtfully. Maynard was watching him. "Especially now there's some actual good stuff to look at."

"All right, look." Maynard reached for his wallet. "I'll chuck in twenty. You give us half the stick. We'll keep the mag. What do you reckon?"

Boof was calculating, the strain of it written all over his face.

"Sounds good," said Reese.

"No worries," chuckled Tommy. "You better get back there, she's gunning for you. Tell her you flogged a fuckin lolly or something. Don't tell her you saw us."

"I'm not going home," Boof grinned as Maynard laid the twenty dollar note his hand. He scrunched it in his fist and shoved it into his pocket. "I'm going to see Magnus. Anyone wanna come for a ride?"

"I'm coming," Reese said quickly. "A quarter of that stick's mine. More than a quarter."

"Yours and Jakes," Boof said. "You coming, Cupcake?"

"Nah, I might go and eat something."

Reese frowned. "Come and get stoned with us, bitch."

"Maybe later on."

"We'll save you a bit," Boof lied.

"Should we meet you back here in like, half an hour?" Reese asked Maynard.

"What about back down the mill?" Tommy said.

Maynard clapped his hands. "Hell yeah! That's a primo spot for a joint!"

"We can try and get up on the roof."

"Where's this?" Reese asked.

The older boys gave them directions and, with the mission planned, they parted ways.

Brad

The clatter of his trucks, the spin of his wheels, the clack of his nose and tail. The savoury scent of succulent skunk. It all soothed his brain.

A little.

Brad kicked and pushed. His ollies were higher, his front-slides sharper. He had a good sweat on. His legs were tired and his t-shirt was damp.

He pushed into the shade and sat on his board, catching his breath.

The buzz from the death had long worn off. It never lasted long. He could cheat it out a bit with a cigarette though.

He patted his empty pockets and then hung his head, sighing; he had left his smokes at home. A flush of bright, uncomfortable frustration electrified his skin. He wanted more than a cigarette.

There's a crop around here. A decent sized one, too.

He eyed the fences that surrounded the carpark. They were all made of the same smooth grey seven-foot timber palings, with the crossbeams hidden on the side.

Hard to climb.

Hard… but not impossible.

He stopped and shook himself.

Jesus, dude. Are you that desperate? Jumping fences, looking for a crop to rip. That's the sort of shit…

He didn't want to finish the thought, but forced it to come anyway.

That's the sort of shit addicts do.

Sighing, he picked up his board and walked down the driveway, leaving the heavy scent behind. There was more death at home.

A few days off it will do you good. Maybe a few weeks.

He knew from experience that he had at least another three days of hard cravings before it began to be okay to not have any dope. A month before it was *really* okay, but…

Three days. He grit his teeth and kicked at weeds, skulking down South Street towards his house. *Three days.*

When he saw the silver Saab parked neatly in the carport, he stopped and scowled.

Mum's home early. He rubbed a dusty eye with the palm of his hand. *Fucking perfect.*

He paused next to the Saab and considered making a break for it. He could skate back into the town, go and check out the half-pipe in Royal Park…

But I don't have my rollies. They're sitting on the kitchen bench.

He groaned again. Maybe that's why he could hear cupboards slamming and crockery cracking about. She hated the fact that he smoked.

Steeling himself, Brad went inside.

She was blustering around between the breakfast bar and the sink, emptying a measuring cup full of rice into a plastic bowl, dropping the cup into the sink with a clatter. There was a pot steaming on one of the hotplates.

When she noticed him standing there, she froze, one hand on the bowl. After a long moment, she crossed the room and gave him a brisk peck on the cheek.

"Hello sweetness… oh Bradford, have you showered today?" Her nose, small and expressive, wrinkled at him.

He hadn't, but it didn't matter. "I've been skating."

"What a surprise." She rolled her eyes and walked back to the sink. "Did you hand your resume in at the skate shop like you promised?"

"They're closed today."

"They're *not* closed today, Brad, I drove past there on my way home from work and the door was *wide* open."

Her voice seemed to pass straight through his flesh and grate his bones.

He took another deep breath, flicked the kettle on and sat down.

"There's only a couple of weeks of holidays left. If I get a job now, I'll have to quit when school starts."

"College kids can have jobs, you know."

"I guess. Why aren't you at work?"

She didn't answer. There was a wooden chopping board laid out on the breakfast bar and she laid half a dozen spring onions across it.

"So what else were you up to today?" She asked, not looking at him. Her knife went up and down. The kettle rattled on the bench behind her.

He snagged his rollie pouch from the edge of the fruit bowl and started rolling a cigarette. She glared at his hands but - for once - didn't say anything.

"Just went for a skate."

"Well, I know that much. What else?"

"Nothing. Skated around the post office. Got some chips. Found a new spot just up the street where I can jam. Probably only on weekends though."

His rollie was done, seamlessly rolled, perfectly manufactured. He admired it in his fingertips.

"So you *did* go to the shop? Down on the main road just here?" She pointed towards the front door with the knife.

The pot on the hotplate was boiling now. So was the kettle. Steam drifted through the bright kitchen's late morning light.

"Yeah, I got some chips, but I only got to eat about half of…"

"From Sam's?" Her eyes were intent.

"What?

"Did you get the chips from Sam's?"

"They don't sell chips at Sam's. They don't do any hot food."

"Oh. Did you go in there though?"

"No. Why?" The kettle had flicked itself off, so he stood up and made his coffee - two teaspoons of instant, two teaspoons of sugar, an inch and a half of milk.

She watched him toss his teaspoon into the sink and sit down again.

"I heard the man at the service station talking about it just before I came home."

"And what did he say?" He stood again, parking the rollie in the corner of his mouth, picking up his coffee mug.

"Well… he saw some kids running out of the shop. Some boys. Running like they'd stolen something, then riding away."

She can't be serious.

Brad took the rollie back out of his mouth, unlit. His spine was tingling.

"And you thought it might be me."

She tossed her head back. He recognised the gesture, had seen it many times before. It reminded him of a flighty horse. It meant she was spoiling for an argument.

"That's *not* what I said, Brad."

"It's what you were thinking though."

"No."

"Bullshit."

"Bradford!"

He skolled the rest of the coffee, glaring at her all the while.

"The men were saying they saw some boys on bikes and I thought…"

"Bikes? I don't even *own* a fuckin bike, mum."

"I thought you might *know* something. Something that could help."

"Bull*shit.*"

"Brad, *please* don't speak to me like that."

"You think I'm a thief. Stealing eggs from the fuckin grocery shop."

"Brad, I *don't* think you're a thief."

"Then what? Why even bring it up?"

She turned away from him and poured rice into the boiling pot on the stove. Her shoulders hung, tired.

"It stinks in here."

"What?"

"It *stinks.* Like the old kitchen used to, whenever *you* ran out of dope."

He didn't have an answer for that.

"So I thought… maybe you didn't have any money and…"

"Junkie shoplifts to fund drug habit, I get it." She wouldn't look at him, so he leaned into it. *"Thanks,* mum."

She made a sound that was both a sob and a scoff. "I didn't mean it like that."

"Bullshit." He shoved his tobacco pouch and lighter into one pocket, his wallet into the other, and strode towards the hallway door.

She put down the tea-towel she'd been wringing and followed him towards the front door.

"Brad, the kitchen *reeks.* I hoped when we moved here that you might… but you could at *least* have the decency to do it outside so that *my house* doesn't smell like a wet bloody ashtray all the time…"

Her voice followed him through the front flyscreen door, which closed behind him with a bang. His skateboard was leaning against the wall next to front door. He scooped it up and jumped the three steps down to the path. By the time his mother reached the front door, he was already skating back up South Street.

Just a goddamned thief. A thief and a druggie.

He kicked, pushed, faster. When he reached the entrance to the carpark, he popped an ollie and stomped down a frontside powerslide that shot him smoothly up the driveway.

Ha, no way.

As pissed off as he was, he had nailed a trick that he usually struggled to land. The combination of sobriety and the adrenaline caused by another fucking ragging from his mother was doing wonders for his skating.

Druggie thief.

Brad threw himself into it.

His wheels were a constant hum. Every ollie was a few inches higher. Every kick flip slammed solidly into place. In no time, he was sweating again. Every manual was perfectly balanced. He hit flow state, he was in the zone, he was on point, he was not paying the slightest bit of attention to skating.

The smell of weed was heavy in the air, sweet and warm and homely.

It mixed with the sunshine, filling his lungs with delicious, teasing, empty scent.

On one hand, it was a balm for the burning in the back of his mind.

On the other, it was salt in the wound.
It smelled so *goddamned* good.

Stephanie

A loud cry bounced off the shop walls, startling her. Stephanie turned to see a young woman standing at the lolly counter. One of her hands rested on the handle of a worn-looking pram, while the other gripped an adorably blonde toddler by the wrist. It was the toddler who was shrieking. Shrieking and pointing at the *Freddo Frogs*.

The woman knelt next to the child, speaking intently into its ear. The baby shifted in the pram.

She's just a few years older than me.

Stephanie had tried to make herself invisible all afternoon, sticking to the fringes of the shop; the pet food corner, the storeroom, the shelves of packaging nestled behind the gifts and home décor.

David, on the other hand, seemed to have plenty to do; he hung around the aisles, at ease in his domain, rearranging the peaches, refilling the dairy fridge, weighing sausages.

But the young woman was heading for the lolly counter and Julie was nowhere to be seen, so Stephanie blew her fringe off her forehead, put down the tinned pineapple she was stacking, and summoned the friendliest smile she had.

Just keep going.

The toddler gazed up at her, blue eyes bright below blonde curls, its sticky fingers in its mouth. The baby sleeping in the pram was infinitely delicate, a few months old at most.

The mum bought a few things; milk, crumpets, mince, Winfield Blues, a small block of cheese. No *Freddo Frogs* though. Stephanie rung everything up - $13.20. Once the woman took the single tenner and three coins out of her purse, there was only a bit of silver left.

Nine hundred and forty-eight dollars.

"Hang on."

Stephanie snagged one of the little white paper bags hanging on a piece of string in the lolly cabinet.

She threw a couple of lollies from each tub into the bag, sat three *Freddo Frogs* on top, and handed it to the young woman.

The mum frowned; the toddler was already reaching for the paper bag, its eyes wide, its lips slack.

"I didn't ask for… I can't…"

"On the house," Stephanie said.

"Lolly mum?" said the toddler.

The woman shrugged. "Thanks."

"Mum!"

"They're your favourites, aren't they Danny." The woman selected a chocolate frog from the bag and handed it over. "What do you say to the lady?"

The kid didn't look up from its chocolate frog and the woman hustled it away, giving Stephanie a tired smile over her shoulder.

Stephanie watched them go, then sighed and went back to her tins of pineapple.

Julie reappeared from nowhere and went straight back to leaning on the lolly counter, humming *Cornflake Girl* and staring out into space, not lifting a goddamned finger to help restock the shelves.

Lazy cow, Stephanie thought, but the thought had no heat behind it. She didn't mind being busy and she didn't much feel like talking anyway.

She was glad Julie had taken the late shift.

Nine-hundred and forty-eight dollars.

Just quit. There'll be other jobs, jobs where the boss doesn't make your skin crawl. Maybe Roelf Voss. Or the Busy Bee.

But maybe there *wouldn't* be other jobs. She just didn't know. This was the only job she'd ever had.

She thought about the pile of coins clinking on her doona cover. About the Volkswagen, or maybe a Ford Cortina, or maybe a motorbike that rumbled the very ground. She thought about Dylan's greasy neck and David's small smile… or was it a sneer? She thought about a naked teenage girl with a greying naked man.

A tin slipped from her fingers and clattered off the stack, smacking onto the metal shelf and rolling. She reached for it, but too slowly; it fell to the floor, bounced on its edge, and disappeared under the bottom shelf.

"Crap."

She knelt on the floor and reached under the shelf, patting the dust here and there. The tiled floor was cold beneath her knees. She felt a power cord, and a few stray price tags, but no tin.

Concentrating, she reached as far as she could, her shoulder resting on the floor, and her fingertips brushed something small and hard.

Is that a coin?

She felt around. There were two other coins as well, two-dollar coins judging from the size of…

Suddenly there were legs standing in front her, just inches away. Standing *over* her.

She blinked in surprise and sat up on her knees.

It was David standing over her with that small smile, humming as though he had sipped a particularly fine wine.

Don't look at me like that, she wanted to hiss. *Don't look at me at all!*

"Stephanie," he drawled, his voice deep and relaxed.

He reached out and for one horrifying moment she thought he would stroke her cheek. Instead, he offered her his palm.

"Don't get yourself dirty." His eyes were on her lips. "I'll get it later with the vacuum."

Blushing, she took his hand and let him help her to her feet. He held onto her hand for a fraction too long… long enough for somebody's throat to clear, long enough for Stephanie to spring back, her cheeks burning.

Julie was at the end of the aisle, watching them, her eyes narrowed, her arms crossed.

Julie! Stephanie wanted to say. Nothing came out. *Julie, help!*

David's eyes flicked to Julie, then back to Stephanie. That small smile never faltered.

She wanted to slap it.

So fucking dumb!

He stepped smoothly around her and walked away. Julie's eyes narrowed as he approached but, if anything, her annoyed pout seemed to amuse him even more.

Stephanie pulled her ponytail tight, smoothing some of the loose strands behind her ears for good measure. Her cheeks were still hot.

She shuffled over to Julie.

"What a bloody creep," she murmured.

Julie raised a single sculpted eyebrow, harrumphed, and walked away.

Dylan

They could hear the progress of the fight in the cheers, jeers and heaves of the crowd. The entire building shook when the roars were at their loudest, the very walls stinking of sweat and blood and oil and men.

Dylan kicked a rock, frustrated.

I should be in there.

Being in the crowd would be good… but *he* should be in the ring. He knew it in his blood.

He lowered his boot onto a pebble of broken glass and twisted it, grinding it into the cement.

Ben Campbell was sitting on the concrete and squeezing at a blackhead on his shoulder. There was another cigarette hanging out of his mouth.

"You know those things'll kill you."

"Yeah. Want one?"

"Yeah."

The windows of the mechanic's workshop rattled in their frames. The big bikie, still standing at the door with Ray, was stretching. Ray was pacing back and forth, pausing occasionally to gawk at the black Mustang.

The roaring in the gym upstairs seemed to reach a crescendo, the screaming crowd hitting a fevered pitch.

The fight's almost done.

Dylan imagined what it would be like, standing in the middle of that ring, his taped-up fist held above his head by a short, neat referee. The crowd screaming for *him*. The bag of cash, handed to him while his fist was still raised, Lily rushing over to wrap one of those gorgeous legs around him

If only Luke was here to see it. His brother couldn't help but be impressed.

"Sounds like it's all over," Ben Campbell was looking up at the top floor.

The tone of the crowd had changed from fury to appreciation. There was cheering and applause. For a few minutes voices bubbled away indistinctly, then the gym door swung open and the crowd began to leave.

Most of the bikies nodded to the big bloke on their way out, while some of the others stopped to talk to Ray. A few of the men got into their cars or started their bikes, but more hung around, waiting.

"Come on," Dylan kicked Ben Campbell's foot. "Let's go and have a look."

Ray was talking to a solid young guy in a white t-shirt who frowned when the two teenagers approached. The old man was talking about a boxer he trained in the mid-eighties that nobody had ever given a fuck about.

"Ray," said Dylan.

The old bloke ignored him, still rattling on. Dylan scowled.

"*Ray.*"

Ray stopped, his mouth hanging open. The guy in the white shirt smirked, then clapped Ray on the shoulder and walked off. The old man watched him go with a frustrated grimace.

"Ray listen, can we go up and…"

Ray drove a hard finger into Dylan's chest.

"Now you listen *here,* you little…"

He was interrupted by sudden cheers and clapping.

Rohan had emerged through the gym door, pulling tape off his fists. There was blood on the tape – a considerable amount of blood – but Rohan himself looked unscathed aside from a small cut below one eye. His shirt was pulled open to reveal the sweat and scarlet-flecked tattoos on his chest.

"*Onya Rohan!*"

"Nice work mate."

"Shouldn't fuck with Romeo Rohan!"

Rohan grinned and pumped a fist and they cheered and clapped. Most of the bikies nodding and raising beers to him wore Marauders patches, but there were a few Henchmen in the mix. Another round of cheers went up when Noah stood next to Rohan and put a meaty arm around his son.

"What do you fuckin want?" Ray said to Dylan, his voice low.

"Just wanted to know who won."

"Rohan cleaned him up," said Ray, his eyes scanning the crowd.

"Yeah no shit."

"Yeah well, piss off then with your stupid bloody questions."

Ray shoved past him and lurched towards the gym door, almost colliding with two men who were exiting together. Ray stepped aside to let them past, his eyes low.

Dylan quickly turned his back to the door before either of the men could recognise him. He seized Ben Campbell's shoulder to spin him around too.

"The *fuck*?" Ben said.

"Shut up," Dylan said, looking back over his shoulder. The men hadn't noticed him. "Look, it's that prick who was at your house before. The Sergeant."

"So?

"He's a bloody *cop*. What the fuck is he doing here?"

"He's not a cop you dickhead, he was at my house."

"Yeah and your mum called him *Sarge.*"

"So?"

"So he's a fucking cop!"

"Who gives a shit?"

"I reckon *they* would," said Dylan, nodding at Rohan and Noah and the other bikies.

"Don't," Ben frowned. "Let's just get out of here."

"Bullshit," Dylan laughed, incredulous. He lowered his voice, watching the two cops. They were in the carpark now, leaning on the hood of a white Commodore, smoking and conferring. "I reckon Noah would *love* to know that there are a couple of dirty pigs here."

This time it was Ben Campbell's turn to grab *his* shoulder.

"Just wait a minute, there might be…"

The gym door swung open again. This time three men came out.

Stick Mansell must have been close to seven feet tall. He was a giant mess;

both eyes were swollen shut, blood was smeared across his chin and lips and cheeks, and he walked hunched over as though his ribs were in pain. The Henchmen on either side were both propping him up and guarding him. They guided him toward the car park.

Jesus. Rohan made a mess of him.

Some of the Marauders called out to the bleeding giant.

"Bloody *top* show mate."

"Good on ya, Stick."

"Next time, buddy, next time."

Stick Mansell's head rolled on his neck. Whether or not he heard their commiserations was anyone's guess.

Rohan and Noah watched the trio limp away before turning back to their raised beers. Hands were still clapping Rohan on the back and Noah was grinning widely.

There was another bang as the gym door opened again – Stick Mansell wasn't the only one being carried out.

Lily's long calves bounced on Pasco's thick forearms, a ragdoll with her head resting on the strap of his backpack. He swung her effortlessly through the doorway.

"Christ," whispered Ben Campbell. "She's hammered."

"You're not wrong."

Lily's eyes were open, but glassy and out of focus. There was something on her lips.

She must have puked.

They watched as Pasco quietly carried her through the crowd back to the Mustang. Neither Rohan or Noah paid them any attention... but the two cops certainly did. Their heads turned, following the progress of the old bikie with the semi-conscious teenage girl in his arms.

"Come on," Dylan hit Ben in the arm. Without waiting to see if Ben would follow, he marched over to the Mustang where Pasco was lowering Lily onto the backseat.

Pasco saw him approaching and scowled.

"Get out of here, you little shit!"

"Wait…" Dylan started but Pasco took a couple of steps towards him and growled.

"She told you to fuck off and now you think you can catch a bloody eyeful, why don't I…"

"Wait, Pasco!" Dylan was backing away, his hands held up defensively. "I gotta tell you something."

Pasco sneered, but he stopped advancing. "What do *you* gotta tell me?"

Dylan swallowed. Ben hadn't followed after all. He was standing back, watching with his arms crossed.

Bloody Mummy's boy.

Dylan stepped closer to Pasco, lowering his voice.

"Don't look, but those two blokes leaning on the white car… you know them?"

Pasco's eyes narrowed, but he didn't look in the men's direction. "Do *you* know them?"

"Yeah," Dylan lowered his voice even more. "I've seen em before, just today. Heard someone call the tall prick Sergeant."

Pasco blinked at him. "Sergeant?"

Dylan nodded. "That's what she said. Called him Sarge, Sergeant. Mouthy fuckin pig, he is."

Pasco's eyes never left Dylan's face. His voice was low and serious. "You reckon he's a cop."

"Yep. Both of them."

Pasco sighed, exhaling through his nose like a bull. "You sure, boy?"

Dylan swallowed. He was pretty sure, so he nodded.

"They're cops."

Pasco swore and shook his head. He chewed his lips for a moment, then seemed to come to a decision.

"Right. Wait here." He walked back towards Noah and Rohan. "And *don't* look in that fuckin back seat."

Ben Campbell was shaking his head when Dylan walked back over to him.

"The fuck did you say?"

"Told him who they are," he resisted to urge to sneer in the cop's direction.

"Dickhead!" Ben grabbed Dylan's arm in a tight grip. "You didn't tell him they were at my house, did you?"

Christ, Benny's stronger than he looks. "I'm not a bloody idiot."

"Aren't you?" Ben let him go, but he looked pissed.

"What's your problem man," Dylan leaned in close. "He's just a dirty pig."

"A dirty pig who knows where I live. And you too, remember? He knows your fuckin name."

Oh shit. He *had* forgotten about that. *It doesn't matter.*

"He won't know it was us."

Pasco was conferring with Noah and Rohan, the three big men nodding and giving the two cops the side-eye. After a moment, Noah waved over another big bikie, this one wearing a Henchmen patch. He joined their discussion for a few moments, then patted Rohan on the back and went back to his crew.

None of them looked at the two men in the car park, not even a glance, but Rohan was rolling up his sleeves. After a few moments, several bikies quietly gathered around him, Marauders and Henchmen both.

"Let's get the fuck out of here," Ben Campbell said quietly. "Come on man."

"What? Bullshit! I wanna see what happens!"

Ben grimaced and spat on the ground while Dylan bounced on his toes.

Noah spoke into Rohan's ear. The younger bikie laughed and took something out of his back pocket; a yellow envelope. He twirled a finger at Pasco to turn around, then put the envelope into the front flap of the other bikie's black backpack. He zipped it up tightly and clapped Pasco on the shoulder. Noah nodded and handed Pasco his car keys.

The stout runabout nodded his goodbyes and walked back over to the Mustang, giving Dylan the barest glance as he passed, then climbed into the driver's seat.

Yeah thanks, no worries, thought Dylan, but the sourness was faint. He was pleased.

Pasco would remember – Dylan had done the Marauders a solid.

Mad bastard owes me one.

The Mustang's engine roared to life. Most of the shaved and tattooed heads in the carpark turned to watch Pasco drive across the gravel and turn slowly onto Herbert Street.

"Spin 'em *up*, Pasco!" A lone voice called out.

Noah frowned, unimpressed. Nobody else egged the Mustang on.

As soon as the growling car was out of sight, Rohan and four of the bikies turned, their faces intent, gravel crunching beneath their brisk boots.

By the time the two cops saw them coming, it was already too late.

Without breaking his stride, Rohan stretched out like a champion fielder making a long-distance throw… then his fist rocketed forward and smashed into Sarge's face.

A sickening *crack* rang out through the car park.

Sarge dropped like a stone.

The other man – the other *cop* – stumbled back with a shocked expression.

"What the *fuck* are you…" he subsided, wide-eyed, as bikies surrounded him.

Sarge, dazed, tried to sit up but Rohan stood over him, bent at the waist, glaring down with fire in his eyes.

"Fuckin *pig!*" He kicked Sarge in the ribs with a dull thud. "I said, are you a fuckin *pig?*" He drew back his foot to kick again.

"He's not a cop!" The other cop shrieked in a high, shaking voice. "We were invited here for the…"

"Shut the *fuck* up!" Rohan pointed a finger at the man's chest, but his eyes didn't leave Sarge on the ground. "Give me your wallet."

"What?" Sarge's voice was faint. He raised a hand in front of his face. "I don't…"

Rohan punched him and the cop's head was driven into the gravel with the sound of an egg cracking.

Dylan clapped his hands together, almost dancing on the spot. "Yeah! *Fuck* yeah!"

"*Stop! He's not a cop!*" The other cop yelped.

"Fuckin bullshit," Rohan muttered. He seized Sarge by the hair, lifting his head, raising his fist.

"*No!*" The other cop lunged… but the bikies were waiting for it. A knee thudded heavily into his side and when he bent over, a fist slammed into the side of his head. The cop's knees buckled, but he managed to stay on his feet, wheezing. "Get *off* him, you fuckin…"

"Clean him up, Rohan!" Dylan snarled. He had wandered closer, could see the gravel dust mixing with the cop's blood. "Fuckin *kill* the prick!"

One bloody fist raised, the other gripping Sarge's hair, Rohan looked over and met his father's eyes.

Noah gave a single, deliberate nod.

The cop's partner thrashed against the tangle of tattooed arms that held him back.

Rohan's fist came down, smashing into Sarge's face with a sickening, wet splatter.

The poartner, grunting wordlessly now, slammed his heel down on one of the bikie's feet and was rewarded with a yowl of pain. The arms around him loosened for a moment, and that was all it took - the cop swung an elbow, catching another bikie's throat, and suddenly he was free. He advanced on Rohan, who still had Sarge's bloody head in his grip.

"Shit!" growled Dylan. *"Fuck!"*

Curling his fists, he charged.

There was a flash of surprise across the cop's face but he recovered instantly, lifting a foot to catch Dylan squarely in the chest.

"Ooof!"

Dylan was lifted off his feet, his chest collapsing inwards. He fell backwards onto the gravel, landing with a yelp of pain, trying to breathe. Through blurry eyes he saw the cop throw a punch at one of the bikies.

Dylan snarled, despite the pain. Moving stiffly, he lifted himself onto an elbow and was about to climb to his feet when a pair of rough hands seized him under the armpits.

"Fuck *off,* Benny!" Darcey wheezed. "Let me *go,* you fuckin…"

But it wasn't Ben Campbell picking him up off the ground. Ray was dragging him to his feet, away from the fight.

"Stupid fuckin *boy,*" the gym owner was hissing in his ears. "Get out their way."

The bikies had surrounded the panting cop, who was crouched into a fighting position, his eyes darting wildly around the circle that was closing around him. Sarge lay on the ground a few feet away, motionless. Rohan's fist was dripping scarlet.

"Let me *go!*" Dylan kicked and tried to roll out of Ray's grip, but the old bloke's hands were immovable. "Ray, let me *help* em!"

"They don't need *your* help boy."

"Let me *go!*"

Ray clapped him around the back of the head and Dylan's skull rang out. "*Ow!*"

"Shut up! Stay out of the way!"

The cop threw a couple of desperate punches, which the bikies easily dodged. When he tried to grapple the nearest Marauder, another one stepped up and punched him, *hard*, in the back of the head.

The cop sank to his knees and Rohan drove his heavy boot into the man's face.

The bikies all took a step back as the cop collapsed, boneless, onto the gravel.

There was a moment of silence.

Then the bikies began to chuckle and clap each other on the back.

Ray's hands loosened and Dylan shrugged them off, spinning to face the old man.

"What the *fuck* did you do that for?" His breath was coming back, but his chest still hurt like hell. "I was gonna..."

"You were gonna get your arse kicked," Dylan growled, unimpressed.

"Bullshit," Dylan spat.

Some of the bikies glanced over.

Ben Campbell was saying something in his ear, but Dylan ignored him.

"*I* fuckin spotted them. *I* could have sorted them out."

"You reckon?" Ray grinned, but it was a mean grin. "You're not your brother, little Dylan."

"Dylan?" One of the bikies said. "Luke Dylan?"

Rohan was watching now too as he walked back over to join his father.

He was rubbing his right fist, smearing the cop's blood over his knuckles.

Ben Campbell was pulling at his shoulder, but Dylan ignored him. He spat on the ground.

"Luke's me brother."

"That fuckhead who ran over the little kid is *your* brother?" The bikie sneered, crossing his arms. "Big tough cunt, he was. I heard they put him in a skirt. I heard he's the loosest bitch in Risdon."

The other bikies laughed.

Fury rushed over Dylan. His cheeks burned. He bared his teeth and snarled.

"He'd put *you* in a coffin, asshole."

The bikies laughed again.

"Let's go man," Ben was whispering. "Just leave it, let's *go!*"

"Get him out of here, for fuck's sake." Ray was shaking his head.

Dylan scowled at the bikies but let Ben led him away. Rohan watched them go with his eyes narrowed.

Ray followed them over to the edge of the carpark, fists on his hips.

"You never let me fight, Ray," Dylan was complaining. His chest was throbbing now and moving made it worse. "You're a fuckin old woman."

"And you'll be a fuckin dead dickhead if you don't smarten up," Ray hissed. "Just get out of here… and stay away for a few weeks."

"What? Where am I supposed to train? What about the fights?"

"Come back when you've got some *hair* on your balls and *brains* in your skull. And stay away from the Marauders, you fuckin halfwit."

Dylan spat between the old man's feet and stormed away.

Maynard

The cigarette was burning his fingers, so Maynard flicked it. It skittered across the cement of his backyard like a white cricket, bouncing this way and that. He stared at it, trying to ignore the thin film of sweat that kept forming above his lip, the butterflies in his stomach, the… the other feeling.

He shuffled uneasily on the back doorstep.

Think about something else, anything else.

Looking off at the treetops in the distance didn't help. The hardness in the front of his jeans felt permanent, implacable.

Just don't fucking stare. Don't stare!

On the other side of the yard, Tommy was sitting on the cement and leaning back against the shed. He was engrossed in the porno. Engrossed and… aroused. He made no effort to hide it, stretching out his legs, pointing his hips at the sky.

Maynard scraped the back of his Puma sandshoes on the concrete, trying to stop his eyes from flicking back to that… to that… *to that bulge.*

He shivered.

What if I could… what if I could just…

"Jeeeesus," Tommy drawled suddenly. His cheeks were flushed, his eyes lidded as if he were already stoned. He turned the magazine around so Maynard could see. "Look at this!"

The picture was a mid-shot of three women. They were all topless and tanned with high perms and bubble fringes. The one in the middle held up a white soft-serve ice cream in a classic waffle cone while the other two pushed their tongues against it.

Maynard let out a soft whistle.

"Bloody lucky ice cream," Tommy nodded, turning it back around.

I can't take it.

"Maybe we should head off," Maynard said with a dry mouth. "Boof and Reese will be down there soon."

"Yeah," Tommy nodded, obviously reluctant. "Yeah I suppose. Wish I could take this home."

"Don't reckon Lorraine would be too impressed."

"She can fuck off," Tommy muttered. "Where will you put it? Under your bed?"

Maynard laughed, standing. "No, Christ. Mum'd kill me. Come in here."

He drew the steel deadbolt on the shed door and waved Dwayne inside. The shed was of a decent size, lined with a long workbench on one side and a peg rack of rusty tools on the other. Maynard's grandfather had been a carpenter - and a good one - but had never taught his daughter or grandson any part of his trade and so the tools hung out here, abandoned.

Out of place in the old workshop was a stack of clean looking cardboard boxes, some odd pieces of furniture wrapped in clear plastic, some rolled rugs in a stack, more tools, cartons and garbage bags. There was a weight bench that looked brand new and a long steel cabinet with a lock on its handle.

Greg's stuff. Maynard's new stepdad had moved in over a year ago, but half of his belongings were still sitting here unpacked. Greg wasn't his mum's first boyfriend; it might be years before his model cars and Richmond posters made their way into her house.

Greg was a short, energetic bloke with a bald patch and a big mouth. He never seemed to hold down any jobs for long, but he didn't have trouble getting new ones either.

He's good at first impressions, Maynard's mother had said once. *But that just makes everything that comes afterwards so much more of a disappointment.*

Maynard reached up and touched the top of a skinny wardrobe that sat in the corner of the shed. He ran his fingers along the top, then blinked at the thick dust on his fingertips.

"Don't put it up there," Tommy scoffed. "It'll get fuckin filthy."

"It's already filthy," Maynard said. "It's just a bit of dust."

Tommy clicked his tongue. He looked around the shed, then reached down to the long steel cabinet and tried the handle.

"You won't get that open, it's Gre…"

But the cabinet *did* open, the steel door swinging easily on well-oiled hinges. Maynard stared, lost for words.

How have I never tried to open that? It didn't matter.

There were three rifles in the cabinet.

Three sticks of gleaming iron and polished wood.

"*Fuck me,*" Tommy breathed. "Look at the firepower!"

They were Greg's hunting rifles, used for exactly one week a year when Greg would join his brothers in the chase for stags out near Karoola.

"Buggered if I knew that cabinet was unlocked," Maynard said, eyes wide. "I don't reckon Greg's noticed. The old bird would lose her mind."

"We should bring one with us," Tommy said, excited. "We could set up some targ…"

"Nope," Maynard said quickly, shaking his head.

"Come *on,* man!"

"No fuckin way!"

"Come on, just a couple of shots each."

"It'd be way too loud," *And I'd get the blame.*

"Bullshit," Tommy scoffed, but his grin never faltered. That grin was contagious, even when he was disagreeing with you. "Not at the mill. Remember that big room, the warehouse? No one's gonna hear it."

"What about all those houses down there? *All* of them would hear it."

"Nup."

"Course they would. A twenty-two's not quiet."

"They're not *that* loud."

"How many times have you fired one?"

Tommy chuckled again, but it was tinged with embarrassment now.

"Heaps of times."

"Yeah bullshit. How many times?"

"All the time, every day."

"You've never shot a fuckin gun in your life, swamp donkey." Maynard clicked his tongue, shaking his head. "You couldn't shoot in a sock."

"That's why we've gotta do it! We can't get out bush, the Railyards are too close to town, there's always people at Invermay Park, Heritage Forest is too quiet… that mill is fuckin perfect!"

"Yeah. Until we get caught and I lose Greg's rifle. He doesn't even know I know about them."

"Then he'll never know it was missing. We'll just put it back before he gets home. Easy."

"And what about the bullets? He'll notice they're gone."

"He won't notice two bullets. Look, there's a few boxes of them in here."

"Two shots you reckon."

"One shot each, in the warehouse. Just to have a crack."

"They'll hear it all the way down in bloody Riverside. The cops will be there in five minutes."

Tommy rolled his eyes. "Nobody's gonna call the cops. There's factories all round there. They'll all be used to loud noises."

He's right. Maynard sighed. *He's always right.*

"We should go now," said Tommy, watching him carefully. "Before people start knocking off from work."

"Now?"

Tommy shrugged again and grinned again.

"Why bother? You wanna say you've fired a gun?"

"Don't you? How many times have *you* fired one?"

Maynard looked into the distance, grimacing.

"Exactly. None. Don't you want see what it's like?"

Yep, Maynard thought. *I do.*

"Course you do." Tommy rolled his eyes. Without warning, he punched a hard fast fist into Maynard's bicep. The sound of it cracked across the roof as Maynard gasped and grabbed his arm.

"Oh you *prick!* You *little shit!*" Maynard spat. A grin was spreading on his face despite his throbbing arm. Tommy was laughing, leaning back into it.

"Sting like a butterfly."

"Sting like a fuckin piss-ant…"

Tommy brandished his fist again, eyes wide. Maynard turned to face him, raising his own knuckles.

They faced off, grinning, dancing around each other in a small circle, ducking and jabbing, faking this way and that, swinging slow roundhouses and twitchy uppercuts, scowling and laughing.

They had never fought for real, *would* never fight for real. In a *real* fight Tommy would have torn him to pieces and they both knew it.

In desperation, Maynard threw his arms around the taller boy and pushed with his shoulder, almost lifting Tommy off his feet. Tommy laughed and wrapping his thick arm around Maynard's neck in a tight headlock.

Maynard wriggled and gasped, but Tommy's grip was far too tight.

"All right, all right!" Maynard tapped Tommy's forearm and Tommy let him go, chuckling.

"Dead in two minutes."

"Stunk to death," Maynard wheezed. His head was filled with Tommy's musk. His hardness was back with a throbbing vengeance. "Try it again and see what happens."

But Tommy was done wrestling.

He bent down and picked up the rifle, cradling it reverently.

"To hell with Greg." That infectious grin.

He held the rifle out to Maynard, a twinkle in his eye.

"Let's go and have some fun."

Maynard couldn't help but grin back.

Brad

He pushed his board to the far side of the carpark, where the tall timber fence made some shade. Fishing out his tobacco pouch, he leaned back against the fence, as cool as a cat.

Brad had seen only a few living marijuana plants over the years, most of them immature or half-dead things his old friends had grown in their backyards or bedrooms... but he knew that heady scent, that savoury tang.

Near the fence the smell was even stronger, *riper*, more enticing, teasing at his brain with its familiarity, its promise of numb contentment.

There *had* to be plants growing in one of these yards.

I'm a druggie, not a thief.

It smelled *so... so... fucking amazing.*

It's Saturday afternoon, maybe there won't be anyone home.

He shook his head and lit his smoke.

It's not worth it. Magnus will come through. He pulled a sharp, gusty draft through his nostrils. Smoke drifted up from between his fingers. The taste of tobacco with only a ghostly hint of weed... *goddamn it.*

He propped his skateboard against the timber fence, wheels facing out, to use as a makeshift stepladder. Balancing carefully, he stepped on to the trucks, then pulled himself up.

The backyard he peered into was a concrete rectangle with a Hill's hoist, a white plastic picnic table and little else.

Not it. He climbed down.

The place next door was different. A green Colourbond shed filled most of the backyard, a double garage, or maybe a workshop of some kind. There was a three-foot gap between the shed and the fence he was perched on that made an alleyway lined with bluestone. There were no windows or doors along the back of the shed, but the whole building was wrapped in a sharply sweet scent.

This is it. There are plants in that shed.

He stepped down from his skateboard and moved along the fence a bit before climbing up again.

From here, he could see that the shed had a closed door on this side, but still no windows. A concrete path led from the shed to the back door of a ramshackle weatherboard house which filled the entire front of the block; there appeared to be no access to the backyard, save through the house itself. The shed wouldn't be visible at all from the street and could only be seen from behind it if you climbed up the fence using a skateboard for a stepladder.

Out of sight, out of mi...

Suddenly a series of hollow metallic clanks rang out from the shed, followed by the sliding rattle of a steel deadbolt. The shed door opened. A large shape emerged.

Shit!

Brad ducked behind the fence, desperately keeping his balance on the skateboard.

He heard heavy footsteps. A man coughed and cleared his wet throat.

He'll hear me. Head down, fingers lightly gripping the top of the fence, Brad held his breath. *He'll see me.*

Footsteps moved away from him towards the house.

Brad waited a moment then slowly lifted his head to look over the fence, just in time to see a man's wide back disappearing into the weatherboard house.

The shed door was wide open. A padlock hung impotently from its latch.

Now or never.

Never. You're not a junkie, or a thief. Never.

But the smell drifting from that shed door was rich and ripe and warm and sweet.

He followed it over the fence.

The bluestone path with a crunched beneath his sneakers when he landed. The moment he touched the ground, a sense of *otherness* came over him; he was an intruder here, an interloper, out of bounds, beyond the pale. Adrenaline tingled through his limbs and made his heart race. His senses were electrified, his breathing uneven.

I shouldn't be here.

But here he was, creeping and silent and starting to sweat.

The smell of dope was thick and cloying and it mixed with his surging blood to make his head light and his body weightless. As if in a dream, he crept over to the open shed door and slipped through it with a glance at the weatherboard house,

Fast, I've gotta move fast... oh, fuck me.

The plants were *magnificent.*

There were maybe twenty in all, tall and green and bursting with life, a jungle neatly arranged on orderly wooden trestles, serrated leaves and thin stalks and clumps of nuggety, sticky-looking flowers.

This is a serious fucking setup. This is industrial.

He tried to take it all in – the bright rectangular lights blazing above the luscious cloud of greenery, the water tanks with pipes and hoses, the manicured branches hanging by the dozen at the back of the...

The girl sleeping on the black vinyl couch.

Brad froze, his heart in this throat.

She might have been a Greek statue. Pale and motionless, her elegant fingers dangled off the side of the couch. Her long hair was spread over a *Pantera* singlet, her black skirt was crumpled, her legs long and strong. Her lips were dry and cracked and her eyelids were so dark they looked bruised. If she was older than him, it wasn't by much.

She's gorgeous.

His breath was stuck in his chest. He couldn't move.

If she opens her eyes, I'm dead.

Blood pounded in his veins and his ears. He waited.

She didn't open her eyes.

This is bad. Get out of here.

It took some effort to look away from that ticking timebomb of a sleeping beauty.

There was a coffee table near the couch with a bunch of empty glasses, an overflowing ashtray, a tall four-chamber bong and a small set of digital scales... but no bud. A black backpack was leaning against the table, presumably the girl's.

He scanned the shed without moving. The huge plants were flowering and ripe, but it would be weeks before the buds were dry and ready to smoke. There were seedlings on a shelf near the back that were months away from even flowering.

There's gotta be something smokable in here, quick!

On the workbench at the side of the shed sat a stack of pots, pruning shears, wire and bamboo, more scales and scissors and a giant wooden toolbox. The toolbox had a padlock on the front – an unlocked padlock. He tiptoed over to it.

No way, no fucking way...

Swallowing, Brad reached out a gentle hand and unthreaded the padlock from the box's latch. With another glance for sleeping beauty, who hadn't stirred, he pushed the latch open and lifted the wooden lid.

Sandwich bags, dozens of sandwich bags, each one of them stuffed with dried, cured, sticky, stinky marijuana. The dope was pale green with crystalline orange hairs, nuggety and dense, carefully trimmed and packed.

Brad exhaled. Some of the tension dissipated from his body.

There was – *finally* - a bud in hand.

Grab it and go. Go!

But there was far too much to shove in his pockets. Too much to carry and jump a fence with. His throat clicked with dryness as his eyes settled on the girl's backpack.

Sorry, gorgeous.

Creeping on his fastest, lightest tippy-toes, Brad gently picked up the girl's bag. Her eyes didn't flicker. The deep rhythm of her breathing didn't change.

He stepped away again – the backpack was lighter than he expected – and pulled open the zipper without thinking.

The zipper rasped loudly, like a record scratching, piercing the silence of the shed.

There was a sigh, and the couch creaked.

Brad froze, his heart in his throat.

To his horror, the girl shifted and stretched.

Then her eyes opened and fixed on him.

Those green eyes, bleary with sleep, blinked a couple of times, looking him over. Her breathing settled back into a calm rhythm. A slow smile touched her lips.

"Cute," she murmured.

Her eyes closed again, but the soft, sleepy smile remained.

Brad shivered in disbelief.

Cute? Me?

A hysterical laugh bubbled behind his lips.

Abruptly he could feel his feet again. He shook his head to clear it and stepped lightly back to the wooden toolbox.

He was careful putting the first couple of sandwich bags into the backpack but moved more and more urgently with each handful.

Five bags… eight bags… *there must be more than a pound here…* eleven… *maybe I should leave a few.*

But his hands were moving too quickly, his blood pumping too loudly… and then the toolbox was empty. The backpack zipped up smoothly and slipped easily over his skinny shoulder.

In for a penny. Time to go.

He spared a last glance for sleeping beauty, trying to fix her in his mind, hoping he might see her again someday and praying that he wouldn't.

Cute. She said I was cute.

Smiling, he turned to leave… and froze.

A German Shepard, sleek, huge and powerfully built, was sitting in the shed doorway watching him, its head cocked, its eyes fixed.

It probably weighs more than I do. For a moment, he though he might be sick.

The dog stood up and Brad's mind went blank.

Time slowed down.

The monster padded over to him, its muscular bulk shifting beneath thick, healthy fur.

Brad didn't move, didn't blink.

Its big muzzle pressed against his hand, snuffling into his palm.

Red collar. Midget. Suddenly, he could breathe again. *No chips for you this time, girl.*

Slowly, ever so slowly, Brad ruffled the dog's ear.

She grinned at him, her tongue hanging out.

The shaking in his hand subsided as it became clear that she wasn't going to rip it off. She snuffled at his palm again and he stroked her, the gentlest pat any good girl ever got. Brad's knuckles were suddenly limber, his fingertips soft and familiar, and he channelled all the love he could muster from the universe down his arm directly into the fucking dog's goddamned skull.

You're gonna let me past, aren't you girl, such a goo...

The dog abruptly spun around and tore away, her paws clattering over the concrete as she clambered out of the shed.

Go. Go!

Brad's legs were weak, but they moved.

Two steps brought him to the shed door. He poked his head out, eyes wide; the dog had sprinted to the house and was skipping around.

Somebody was coming.

GO!

With the strange, delicate gait of a ballerina, Brad leaped towards the fence as fast as he could, the back of his neck tingling.

Almost there, almost there...

"Oi! *Oi!*" A door slammed. "You little *fuck!*"

Barking abruptly filled the air, followed by the quick click of paws.

"Get 'im Midget!"

Pasco. Mad bastard.

Brad's stomach turned to water. No longer sneaking, he threw himself at the fence in full flight and scrambled up as quickly as he could.

"Fuckin *get 'im!*"

Oh shit oh shit oh...

A deep, angry growl became a snarl as Midget closed in on his dangling foot.

Bloody turncoat.

Brad threw a skinny leg over the top of the fence, looked up for just long enough to meet the eyes of the huffing, red-faced bikie who was furiously ambling towards him... then let himself fall.

He slammed into the dirt a few feet away from his skateboard. The wind was knocked out of him, but only for a moment – he had taken enough dives to shrug this one off.

Midget slammed into the other side of the fence, barking and growling, her paws scratching for purchase on the timber. Furious barking filled the air, punctuated with curses and shouts.

Brad pulled the backpack tight on his shoulder, snagged his skateboard and *ran.*

He sprinted for the nearest exit, carrying his board; this was no time for skating on gravelly footpaths.

Shit wrong way!

The other exit would have spat him out not far from his house, but it was too late to turn back. As he dodged around the boom gate and onto Little Green Street, he glanced back the way he had come.

Midget was barking furiously, but nobody was watching his retreat.

Pasco's a mad bastard... but he couldn't climb the fence, the fat fuck.

Without a back gate, it would take the bikie a few minutes to get around the block.

Go. Get home now.

Brad jogged towards Bryan Street. If he could make it to South Street he could skate at speed. He would be safe at home before Pasco even made it to the corner.

Get home and fucking stay there.

A loud roar made him jump as if goosed.

It was rumbling up Bryan Street like a landslide, shaking the very footpaths and getting closer by the moment.

Brad's steps faltered. He clutched at his board.

A dozen bikies on Harley Davidsons were bellowing their way towards him.

They'll see me. They've already seen me.

It was too late to run. Too late to move.

He simply stood there as they approached.

The leader was young and tall and… *is that blood?* His motorbike screamed as it closed in on Brad… then passed him without slowing.

The other riders followed behind him at a respectful distance. A couple of them sneered at the young skater shrinking into the footpath, but most ignored him.

Brad turned to watch them go, his knees as stiffened to marble. The bikers turned the corner at the bottom of Bryan Street. Brad heard them pulling up, the engines cutting.

Pasco's. They've stopped at Pasco's.

Mad bastard. Even the other bikers won't fuck with him.

His stomach lurched.

Not Pasco's house. The clubhouse. The bikie's clubhouse.

He had just ripped off the Marauders Motorcycle Club.

Panic shook through him. He turned back, ready to sprint and never stop sprinting… only to find that another motorbike was coming, following the others.

The huge Harley cruised up the centre of Bryan Street, its fat wheels at home on the cracked bitumen. It slowed a little as it approached Brad, its gleaming lines of black and silver catching the afternoon sun.

Unable to help himself, unable to move, Brad met the bikie's eyes.

He was in his fifties, helmetless, enormous. Grey hair flapped out behind him and blue tattoos snaked up his thick arms.

With the barest shadow of a smile, the rider nodded to him, a respectful acknowledgement, a wolf greeting a cub.

I see you.

Brad nodded back, purely on reflex.

Then the Harley was gone, burning down Bryan Street, turning right into Herbert Street the same as the others, the roar of the engine still rumbling the footpath.

Brad turned and ran.

Jake,

Damn those sausage rolls smell good.

Every afternoon Milky would wheel four tall metal cooling racks into the backyard. The skinny baker in the white singlet would push the rumbling racks onto the uneven concrete of the driveway where the pastries could cool in the open air.

The six-foot-tall racks each held over a dozen metal baking trays filled with freshly baked sausage rolls, hedgehog slice, Cornish pasties, brioche buns, apple tarts, vegetable scrolls and eight varieties of meat pie.

Jake tried to ignore them. You would think that after a lifetime of hanging around fresh pastries and cakes the temptation to nick one would wear off, but it never did. He did *try* to restrain himself. The bakehouse was his, but the pies were Lynn and John's, so Jake ignored them.

Most of the time.

His stomach rumbled. The *Marauders* had just ridden past the mouth of driveway, with big Noah at their tail. No doubt they were about to tuck in to some pies and tarts themselves.

That I helped score for them. Which made extra money for Lynn.

He thought back to Noah at his bedroom window, to the boss bikie's hard, square face listening to the softly mystic, vaguely horny strains of *Enigma* coming from Jake's stereo.

Wait until he finds out I flogged a porno.

A wave of embarrassment and shame rolled through his stomach, making it rumble again.

Fuck it. He closed in on the racks, nose twitching. *I'm just gonna take one.*

With two warm sausage rolls in his hands, he sauntered up the driveway towards Bryan Street. If somebody came out of the screen door now, they would see only his back, not the delicious fresh pastries in his hands.

He quickened his step a little anyway, striding as though he were on an important errand, perhaps for his grandparents, out of the driveway into Bry…

Something crashed into him, hard, knocking him clear off his feet.

After a weird weightless moment, Jake landed heavily on the bitumen. Black gravel twisted painfully into his side. There was a clatter of wood. The sausage rolls were gone, strewn into the gutter. He'd only managed a single bite.

Groaning, he rolled onto his back. He had managed to take most of the fall on his side, instinctively tucking his elbow away, and his breath came back quickly enough. All those years of football might have been worth something after all. Still, he was scraped and bruised and would be stiff tomorrow.

He heard a mutter and raised his head to see.

A bloke around his own age was lurching to his feet, clutching at a backpack. He had dropped a skateboard too – it was laying upside down, the wheels spinning with a smooth whir. The skater checked the backpack, looked back the way he had come, then scowled at him, rubbing a wrist.

"What the *hell* man? That fuckin *caned*." He was skinny, scruffy, and his eyes were bright.

"Fuck mate, I didn't hear you." Jake got up, brushing down his knees. "Are you all right?"

"Why don't.…" the skater blinked at him with a surprised expression, then took a deep breath. His face was pale. "Yeah. I'm fine. You?"

"I'll live. Were you skating? I didn't hear you."

"Nah" the skater shook his head. "I was on foot, I…"

He broke off, looking down Bryan Street with an odd expression.

Jake heard the throaty rumble of a Harley Davidson. Others joined it in a guttural chorus.

The Marauders.

Eyes wild, the skater hefted his board, clearly about to bolt.

He's scared of them, Jake realised. *Does he think they're after him?* He wouldn't be the first kid to regret mouthing off to the *Marauders,* but they wouldn't give a shit about some skater. Would they?

They're not all like Noah. Jake had heard the stories just like everyone else. Some of the bikers were bordering on psychotic.

This skeezy-looking skater might make it to the corner of South Street, but the *Marauders* would see him, and they would catch him.

And then what? If this kid was older than Jake, it wasn't by much. *It's none of my business.*

"Wait," Jake told him. He gestured down the driveway. "In here. They won't see you."

There was a space behind the gate that was invisible from the street. He had ducked in there himself, more than once, when Dylan or the police or the pretty blonde girl from Green Street went by.

The skater looked at Jake, surprised again, but he hesitated.

"Behind here, quick." Jake skipped into the driveway.

The skater hesitated, then followed Jake behind the gate with a grateful nod.

They boys stood like statues as the *Marauders* growled closer. The motorbikes slowed down as they reached the wide intersection, with some splitting off down South and Doolan while the rest continued down Bryan Street.

Looking for somebody. Jake looked the skater up and down. *Looking for him.*

The kid was half a foot shorter than Jake. His clothes looked like good quality brands, but they were oversized and unwashed, dishevelled. He reeked of cigarettes. He was looking into space, obviously listening to the progress of the motorbikes.

When they had made a bit of distance, the skater poked his head out of the gate, peering after them. He exhaled slowly and turned back to Jake.

"Thanks man." He pulled a tobacco pouch out of his pocket. His hands were shaking.

"The *Marauders* are after you."

"Yeah." The skater frowned into his pouch. "Yeah, I guess so."

"It's all right man, I know what they're like. Most people try not to piss them off, hey."

"I wasn't *trying* to," the skater shrugged. "I… their dog chased me when I was skating past, so I kicked the goddamn thing. They got all pissed off, fuckin turned around and chased me."

"You kicked Midget?" Jake whistled between his teeth, sitting down and leaning back against the warm bakehouse wall. "That'll do it."

"It… *she* was chasing me."

"Yeah man. She's their guard dog. Dumb as a fuckin hammer. Did she get out?"

"Must of. I come out up that little street and… *listen.*" He held up a hand, cocking his head.

Jake listened. That same obnoxious gunning was coming back towards them. He watched Brad's face as the bikes split off into different directions again, fanning out.

"Don't stress too much, man, but… maybe keep a low profile for a bit."

"Yeah, I fuckin reckon." The skater chuckled but it sounded thin.

He offered the tobacco pouch to Jake, who shook his head. The skater shrugged.

"Thanks for letting me duck in here man, they would have spotted me for sure."

"It's all right. Some of them are okay but some… you don't want to fuck with." Jake shrugged. "You live around here?"

"Yeah." The skater lit his cigarette and extended a hand. "Brad."

"I'm Jake."

They shook on it. Brad exhaled a thick plume of grey smoke.

"We moved in down the bottom of South Street a few months back."

"Near the laneway, Litte Ray?"

"Yeah, right across from it."

"You're more or less neighbours with Boof and Tommy then."

"Maybe," Brad shrugged, then tilted his head. "Oh, hang on… two brothers?

Tall blonde one? And the other one's built like a brick shithouse."

It was Jake's turn to chuckle. "That's them. And you've probably seen their mum hanging around too."

"Their mum? Shit, I don't know."

"I'm surprised you don't hear her from your place."

"Maybe I do." Brad said thoughtfully. He looked down the driveway at the pastry racks in the backyard, the row of sheds where Jake's great-grandfather had kept his Clydesdales. "Is this your place?"

"Yeah."

I'm not gonna invite you in, buddy. He thought he might like this skinny, raggedy skater… but he sure didn't trust him. *Not yet.*

"It's a good backyard for skating, all this cement."

"I've never really tried it to be honest. Got my BMX."

"Yep, yep, as long as you can get around, right? I used to…"

Another motor thrummed up Bryan Street, but it was slowing down.

"Christ, is that them *again?*" Jake poked his head out of the driveway and peered down the street.

Brad's face was pale. "They must love that fuckin dog."

"Shit." Jake recognised that bike, that bikie.

He was coming.

"Stand over there."

"What?"

"*Just…* just stand back there. Don't fuckin move."

Brad skipped out of sight.

The Harley rolled across the top of the driveway.

It was Romeo Rohan, Noah's mountainous son, and Rohan looked pissed off.

Keeping his expression carefully neutral, Jake gave the stony-faced biker a weak wave.

"Rohan. How'd the fights go?"

"Do you know some skater fuck?" Rohan growled. His bike chuttered. "Would have just come past here."

What will you do when you find him?

"No mate." He didn't look at Brad, standing just behind the gate. "Don't know any skaters."

"Didn't see one? Just a minute ago?"

"Haven't seen anyone. Except you blokes."

"Right." The big bike revved. "You fuckin see him, a fuckin skater with a *black backpack*, you fuckin come and tell me or dad, right?"

Jake nodded. He lifted a hand as the chortling black beast rolled away.

In a few seconds, Rohan was gone.

"Jesus." Brad let out a relieved sigh. "Thanks man. Can't believe that fuckin nutjob listened to you."

Jake nodded, but he was distracted. The motorbike growled its way out of earshot.

I've gotta fuck him off, if they see him here now...

Brad coughed nervously.

"Hey… do you smoke weed? I could roll us a joint. To say thanks."

"Oh yeah," Jake said, trying to sound casual.

Brad reached for his tobacco pouch.

"Not here though. This is my house man. People come and go from the bakehouse all day."

"Oh," Brad slumped a little. "Right."

"Look, I was gonna go and meet Boof and Reese in a minute anyway. Someone found this burned-out mill and we're gonna try and get up on the roof. Maybe you should come."

"Um." The skater looked down. "Nah man, think I'll go and lay low for a bit, you know, like you said."

"You'll be right man, nobody else'll be down there. Just leave your deck here, maybe. And I'll lend you a different t-shirt."

"A burned-out mill?"

"Yeah, it's like a big old factory. Plenty of weird spots for a joint, and you'll hear these bikies coming from a mile away."

Plenty of places to hide.

Brad considered. "Who's gonna be there? The blokes who live near me?"

"Both of them. And another dude from just around the corner. C'mon man, good way to meet the boys, and we're used to avoiding these fuckwits. Just leave your deck here, because that's the giveaway."

Brad nodded thoughtfully, and a sideways grin slowly spread across his face.

"Yeah. Shit. Righto, man, let's do it."

Maynard

Maynard was jumpy.

We stick out like two pimples on a pumpkin. Two pimples with a gun.

There were parks all the way along Forster Street – the reserve on the corner of Invermay Road, the bowls club, Invermay Park and then the Railyards. On the other side of the Railyards, the flood levy ran for about half a kilometre before Churchill Park Drive gave way to Heritage Forest. You could probably walk for an hour without seeing another person, but *if* you saw someone else you would probably remember them.

Especially if they were carrying a long rifle with a black iron barrel.

Maynard scowled. The rifle's wooden stock felt greasy in his hand. It seemed heavier than it should be.

I shouldn't have let him talk me into this. I let him talk me into too much.

If only *he* could take the lead, just once.

What would I do? What would I want him *to do?*

He shied away from the thought.

"We could aim for the top of that," Tommy said. He nodded at the towering brick chimney that loomed over the next block like a shot tower. At its very top were three small chimney crowns that *would* make pretty good targets.

"Settle down, sniper. Start off with not shooting yourself in the foot, maybe."

"How many rounds were there?"

Maynard rolled his eyes. "Two, I told you."

"Bullshit. How many did you really bring?"

"I fuckin brought two!" Maynard waved a hand at him. They kept walking. "One shot each in the warehouse, then we take it back."

"We can't just do one."

"One each."

"You bought more bullets though, didn't you."

"Fuck off!"

"I'm just saying. Because you did."

Maynard swore.

They reached the vacant land that surrounded the mill and quickened their pace, heading for the shaded alley between the mill and the white woolstore.

Maynard looked around nervously, craning his neck this way and that.

"Nobody's gonna hear it, man." Tommy was bouncing on his toes. "There's nobody around for miles."

"There's still people working over the back there. And the main road's not *that* far away."

"How loud do you think it's gonna be? We'll be inside, don't forget."

"Yeah, so we won't see if anyone's coming."

Tommy considered this. "Maybe we should get up on the roof."

"What, so you can jump off?"

"Don't be like that, Maynard."

"Listen."

Tommy was still. There was revving in the distance, a V8 or a motorbike. Somebody was burning down Forster Street towards them.

"That's a Harley." Maynard spat on the ground. "Bloody bikies."

"So? We've got hardware, remember? He's not gonna mess with us."

"You're hardcore. You should start your own gang."

"Yeah and you should start a fuckin boy band."

The roaring veered off into the streets and faded out of earshot.

Maynard and Tommy climbed back through the loading bay doors into the mill. It was much the same as they had left it earlier; dusty, quiet and still.

Tommy went straight to the warehouse door, but Maynard hesitated, hefting the rifle on his shoulder.

"How long do you reckon Boof and Reese will be?"

"Ages."

"Then we should find something we can set up as a target."

"Who's the sniper now? You're not gonna hit anything from the other end of the warehouse."

"We might as well aim at something."

They fossicked around the workshop, kicking a few scraps of timber around the floor until Tommy shuffled something with his foot.

"Here we go." He held up a rusted circular saw blade the size of a dinner plate.

"Shit that's easy." Maynard chuckled. "Can't you find anything smaller?"

"I don't need no guns anyway, I'm going ninja style." Tommy flung the round blade frisbee-style. It sailed through the air, spinning like a record, then clashed into the workshop wall and fell to the concrete floor with a clang that made Maynard's back clench.

There was a dozen or more blades sitting on the dusty floor. Maynard collected most of them while Tommy flung a few more at the wall, a Chickenfeed Apollo with his junkyard discus. He grunted as the saws bounced off the hard timber.

"Come on then."

They went into the warehouse. Motes of dust and ash floated through the cavernous space, catching the orange light that streamed in through the high ceiling's skylights. Tommy gazed up at the timber balcony that ran around the warehouse's high walls.

"Why don't we go up there?"

Maynard frowned and walked back to him. "You reckon?"

"Might as well."

"What if we have to bail?"

"What difference will it make? If we're sprung, we're sprung."

"All right, let's do it and get out of here."

Tommy laughed his easy laugh. "Nobody's gonna call the cops, I promise."

"Well, come on then."

They climbed the old steel staircase, their footsteps echoing through the warehouse, then walked along the shifting balcony until they reached the far end.

Maynard examined the wooden railing and found nails sticking out at odd intervals on its outside edge. Each of the saw blades had a small hole in its middle, so when he slipped one over a nail it hung there easily.

"Nice work," Tommy grinned.

There were plenty of nails, so they hung the blades all along the railing. Tommy put his finger on the edge of one and set it spinning. The blade spun quickly for a few moments before it wobbled off the nail and dropped to the floor below. It landed on the concrete with a spangle, bouncing off its edge then rolling a few feet before clattering over.

"Well, that's one less to aim for," chuckled Tommy sheepishly. "At least we know that if you hit one it'll come off."

"That's pretty sick. You might even win a panda bear," Maynard chuckled. Tommy's expression was blank. "You know, like the thing at the Regatta. Where you shoot the tin ducks and win stupid shit."

"Never been," Tommy shrugged.

Never been to the Regatta. Of course. Rides and games, food and show-bags… Lorraine would never fork out for such a good time. *I'll take him to the next one. If we're not in jail.*

They walked back to the other end of the warehouse, the balcony creaking below their feet. When they were in position, Tommy rubbed his hands together, eyes alight.

Maynard held out the rifle and Tommy took it with reverence. While Maynard fussed around looking for the bullets, Tommy put it to his shoulder and looked down the barrel at the blades in the distance.

"Bam," he whispered.

"Um," Maynard said. He could feel his cheeks burning and hoped it wasn't too obvious in the warehouse light. "I'm… I don't know how to load it."

"Oh. Shit." Tommy lowered the rifle, his face blank. "Don't they like, crack in half so you can put the bullets in the barrel?"

"That's a shotgun I reckon. Look, there's no hinge or anything."

Tommy passed the rifle back to Maynard, who inspected it closely.

The rifle's black iron barrel and polished timber stock seemed heavy and serious. It was well-maintained and in good nick, smooth curves of timber and steel punctuated by various notches and a low sight. There was a switch behind and to the side of the trigger, close to where your thumb might rest when you were aiming. There were no hinges or panels, nothing that would open or slide.

"I don't know. Shit."

"Maybe just drop them down the barrel?"

Maynard shook his head. "That's like the old fuckin muskets, with the brush to push the gunpowder down. Or a cannon."

Tommy chuckled sheepishly. "Maybe we should go and find that bikie and ask him."

"Hang on." Below the barrel was a shorter, thinner barrel plugged by a screw cap. Maynard twisted the cap with his fingertips and was pleased to find it turned easily. He unscrewed it all the way and pulled out the long, thin rod that was attached to it.

"Ooh aah! Maybe you drop the bullets down that one."

"No look," Tommy said, pointing at the bottom of the shorter barrel. There was a slot near the timber stock a few inches in front of the trigger guard. A bullet-sized slot. "Pop it in there, I reckon."

"Clever dick," Maynard grinned. He passed the rod to Tommy and pushed one of the rounds into the slot. It slid comfortably into the barrel, so he popped another in, and since Tommy was still examining the rod, added another two for good measure.

A couple of bonus ones, he thought, imagining Tommy's pleased, grateful grin.

The thin rod eased back into place and he twisted until it was snug.

"Locked and loaded."

"Fuckin righto!" Tommy beamed and clapped his hands together. "Giddy-*up* old son!"

Maynard flicked the safety switch back and forth with his thumb. Pushing it forward made a small red dot appear. He flicked it off.

"Come on!" Tommy was near bouncing on his toes. "Show us what you've got, Dirty Maynard."

Maynard scoffed and licked his lips. Butterflies drifted through his stomach as he stepped over to the railing and lifted the rifle to his shoulder.

Looking down the barrel, the rotary blades were the size of coins, taunting him from the other end of the empty warehouse.

"A thousand bucks if you get one," Tommy said.

Maynard balanced the stock more comfortably against his shoulder, lining up the notch on the barrel with one of the blades. He settled his feet and held his breath, pushing the safety switch with his thumb. It flicked forward so he could see the red dot and suddenly the rifle seemed heavier, more alive in his hands.

His head grew light as his focus narrowed and his finger found the rifle's trigger...

"*Bam!*" A voice from below, loud and boisterous.

Cops! It's the cops!

"What a fuckin *find!*"

He saw the panic in Tommy's eyes as the workshop door directly below them swung open hard enough to crack against the wall. Stepping back from the rail, adrenaline flooding his body, Maynard pointed the rifle's nuzzle towards the ceiling.

Caught, I'm caught!

Tommy was easing over to the balcony, peering over the edge.

"... set up a basketball ring up in here, couple of lights and we could play *whenever.*"

That's not the cops. That's Reese.

Tommy's shoulders sagged and Maynard felt his knees waver as relief rushed down his spine.

"Yeah man, you could run a two-on-two tournament, five bucks entry, winner takes all."

The top of Boof's head popped into view. Neither of them looked up to the balcony.

Tommy mimicked wiping sweat off his brow.

Maynard rolled his eyes and shook his head.

Another second and I would have fired.

Tommy held a finger to his smirking lips, a twinkle in his eye. Boofhead and Reese were pointing out where the scoreboard and beer taps might go.

Tommy turned back to the railing and unzipped his jeans.

Maynard gasped, but managed to stifle a giggle.

"…and you can choose between Jordan or Shaq for a teammate," Boof had the bit in his teeth. "We can get Nike to build one of those glass floors with the… what the *fuck?*"

A stream of piss arced through the air a couple of feet away from his head, thundering onto the concrete and splashing on his filthy Pumas.

With a disgusted yelp, Boof stumbled backwards into Reese and together their eyes followed the yellow ribbon of piss up to the balcony where Tommy was laughing, dick in hand.

"You fuckin *fucktard!*" Boof squealed. "You almost *pissed* on me!"

Maynard laughed so hard that he doubled in two and even Reese was smirking – *his* shoes hadn't been splashed, after all. Tommy chuckled as he cut off the flow in three shorts bursts.

"Put it away you gimp." Boofhead glowered. "What are you even doing up there with your cock out?"

"What are *you* doing down there in the toilet?"

"Is that a *gun?*" Reese was pointing, disbelief in his voice.

"That's what your mum calls it," said Tommy.

Maynard quickly lowered the rifle, but it was far too late.

"Bullshit!" said Boofhead in a hushed tone. "That's your stepdad's rifle, isn't it. We're coming up."

"Hang on, don't bloody come up here," Tommy complained, but it was no good. The other two boys were heading for the steel stairs. "*Shit.*"

"Well, we can't fire it now," Maynard muttered. *And thank Christ for that.*

"Why not?"

"Not with *them* here. They'll go bragging about it all over Invermay."

"Greg won't find out. Just tell 'em to piss off."

"Nup. They'll both want a go and then we'll all be bloody shooting."

"But there's only two bullets, right?" Tommy said with that infectious grin.

Maynard groaned and Tommy laughed again.

"I knew you were full of shit."

Reese came barrelling along the balcony with Boof at his heels. "Can I've a look?"

Maynard shook his head, holding the rifle tightly against his chest.

"Nah, we only just got it out."

"Is it loaded?"

Maynard and Tommy looked at each other.

"Fuckin hell!" Reese's eyes were wide. "It *is*, isn't it? Are you gonna fire it? Can I have a go?"

Tommy rolled his eyes. "We only bought two rounds, one each."

"Bullshit," Boof countered.

"How would you know?" Tommy frowned at him.

"You wouldn't knock it off and bring it all the way down here for one shot each."

"We did though," Maynard scowled.

"Come on man," Reese implored. "Just give us one crack at it."

"Nup." Maynard was resolute. "I'm having one, then he's having one. Then we get the fuck out of here."

"Why?" Reese sulked.

"In case the cops come," Tommy said quietly.

"Cops," Reese scoffed. "Nobody's gonna hear it down here."

"How would you know?"

"It won't be that loud."

"Let's find out." Maynard put the rifle on his shoulder again and picked a distant blade.

"Hang on," said Boof. "What if we…"

A *crack* rang out through the warehouse, echoing off the walls like sharp thunder.

Boof skipped backwards and Reese put his hands over his ears. Tommy clapped his hands together with a hoot.

Maynard lowered the rifle, looking at the far wall. None of the blades moved.

"Shit," he scoffed. "Not even close."

Maynard flicked the safety switch back on. *I'll have a sore shoulder tomorrow.* The stock had kicked much harder than he'd been expecting.

"No good, Robin Hood!" Tommy was bouncing with excitement.

"Fuck that was loud," Reese chuckled.

"Yeah," Maynard admitted. "Maybe we should wait a bit before your turn."

"Yeah. Probably." Tommy rubbed his hands together. "How'd you blokes go anyway? Was Magnus home?"

"Sorted," Boof patted his pocket. "Christ, his house stinks."

"What if we go smoke a joint on the roof?" Maynard suggested. "We'll be able to see if anyone's checking us out that way too."

"How do we get on the roof?" Reese asked.

"There's a manhole." Tommy pointed out the ladder at the end of the balcony.

"Trust you to sniff out a manhole," Boof rolled his eyes.

"You gonna come up, Boof?" Reese said.

"Yep," He was watching Maynard inspect the rifle. "Jake'll probably turn up too, don't forget. Don't leave that down here."

"Wasn't going to," Maynard said. "She doesn't leave my sight, cocko."

"Righto, come on then." Tommy led them over to the ladder. A few hard shoves and the manhole popped open with a squeal. "If the cops show up, we can shoot em."

"You'll shoot in your pants," Boof scoffed.

They filed up the ladder into the afternoon light.

Stephanie

Eventually, miraculously, it was 4pm.

Thank goodness.

Stephanie untied her blue apron and hung it on the wooden peg in the storeroom, then collected her jacket and took out her ponytail.

On the way out, she waved goodnight to Julie. Julie didn't acknowledge her. She stood motionless behind the main counter with her arms crossed over her blue apron.

What's up her arse? He's *the one that's in the wrong!*

He was behind the photo counter, polishing a lens.

What a lurk.

Stephanie kept her head held high as she walked past him but couldn't bring herself to meet his eyes.

"Bye David." She hated the high falsetto that made her voice tremble.

"Stephanie," her boss said, the polishing cloth gliding in a smooth circle. "We'll need help closing tonight. You'll be back at six, please." It wasn't a question.

She froze, a deer caught in headlights. "Tonight?"

"Is that okay?"

Now Julie spoke up. She frowned at David.

"I thought *I* was closing up toni…"

"I want both of you," he said without looking up. "There's a bit of stocktake, and Barb's gone home for the night."

Julie was scowling at Steph now.

Nine hundred and fifty dollars.

David had lowered the cloth and was watching her eyes.

"Can you do that for me?"

Just keep going.

"Okay. Um… okay. Back at six then."

Her smile was more of a grimace.

His was more of a smirk.

She walked out of the shop and now anger bubbled out of her. She let it come, snarling at the wire rubbish bin, scowling at the family walking into the fish and chip shop, clenching her fists tight, fuming.

Goddamned bastard of an old prick… prick! So… fucking… *dumb!*

The roar of an engine, loud and obnoxious, rumbled the street and rattled through her chest. She clenched her teeth and let it flow through her.

It matched her mood. It felt *good.*

She watched the motorbike roar off the main road and tear up Bryan Street, its rider an angry blur. By the time she had turned the corner it had disappeared, the growl fading away.

Back at work in a couple of hours. She sighed. *At least I can clean my shoes.*

She had never realised how much of a creep David was, but now it seemed so obvious; smiling his sly smiles, leering amongst the lollies, rocking his hips back and forth, gasping as she spilt milk all over the floor, watching it drip from her fingers *oh no…*

Stop it! He's dumb, gross! You're gross!

She squeezed her eyes shut, stomping up the footpath.

Just pretend it never happened. Just pretend that it was you in that magazine, that you were tou…

She pulled up abruptly, her loose hair flicking against the back of her neck, her stomach sinking.

Ben Campbell was standing out the front of his house, leaning nonchalantly against the rusty wire fence. Worse, Dylan was with him, standing a bit further down Bryan Street. He was facing away from her, his fists on his hips, his acid wash jeans snug around his hips. In her fury, she hadn't noticed them.

God, not today. It was too late to backtrack down the block and walk the long way home… wasn't it?

If I can get back to the church, I'll duck around the…

But Dyaln had already turned and when he saw her standing across the street, his face lit up.

"Hello gorgeous!" Dylan grinned, hands on his hips, that hyena arrogance in the jaunty cock of his head.

Ben nodded at her, distracted.

Ben won't let him do anything, Stephanie told herself, with no idea whether it was true or not.

She kept walking.

"She's always so quiet, this one," Dylan marvelled. "I don't reckon she'd be quiet in the sack though, eh Benny?"

"Leave her alone, man." Ben frowned down the street. "He's doing another blockie."

Dylan scowled. "Oh well, it's none of our business, he can ride wherever he fuckin wants. Oh hey… *hey!*"

As Stephanie tried to sidle past, he skittered across the street and stood on the footpath in front of her, blocking the way.

Oh piss off.

Close up she could see the sweat stains on his white singlet, the purple acne scars around his cut shoulders, the acid wash jeans so tight they looked painted on.

She took a step backwards and put her hands on her hips.

"What do you want?"

He leered. "You know what I want."

"Some high heels to go with those jeans?"

Ben snorted laughter. Dylan's cheeks flushed. He licked his lips.

"If you don't like em, come and take em off for me."

"I'll be right thanks."

"You will be after I'm done with you."

He advanced. She matched each of his steps with a backwards one of her own.

"Not interested, Dylan." Her heel scraped against something – she had backed into a fence. Its pointed palings pressed into her lower back. "I'll scream my fuckin head off."

He pulled up short, then shook his head and laughed.

"That's cute baby. You can scream my name out if you want, I don't mind."

"Dylan, I'm not fuckin joking."

"Shh… *gorgeous.*" He came in close to her. "You been teasing me for years, waving that little arse up and down the footpath. Let's just fuck a few times, get it out of our sys…"

A guttural growl, a rumble like thunder, and a motorbike appeared on the South Street intersection not fifty metres away.

The rider clocked them, clocked Ben standing nearby, and twisted the throttle. He covered the distance between them in moments, pulling up at the gutter with his front wheel pointed at the space between Stephanie and Dylan.

The Harley was so loud she could barely hear herself think. The engine's beat was fat and powerful and she could feel it her belly.

Run, just run!

No. Running would be a mistake.

The bikie eyed them both as he shut off the Harley's engine and the roaring choked away. He kicked out the bike's stand with a heavy black boot, then reclined on the leather seat, appraising them.

Those tattoos. He's the one I saw earlier.

Dylan had taken a step back from Stephanie and pushed out his chest.

"How you goin, Rohan?"

Nobody messes with Rohan's girlfriend. Stephanie's eyes were wide. *This* was Lily's boyfriend?

"All right *mate*, how *you* going?" The bikie's voice was deep and calm, but his eyes glared at Dylan, bright and wide.

"Cleaned up that bloody cop earlier, eh, nice work I reckon." Dylan swallowed. "Good thing I spotted him, eh?"

"You know a bloke on a skateboard? Fuckin young bloke?"

"Who wants to know?" Ben called out, making all their heads turn.

"*I* fuckin wanna know." The bikie looked Ben up and down, then turned back to Dylan. "Seen him in the last ten minutes or so? Dirty looking little fuck on a skateboard."

"Nup," Dylan shrugged. "Dunno. Sorry mate."

"Don't know any skaters," Ben added.

"Hey Rohan, do you reckon since I helped you fellas with that…"

Rohan scowled at them, then turned to Stephanie.

"What about you, girl? You see a skater?" He blinked at her. "I know your face. Why do I know you?"

Nobody messes with Rohan's girlfriend.

"I'm friends with your girlfriend, Lily," she told him.

It was only half a lie. Everybody in her school knew Lily. And they *had* been friends, good friends. For a little while. In grade four.

Rohan considered this, then nodded.

"She's not my girl anymore. What's *your* name?"

"Stephanie."

"Is this cunt giving you a hard time, Stephanie?" He eyed Dylan, his hands flexing into fists, relaxing, flexing.

A flush of excitement spread up Stephanie's spine.

"Not anymore."

Rohan smirked, but when he met her eyes, his face softened for a moment. Stephanie felt another flush of excitement, this time in her lower belly. *His eyes!*

"If he gives you any shit, you come and see me. Got it, Stephanie?"

Nobody messes with Rohan's girlfriend.

Rohan doesn't have a girlfriend.

He held her gaze until she nodded, then he raised a finger at Dylan.

"Got it?"

Pouting, Dylan nodded. The bikie's scowl returned.

"I know who you are, Matthew *Dylan*. You want to run with the big boys."

"Ray said that if I…"

"You know this fuckin skater or not?"

"There's no skaters here," said a new, deeper than a oil well.

Rohan stood up a little straighter.

Allan Campbell was standing a few feet away, polishing a long steel wrench with a rag. He didn't look at the bikie.

"He would've gone past in the last ten…"

"He's not here," Allan repeated. "What'd he do?"

"He took something that wasn't fuckin his." Rohan's jaw worked furiously for a moment. "He was seen just here about fifteen minutes ago so he hasn't fuckin gone far."

Stephanie saw Ben and Dylan share a look, but Rohan didn't notice – he was watching the wrench in Allan's hand.

"No skaters here." Allan's tone was immutable. "No thieves either."

"Nah, only fuckin hookers."

Now Allan looked at him, his eyes fixed and unblinking.

Scowling, Rohan straightened up his bike and kicked the stand away. He pointed at Dylan.

"You see him, you fuckin come and tell me. I'll give you an ounce of weed." He considered.

"You *bring* him, we'll talk about the fights. Right?"

"You'll let me fight?" There was wonder in Dylan's voice.

"Just fuckin find him."

Go, go now, before he *does*.

Stephanie began striding away from them towards the corner. She could feel their eyes watching her go, but none of them called to her.

Just keep going.

A moment later the Harley roared to life again and revved a few times, screaming like a banshee. By the time it had pulled away from the gutter and started down Bryan Street she had put a good distance between herself and the Campbell's place.

She glanced over her shoulder as Rohan rode past. He caught her eye and nodded. before his Harley bellowed a furious trail of thunder down Bryan Street.

If he gives you any shit, you come and see me.

She glanced back. Allan and Ben were talking, their faces serious.

Dylan was watching her in the distance, his arms crossed.
She smiled. *So dumb.*

So, so dumb.

Brad

"Oh shit, really?" Brad chuckled, holding the *Faith No More* t-shirt against his wiry frame.

"It's kind of the death metal starter pack, but…" Jake shrugged with a wry smile.

"Nah man, I used to have this exact same shirt. *King for a Day* is a sick album. Thanks, dude."

"All good, just bring it back whenever. Want me to chuck your deck inside?"

This guy's all right. I think.

Brad hesitated. He didn't want to leave his skateboard here. He didn't like being separated from it. But Jake was right - it was a dead giveaway. There were no other skaters around this part of Invermay, not that Brad had come across anyway.

"Can I just leave it out here somewhere?"

"No worries. What about your bag?"

"Nah." Brad's grip on the backpack tightened. "It's got all my shit in it."

"Suit yourself, man. Here, chuck us your board."

Brad hesitated again, but Jake handled the board respectfully enough, checking out the trucks and the wheels as he leaned it against the fence.

Brad took the backpack off his shoulders and held it tightly between his ankles while he changed shirts. He dropped his own t-shirt onto his skateboard's trucks. It felt good to have the familiar snarling dog spread across his chest, as though he had chanced upon an old friend.

This better work.

Jake looked him up and down and nodded his approval.

"Just like a proper swampy. I'll just grab my shit, and we'll go, all right?" He disappeared into the mustard-coloured house.

Brad waited a few moments and, finally alone, lifted up the backpack. The excitement he'd been tamping down bubbled up again.

Finally, some proper dope. In a couple of hours, all this weed would be safely squirreled away in his woodshed. He could sit out there all day and all night, happily laying low, out of sight and out of mind, contentedly blowing smoke, not a worry in the goddamned world.

He pulled the zipper open, spread the bag wide, and the familiar sweet smell washed over him.

Fourteen ounces at least. Maybe a pound. No wonder they're looking for me.

The buds were as thick as his thumb, dense and sticky-looking. And there were piles of them.

So much.

More weed than he had ever seen in one place. Handfuls and handfuls of stinky hydroponic skunk.

Too much. Way too much. I should take it back. Some of it.

With a wry shake of his head, he pawed through the backpack, squeezing its compartments and folds. Along with the bags of dope, there was something chunky in the front pocket.

Feels like a pair of socks.

He unzipped the front pocket and found a bulging yellow envelope tucked snugly inside, clean and crisp and unsealed.

No socks.

Brad lifted the envelope's flap with numb fingers and looked inside.

His heart skipped a beat.

The envelope was full of cash.

Green hundred-dollar bills and yellow fifties, all strapped together with rubber bands to make a single wad as thick as his wrist.

He let the flap close, blinked, then lifted it again.

Thousands of dollars.

Maybe *tens* of thousands.

Oh fuck.

He shoved the envelope back into the backpack. It took several attempts to close the zipper. His head was spinning and light and empty and waves of unreality washed over him.

The weed was bad enough but *this?* This was too much. *Way* too much.

No wonder those bikies were still looking for him.

They wouldn't just *bash* him if they caught him.

What have I done? I need to get home.

There was a loud *bang* a few feet away and he started, but it was just Jake closing his back door.

Brad took a deep breath. When the world wavered a little, he planted his feet by reflex, closing his eyes against the brightness.

What the fuck have I done?

"You all right man?"

"Yeah. Yeah. Just spinning out a bit."

"They'll forget about it when they cool down man."

I don't think so.

"We should get going." He started back up the driveway, but Jake took his arm.

"Not that way. Probably want to stay off Bryan Streets. Allan Campbell's out the front of his house twenty-four-seven."

"Right. Right."

Jake led him through the backyard to a little dead-end alleyway behind the last stable, where he vaulted over the timber fence. Brad climbed the fence after him, but poked his head over slowly, looking up and down South Street.

No motorbikes. No dogs.

"Let's went, man." Jake said from below.

No fuckin chance.

Brad clenched his jaw and jumped the fence.

They hurried along the footpath, Brad clutching the backpack's straps with sweating hands. He wanted to bolt, to sprint as fast as he could, but he had to be content with a brisk walk. If he ran, he would panic, so he walked as quickly as he could with his head down and his ears open.

Jake, half a foot taller, had no trouble keeping up.

"We should cross the street and duck into the park," Jake suggested. "There's an old dirt lane that runs behind the houses. No way they'd get a bike up there."

"Really?"

"I'll show you."

They came to Monash Reserve, the big grassy rectangle that was once a Jewish cemetery. Jake stepped over the ankle-high concrete barrier into the park, so Brad followed him.

The sides of Monash Reserve were lined with weathered grey timber fences and on the far side was a gap where some of the palings had been removed. Through the gap he could see a leafy, shaded lane, unpaved and littered with old car parts.

"The lane comes out next to Boofhead's house on Little Ray. I don't know what they used..."

A ravenous growl from the end of South Street, the thunder of a Harley Davidson engine drawing closer.

Sprung. Brad's stomach turned to ice and his legs stopped moving. If a chasm had suddenly opened in the ground in front of him, he would have gladly fallen into it.

They got me.

They won't recognise me. Different top, no skateboard.

He didn't believe it.

"Oh shit!" Jake laughed. There was excitement in his voice, the delight of a young boy playing *kiss'n'catch*. "Here we go."

The gap in the fence was thirty metres away. They wouldn't make it. The bike would reach the reserve in moments.

They got me.

"Get down," he hissed at Jake and fell to his knees.

"What?" Jake chuckled.

"Lay down!" Brad sprawled out on the grass, face down.

Jake hesitated, then mimicked him, dropping to the ground with a *thud*.

The motorbike rolled into view, a stallion on a ridge.

It slowed down, the engine taking a breath as the bikie peered into the reserve.

This is it.

Brad pushed his shoulders into the grass, making himself as small as possible.

If the bikie saw them, he gave no indication. The motor throttled again. He sped out of view. They heard him turn down Feral Street.

Jake stood up, brushing himself off and grinning into the distance.

"Bloody hell that worked a treat. I don't reckon he…"

Brad vomited.

The heave caught him off guard. He pushed his knees, tried to balance himself, and vomited again. Shudders wracking his body and he squeezed his eyes closed.

He didn't see me. His eyes watered and his throat was bitter. *He didn't see me.*

He caught his breath. He wiped a sleeve across his eyes.

Jake was watching him, a doubtful look on his face, his good humour vanished.

"You all right, man?"

Brad spat yellow froth onto the ground. "Think I'd better go home."

"Yeah. Yeah, I reckon. We should still go this way." Jake shrugged towards the fence. "Better than the street."

"Okay. Sorry."

"Don't worry about it. You know… they're not gonna kneecap you for kicking their dog."

"Yeah. Probably. I should just go and lay low."

I should go and buy a plane ticket.

They ducked through the gap in the fence and into the green, overgrown lane. Tall trees bordered the uneven shoulders with branches so thick and verdant that the sunlight struggled to break through. Thin blades of grass tickled at their calves. Backyards with fences and gates in various states of disrepair backed onto the lane, private and unknowable. The laneway felt like a secret.

The backpack weighed a ton.

Tommy and Boofhead's tiny cottage hunched on the corner the laneway made with Little Ray Street. There was no sign of the brothers – or, thankfully, their nosey mother.

"My place is just up here, across the street," Brad said as they reached the end of Little Ray. "Wait!"

He pulled up short, then stepped closer to the fence and peeked over the top.

"What is it?"

"Someone's at my house." Brad ducked his head again. "I can't quite see them."

Jake stood on his toes and looked over the top of the fence.

"It's fuckin Dylan. And Ben Campbell."

Just that Van Damme wannabee.

"Thank Christ," Brad sighed. He was about to round the fence when Jake grabbed his shoulder.

"What are you doing?" Jake whispered, frowning.

"They just wanna smoke more fuckin death."

"You serious?" Jake was looking at Brad as though seeing him for the first time. "You're mates with Dylan?"

Brad hesitated.

Am I?

"We hung out today for a bit, got stoned." He shrugged. "He's a bit of a knob, but… he's all right, isn't he?"

Isn't he?

He thought he probably knew the answer to that already… but Dylan already knew where he lived, so there wasn't much point hiding from him.

I need to get home. I can put up with Billy Idol for a bit.

"Dylan's a fuckin douche." Jake was watching him doubtfully. "Sorry if you like him, but… he's always been a bully, ever since we were kids. If he wasn't scared of Tommy, he'd be a fuckin nightmare."

"Why? What did he do?"

"A lot of shit, man. He stole Taylor's Diamondback BMX last year, then when Mick tried to get it back he broke his nose. He threw a wheely bin at Bobby Gardner and cracked his rib. Smashed up Leigh's guitar. None of the girls in Invermay will go near him. He doesn't fuck with Reese because he thinks he can get in Elisha's pants. He doesn't fuck with Boof because of Tommy, so…"

"So he fucks with you." Brad sighed. "He seemed all right to start off with. The first one around here to say g'day. You know."

"I dunno man." Jake raised his hands. "It's up to you. But I might just duck down the hill and piss off, I reckon."

"Wait," said Brad.

He thought about Dylan's sneer.

Do I look like a fuckin skatie?

Then he looked down at the *Faith No More* t-shirt Jake had lent him.

"Fuck him, I'll come with you. If that's still all right?"

Jake grinned. "Yeah man. Let's get the fuck out of here."

They ducked across South Street and took the short sharp hill down to Forster. The scrappy, chaotic Railyards was the obvious route. They crept along rows of old tractor tyres, rotting stacks of timber and abandoned freight cars, staying out of sight.

I've got to offload this backpack.

There were plenty of places around here he could stash the bag… but the idea was laughable.

All that weed. All that money.

His stomach lurched.

"Jake," he said with a sticky dry mouth. "Would Dylan tell the bikies where I live?"

"Shit." Jake thought about it as he picked his way through the weeds and scrap metal. "In all honesty man, I wouldn't be surprised if that fucker sold his own mother."

Stephanie

As soon as Stephanie opened the front door, she knew that her father was home. Not only was his patchy brown coat hanging from the back of the front door, but the miasmic waft of warm beer that followed him like a cloud still lingered in the doorway.

"Stephie?" He was in the kitchen.

She gauged the thickness in his voice the way she might have gauged the freshness of a nectarine. This one was oversweet, not *quite* rotten… but not far from it.

He started early.

She sighed. Some weekends – most weekends – he would break his self-imposed, much trumpeted rule of not drinking before 3pm.

He'll be unconscious by the time I finish work, at least.

"It's only me," she eased the front door closed and sat her handbag down.

Aunt Shirley was in her chair, still wearing her threadbare pink dressing gown and her ancient pink slippers. The old woman didn't register Stephanie's presence, even when she leaned in to kiss her aunt's papery cheek.

She's been sitting in that goddamned chair all day.

Aunty Shirley was far more lucid and vibrant on the days when she took an afternoon walk and maybe spent some time hovering around their bare backyard.

"Why aren't you dressed, Aunty Shirley?"

"How was work, darlin?" her father called out.

"Dad?" She tried to keep the frustration out her voice, it was hard. She was tired. "Why isn't Shirley dressed?"

He appeared in the doorway, a short chubby man with a slack, hangdog face. His white singlet was damp in patches and dotted with gravy, while his belted brown slacks clung to wide hips. A Boag's Draught stubby was gripped in his pale fingers.

"Couldn't be bothered," he wheezed, shrugging his meaty shoulders. "Wasn't doing anything today anyway, was we Shirl?" His voice got louder at the end, the way it did whenever he addressed his Aunt.

"You should still help her get dressed. You *know* it's no good for her, spending all day in her nightie. What if she wants to go for a walk?"

"She's not going for a walk *now*, is she? Not with all those motorbikes tearing up and down the street."

"No, but if she *wanted* to go for a walk…"

"She's not going for a walk," her dad turned back into the kitchen. "She wants to watch *Hey Hey It's Saturday*."

Stephanie crossed her arms, shaking her head. Aunt Shirley was looking in the general direction of the TV, but her eyes were a million miles away.

"I have to do a split shift," she followed him into the kitchen.

"Tonight?" He lowered himself into his chair.

Their kitchen table was almost completely covered by pages from *The Saturday Examiner* – the racing forms. A ceramic ashtray held a smouldering cigarette next to his stubby. The bottom of the ashtray was painted in the likeness of Queen Victoria's silhouette.

"Yeah. David's… David's being a jerk."

"He has to pay you for it though, doesn't he?"

"I suppose." She leaned back against the kitchen counter, narrowing her eyes at the stubby in his hand. "But Julie had already told me I could have the night off. There's a movie I want to watch and I told Aunty Shirley we could play Bridge and he's just…"

"Shirley'll be all right." He took a knock from the stubby and picked up one of the racing forms.

You don't care, as long as you don't run out of horse piss.

"*You* could play Bridge with her, you know."

"Well. I *could…*"

"She needs to *do* something, Dad. She can't just sit around all day staring into space, it's not good for her."

"She's got Michael to talk to."

"Very funny."

Stephanie flicked the electric kettle on and its gurgle followed her little bedroom. Her doona, tucked taught into the side of the bed, was spotless and wrinkle free. After carefully hanging her jacket on the back of her door, she kicked off her sneakers and flopped heavily onto her bed.

So dumb. How could I not have noticed?

David had always been friendly enough, but never *over*-friendly. She couldn't remember ever feeling uncomfortable around him before today. Of course, most of the time his wife or one of the other part-timers was there as well, but not always. He wasn't as intimidating as Barb – she was the one who had given Stephanie the job almost twelve months ago – but she minded her p's and q's around him. They would chat, mostly about the work, and occasionally he would ask how her dad and Aunt Shirley were faring. He had seemed to be a decent boss.

He's a goddamned pervert.

She rolled onto her belly, her chin resting on her forearms.

I should just tell Barb.

Ooh she's tough.

What would Barb do - confront her husband? Call the police? Close down the business they had built together on the word of a casually employed seventeen-year-old?

No. She would sack me.

Nine hundred and fifty.

She looked at the little digital clock on her bookshelf. She had to be back in an hour and a half. Not long enough to really do anything, but too long to just sit around doing nothing.

To hell with David. When I have a car, I can drive over to Sandy's. Or to MacDonalds.

She stretched again.

Or off a bloody cliff.

She thought of bakery Jake, standing there with the stolen porno, and a flush passed through her drifting, dozing body. He could be somewhere looking at the porno right now, right at this very moment.

So dumb.

On the verge of falling asleep, she pushed her hips fittingly into the mattress, her body drifting, the warmth in her belly blooming to match the vivid colours beginning to swirl on the back of her eyelids. Swirling tattoo colours.

If he gives you any shit, you come and see me. Got it, Stephanie?

She turned on to her side and something dug painfully into the top of her thigh, something hard. The coins she had found beneath the shelves.

Nine hundred and fifty.

She dug out the coins. Two bucks fifty, still dotted with floor dust. About ten minute's worth of wages. Ten minutes less that she would need to work before she could drive off into the sunset. Two bucks fifty. It was better than nothing. Wasn't it?

Properly awake now, she sat up on the edge of the bed and reached for the little plastic computer behind her mother's photo.

Just keep going.

When she picked the moneybox up, her heart sank.

START SAVING.

This morning it had been satisfyingly heavy, a serious weight. Now it was light. Empty.

And it didn't say JUST KEEP GOING anymore. Or even BANK TODAY! START SAVING.

Nine hundred and fifty dollars. Her shaking fingernails worked to crack open the panel at the back. *Nine hundred and fif...*

The little computer popped open and a single twenty dollar note drifted down onto the bed.

Twenty bucks.

Her belly was a cold, heavy stone.

Twenty fucking dollars.

She was still figuring out whether to laugh or cry or scream when a wheezing cough from the kitchen set her blood alight.

She stormed into the kitchen, a furious dervish, and slammed the money box down on the racing forms.

Her father's jowls hung slack. He blinked up at her sadly.

"Stephie, I…"

"*Where* is it? What did you do with my money?"

"Stephanie, listen to m…"

"Dad! What did you *do* with it?" Heat was piercing the corners of her eyes. "It's *my* money. It's *my* money that I worked for!"

He looked down at his chubby hands.

"I know, you saved up all those coins. And you've been working so hard. *So* hard."

"It wasn't just *coins*, it was *nine hundred fucking dollars!*"

"I'll pay you back, Stephie."

Now the tears came.

"*Where* is my money?"

When he wouldn't look at her, she sat down at the table and put her heads in her hands.

"It's the power bill," he said in a quiet voice. "It was a bit more than usual this month."

"*Bullshit,*" she shrieked, thumping her fist on the newspaper.

Ooh she's tough.

"Michael?" Came a reedy voice from the lounge room. "Michael is that you?"

Stephanie's fury abandoned her and was replaced by a familiar cold resignation. A tear cut a line down her cheek, but she ignored it. It hardly mattered now.

The horses ran this afternoon.

"It's not bullshit." His slack, hangdog face. "*I* pay the bloody bills, girl."

"You pay them out of *her* pension and my board," Stephanie said dully. "And the power bill's not due until next month anyway."

"How would you know," he stood up abruptly.

"Because I *bloody* do!" She shouted, pushing to her feet as well. "Because I don't want us to go cold again just because *you've* pissed all our money away."

"You think I can't look after you? The both of you?"

"Dad, where is my *money*?" Blood pumped into her face and her throat. "It's my *savings*, Dad!"

He already had his shoes on, and his chins wobbled as he scrabbled his wallet and keys off the kitchen bench.

"It's too much money for a girl your age to keep in her room," he wouldn't look at her. "Almost a thousand dollars!"

Nine-hundred and fif...

"I've been saving it for *ever*," she pleaded. "Since I started work! I've been putting it away, a bit at a time..."

"You've been putting it away while we've been scraping by," he said quietly, unaffected by her anger. He was pulling his coat on, the brown op shop jacket to match his slacks. "While I've been scrounging for coins on the pub floor, you've been stashing all this money. And for what? For what, Stephanie?"

To get me away from here and you and David and Dylan and...

She sat down at the table again, listless.

"It doesn't matter."

"For *what*? What was it for?"

"It was for *me*, Dad. I was saving it for *me*. It's *my* money."

"You see," he said triumphantly, buttoning up his jacket. "Selfish. You could have been using that to help us, to help the family. You only care about yourself."

"I pay half the rent," she said dully. "And half the bills."

"Yep and you keep the rest for yourself, don't you. Bloody magazines, make-up, lollies... just *bloody* selfish."

He still didn't look at her as he put his hat on and walked into the loungeroom.

"Where are you going?" she called, her voice hitching.

"Out."

"Dad! I have to be back at work in…"

"That's *your* problem, isn't it Stephanie. It's not always about you."

"Where's my *money*, Dad?"

He looked at her then, one hand on the front door. "It's too much for a young woman to have squirreled away."

"I *earned* that money Da…"

But he was swinging open the front door, pushing his hat down on his head, breezing back out into the afternoon sun.

And then he was gone.

Stephanie slumped against the door frame, her hands curled into tight, painful fists. Aunt Shirley was watching her with a calm expression.

He has no right.

Maybe she *was* being selfish, but it was *her* money, *her* evenings spent stacking lettuces or sweeping floors or counting tins of peas.

It was mine.

She wiped her face and scowled at Aunt Shirley.

The old woman smiled, her eyes empty. "It's time for tea, Michael."

Maynard

"There are seeds in it," Boof complained. "It's all seed and stem."

They were on the roof of the mill's workshop. Maynard and Boof sat with their backs against the four-foot wall that marked the intersection of the workshop and the warehouse roofs. The rifle was nestled into the guttering behind them, out of sight, out of mind.

Boof was poking his finger into a little plastic scam bag, trying to scoop out the best-looking bits of flower. He held up a thin green stick, a tiny branch with a few thin leaves sticking to it.

"It doesn't look anything like bud."

"It's not," Maynard reached out and took the scrap of weed from him. "That's just leafy stem. I'd be asking for my money back."

"Some of it's a bit better," Boof muttered.

"Should still smoke up, I suppose."

"You finished rolling that joint yet?" Tommy called, grinning and winking at Reese. They were standing across the roof, looking out across the river and the Railyards. "Want me to do it for you?"

"Piss off," Boof called back.

Reese muttered something to Tommy and they both laughed.

"Dickheads." Balanced on Boof's open palm were three Tally-Ho papers, gummed together to form a larger sheet. Boof sprinkled a mixture of rough weed and rolling tobacco onto the paper in a fat line, careful not to spill any of it onto his lap. It looked like a huge caterpillar on a napkin.

"Hope the wind doesn't come up," Maynard chirped.

"Don't say that."

Boof ripped a strip of cardboard off the Tally-Ho packet to make a crude filter. He sat the filter behind the caterpillar, then folded the sheet over the top of it, tucking in the edge, rolling it down into a neat cylinder. After a businesslike lick, he pressed the edge down gently and gave the end a twist.

He passed it to Maynard for inspection; a smoothly seamless, perfectly proportioned joint.

"Fuckin hell, Boof. Nice work."

"Not bad hey."

"You're a man of many talents."

"Yep."

Maynard passed the joint back to him – roller's rights – and Boof lit it up with a yellow Bic lighter.

The scoob caught the flame easily and burned in an even round glow. He took a long, savouring drag, leaning back against the wall and closing his eyes.

Maynard scoffed and was about to point out that bad weed is bad weed when Reese shouted, startling them all.

"Oi! Dickhead!" He was waving his arms over his head.

"Is it Bakery Jakery?" Boof asked.

"I think so," Tommy squinted. "There's someone with him though."

Perfect, Maynard thought, annoyed. *I should have taken this gun home.*

"Who is it?" Boofhead asked, waving the joint in front of Maynard's face.

Maynard took it in his fingers and had a quick toke; it tasted stale and dry.

"Dunno," Reese said. He called out to the newcomers. "What's going on, cupcake?"

There was a reply from below.

"Just go in the warehouse and up the stairs to the balcony," Reese pointed down the alleyway between the mill and the wool store. "You'll see the ladder. The manhole's open."

"His manhole's always open," Tommy grinned down.

There was another reply. Reese and Tommy both laughed.

"We just rolled one up," Reese said. "Come on!"

Maynard waved the joint at Tommy, who skipped over and plucked it from his fingers.

"Who's with him?" Boof asked again.

"Fucked if I know, some bloke." Tommy shrugged. "You'll see in a minute." *The more the bloody merrier.*

He pulled the rifle closer, pushing it tight against the guttering. It would be out of sight unless somebody sat right next to him.

They heard footsteps across the warehouse roof, then a heavy *bang* as Jake jumped down to where they were sitting.

"Oi bitches!"

They all swore at him in greeting until there was a second bang on the roof.

The bloke who stood up was skinny and unkempt, like he hadn't showered in a week. His cheeks were pale, almost gaunt, and his *Faith No More* t-shirt hung from skinny shoulders. Clever eyes darted from face to face.

The stranger focused in on Reese first.

"How's it going. I'm Brad."

Reese stuck his hand out. "Reese. I've seen you skating around."

They shook.

"Oh yeah, you're *that* dude," Boof nodded. "They call me Boofhead."

"That's what they call you to your face," Maynard chuckled.

When the introductions were done, Boof offered Brad the joint.

The skater took it without hesitation and had a long, deep drag, his shoulders rising. After a moment he took it from his lips, blinked at it in confusion, and passed it back to Boof.

"Is that a joint?"

Tommy guffawed laughter. Maynard slapped his knee. Boof and Reese shared an unimpressed glance.

"I knew that prick ripped us off," Boofhead muttered. He butted the joint out on the wall next to his shoulder.

"Swamp weed," Reese explained.

"Right," said Brad, obviously bewildered. "Well, I've got some other gear. Maybe we should give it a spin."

"You beauty!" Tommy laughed.

"Might not throw you off the roof after all," Boof grinned.

Brad looked up sharply.

"He thinks he's funny," Jake apologised.

"Don't chuck me off just yet," Brad shrugged, unconvinced. "Wait until I've sparked one up at least. I haven't tried this weed yet, but it looks all right."

He sat down on the roof and unzipped his backpack, reaching inside carefully. He fidgeted around, eyes distant, concentrating, and when he removed his hand there was a pale green bud the size of a fifty-cent coin in his fingers.

"Fuck yeah!" Reese's eyes were wide.

"That's a nice flower," Tommy agreed.

"You wanna roll it up?" Brad offered it to Boof.

Boof took the bud from him, confused. "All of it?"

"Not all of it dickhead," Tommy admonished.

"Whatever you want to put in it, I guess." Brad shrugged. "Might as well make it a good one."

Reese and Tommy grinned at each other while Boof got to work. Jake stood up and stretched.

"This is a pretty sweet spot," Brad said. He was scanning the horizon, head cocked as if he was listening.

"Yeah," Tommy said. "We only just found it."

"*I* found it," Maynard called out.

We never would have come here otherwise.

Boof rolled his eyes. "There's a room full of old page-three girl posters downstairs. Maynard was hoping we'd all come over and play soggy biscuits."

He put the finished joint into his mouth and lit it while the others laughed.

Nobody asked you to come.

After a couple of draws, Boof's face lit with surprise and his shoulders shook as if he was struggling to keep the smoke in. As Maynard took the joint from his fingers, Boof exhaled with a wheeze and a cough.

"*...fuck me...*" he managed. "*...it's a little bit better...*"

He coughed again.

Maynard took a testing toke. The smoke grated against his lungs, filled his throat with a harsh sweetness.

Brad and Jake wandered back over and Maynard nodded emphatically, passing the joint to Brad.

"Yeah man, that's got some kick to it, cheers."

"It's all right?" Brad took a long toke, considered the joint, then took an even longer drag on it, his eyes closing.

"This is heaps better than what we get." Maynard asked. "Where did it come from?"

Brad gave him a weak grin. "I know a guy."

"Oh right, one of *those*. Do you reckon he could sort us out too?"

He took another long drag. "I can probably get more man, no sweat."

"Sick."

They passed the joint around and everyone had a few tokes. Even Jake, who would normally wave a joint away, had a decent blast on it.

Proper stoned, Maynard thought. His eyelids already felt heavy, his head full of cotton. It felt like he was watching from behind a thin piece of glass, behind something that separated him from the real world. He was an observer with a body, not a real person anymore, not straight.

Not straight.

A strange shiver passed over him. His face flushed hot and bile rumbled in his gut. He pushed his thoughts away.

When the joint was done, Boof stood up and stretched like a bakehouse cat. He bent down and picked up a rusted bolt from the roof, weighing it with his hand.

Moving languorously, he flipped it towards the huge steel silo that clung to the side of the building.

The silo clung like an enormous bell, loud and sonorous, a heavy peal.

Brad scramble to his feet in a panic.

"Fuckin hell," he panted, looking at each of them "That was so *loud.*"

Sketchy. This bloke's shitting himself.

The others were watching the skater with dopey red eyes.

"Dead centre," beamed Boof. "I'm a crack shot."

"Fuckin crack *head*," muttered Maynard. Tommy snorted.

"Gave me a bloody heart attack," breathed Brad. "Jesus Christ."

Nobody replied.

"What is that thing, anyway?" Jake said, breaking the silence. "Looks like a grain silo."

"There's a chute at the bottom, probably to park a truck under," Maynard shrugged.

"It opens there," Reese pointed. There was another hatch on this side of the silo, it's bottom edge slightly higher than the roof they were standing on. "I'm gonna have a look."

Boof climbed to his feet and followed him over with Jake and Brad.

"They'll never get that open," Maynard scoffed to Tommy, his voice low.

"Let's fuck off," Tommy whispered, stoned and cheeky.

"What?"

"Let's go back down. I wanna shoot my shot."

"Now? With the whole of fuckin Invermay hanging around?"

"They don't matter."

"I don't know man," Maynard lowered his voice even more. "This new bloke's a bit dodgy. See how high he jumped just before?"

"So? What's he gonna do? Skate at you?"

Maynard chortled.

Boof had his fingers between the hatch's steel flaps and was trying to prise them open. One side peeled away a little, just enough for Jake to reach over and slip his fingers in as well. Both boys pulled at the flap and the hinge gave a low, dirty groan.

"All right," Maynard whispered. "Let's go now, while they're busy."

Tommy gave him an excited titter and they crept away.

Jake

Jake rubbed his hands on his jeans, but the rust had already stained his fingers. He wiped them again, but only succeeded in pushing the orange dust more deeply into the denim.

Damn. Mum's gonna kill me.

Boof pushed the hatch with his sneakered foot and it moved with a deep iron yawn. The opening was arched like the door of some black church, framing the darkness within. It was maybe three feet wide, just big enough for them to peer though, shoulder to shoulder.

The inside of the silo had an unearthly stillness. The air inside was dry and stale, undisturbed in the years since the fire. The only light was what the hatch let in, and their shadows blocked most it.

"Ooh," said Boof. "A bunch of dirt."

"It's sawdust," Jake pointed out.

"Ooh," said Boof. "A bunch of fuckin sawdust."

"Get out of the way." Reese pawed at Jake's shoulder. "Give us a look."

"Christ, righto," muttered Jake, stepping back to let him in. He rolled his eyes at Brad, but the skater just looked at him blankly.

"Is *that* all?" Reese sighed in disappointment.

Boof grinned, raising a speculative eyebrow at him.

"Wanna do it?"

"What?"

"Jump in."

"No," Reese scoffed. "How the fuck would you get out?"

"There's a funnel bit down the bottom, remember?" Boof stepped away from the hatch and pointed over the side of the building.

The chute that protruded from the bottom of the silo was maybe three metres long, rickety and rusted through in places. The end of it wavered high above the ground, waiting in vain for a truck to park below. It looked like a stiff breeze might bring the whole thing crashing down, let alone the weight of one whole Boofhead.

"See? You could just slide down and drop onto the ground."

"Go on then," Reese smirked, rolling his eyes. "We'll meet you down there."

"I'm not doing it by myself."

"I can't even tell how high the drop is," called Brad, peering into the dark silo.

Boof scoffed. "Like, two metres. At the most."

"And how deep's the sawdust?"

"Another metre on top of that. So it would come up to about…" he put his hand flat at his waist. "It's gonna be soft enough to land on."

"Fuck that," Jake rolled his eyes. "What's the point? To have a slide down the chute?"

"Where did *they* go?" Reese asked, making them all turn.

Tommy and Maynard had disappeared.

"Who cares," muttered Boof. "Gone to root each other, probably."

Abruptly Brad was striding across the roof and snatching up his backpack. The others watched as he checked the zippers, then opened the backpack and looked inside.

"Paranoid," Reese muttered. He raised his voice. "They wouldn't have flogged your gear, mate."

Brad was rifling through the bag's contents. He seemed to hesitate, then took something out of the bag's front pocket and shoved it into his jeans.

His wallet, Jake thought. *Christ, he* is *paranoid.*

"Don't stress man, they wouldn't have touched it."

"I know," Brad clutched the backpack in white knuckles as he sat down on the roof. "I just… it was hard to get this stuff. I don't know anyone up here. In Launceston, I mean."

"Should we have another joint?" Boof suggested.

"Yeah. Yeah, I reckon."

As Brad pulled out his tobacco pouch, Jake came over to sit with him.

"Tell him to fuck off if you want," he said quietly. "You don't have to shout us your weed."

"It's all right," Brad nodded. "Thanks though, man. Do you fellas smoke a bit?"

"They do."

"But not you?"

"Not so much. If we're watching a movie or something sure, but otherwise… it just makes me too… I don't know…"

"Stoned?"

Jake grinned. "Yeah."

"It's not for everyone, man."

"You like it though?"

"Yeah," Brad grimaced. "Way too much. It helps me focus when I'm skating, helps me rest when I'm not."

"Makes sense."

"Are you rolling up or what?" Boof's voice carried across the roof.

"Are you jumping in that death trap or what?" Brad mimicked. Jake and Reese laughed.

"Maybe later," Boof shrugged.

"As if you fuckin will," Reese admonished. "You're so full of shi…"

"What do these dickheads want?" Boof was frowning into the distance. Jake stood and followed his gaze.

"Shit. It's Dylan and Ben Campbell."

"Serious?" Brad's face fell. The Tally-ho sheet was balanced on his knee, already sprinkled with dry chunks of pale green weed.

"Don't stress dude. Just… hang on a tic." He took a few steps forward. "Reese."

Reese didn't look around. He was giving Dylan and Ben Campbell the finger.

"Reese!"

"What?"

"Get rid of 'em."

"What? Why?"

Jake cut his eyes to Brad, who had finished rolling the joint. The skater had his head down.

"Dylan's after him," Jake tried to keep his voice low. "Just fuck them off."

Reese looked incredulous, but he kept his voice low too.

"How? It's fuckin Dylan."

"What's going on legends?" Boof called down in a too-loud voice, letting them know that Dylan and Campbell were close enough to hear.

"Look at these faggots." Dylan's mean voice drifted up them. "You boys sucking each other off up there?"

"Nah, no dick today, sorry fellas."

"Fuckin smart arse. How do you get up?"

"Go right down the other end of the warehouse," Reese pointed down the alleyway. "When you get around the corner, there's a sort of frame thing on the wall you have to climb up."

Jake grinned at the expression on Brad's face. The time they spent looking for the non-existent frame would be more than long enough for Brad slip through the manhole and disappear.

Reese the shark.

"Fuck that." It was Ben's voice. "Hey Reese, you know that bloke who's been skating around South Street? Brad?"

"Seen him round." Reese shrugged. "Looks like trouble."

"You're a fuckin old woman Reese," Dylan cackled. "Have you seen him like in the last hour or so?"

"Don't think so man, why's that?"

"Just wanna catch up with him, that's all."

"Sounds like trouble," said Boof.

"Never talked to him," Reese said. "Bloody skaters, eh?"

"Nah he's all right," said Ben Campbell. "He just likes a smoke."

"Fuckin *loves* a smoke," Dylan added.

Brad, out of sight, shrugged and lit his joint. It was enormous.

"Come on, why you looking for him?" Reese insisted.

"Not us," said Ben.

"Who then? Judy?"

"I said *not us.*"

"Then who?"

"Just fuckin tell him to come and see us, Reese."

"I don't fuckin know him, man. *You* tell him."

"What do you think I'm trying to do, you dickhead."

"You're not telling him, you're telling *me.*"

"Still a smart arse then, Reese. How's that sexy sister of yours?"

"Piss off Dylan."

"What? *What* did you say, Reese? You wanna come down here and say it?"

"Just don't fuckin talk about Elisha!"

"I heard she likes it in the arse. Like a fuckin dog."

"That's not how dogs work, young Dylan," Boof shook his head in disappointment.

"Oh you want a fuckin smack as well, Boofhead? Pretty mouthy aren't you, when your big tough big brother's not around."

"Come on man," Ben Campbell's voice was weary. "Let's keep going."

"Have you fuckin seen him or not?" Dylan demanded.

"Nup," said Reese, disinterested.

"Who you talking about?" Boof asked.

"Yeah you'll be a fuckin smartarse when the Marauders get hold of you. We'll tell em you're his boyfriends."

Reese and Boof exchanged a look.

"The bikies are looking for him?" Reese asked.

"Fuckin hell," Ben muttered. He looked up at Reese. "Rohan said he'd give us an ounce if we found him."

"No shit?" Boof breathed.

An ounce of weed? Jake blinked. *Because he kicked their dog?*

"What did he do?" Reese asked.

Brad was listening. The joint trembled between his fingers.

"Stole something from em," Dylan chuckled. "Fuckin dumb, stealing from the Marauders."

Jake realised he was staring at the skater. The stranger. Reese and Boof were looking back at him too.

Dylan's full of shit.

He swallowed. When he spoke, it was almost a whisper.

"Did you? Steal from them, I mean? What did you…" His eyes flicked to the backpack. "Oh. Shit."

He puked. When the bikie almost saw us, he puked.

Abruptly he wished he was somewhere else, anywhere else.

"Nothing to do with us," Reese called down. He was scowling.

Boof spat on the roof. "Fuckin death wish."

"You're a pussy, Boof," Dylan cackled.

"Come on," Ben Campbell muttered. "Let's keep going."

"You see him, you come and tell us right?"

Reese nodded, arms crossed over his chest. "Yep. We'll tell Rohan."

"Yeah bullshit you'll tell Rohan," Dylan laughed. "Just come and tell *us*, Reese."

"See ya." Boof saluted. "Wouldn't wanna *be* ya."

"Yeah ha ha don't fall off the roof you fuckin clown."

Brad stubbed the joint out on the roof next to where he was sitting. He had smoked the entire thing himself, had smoked it until it was gone. When he stood up, his eyes were glassy and his cheeks so pale they were almost green.

Jesus, he's packing it. Jake's stomach churned. He didn't feel so great himself.
I don't want anything to do with this.

The skater looked at them each in turn.

"Thanks, eh."

There was a sudden clatter on the roof next to them, a pattering of falling gravel, a handful of rocks thrown from the empty lot below.

"Nice one, Dylan!" Boof yelled. "Rock and roll, *dickhead!*"

They heard him cackling.

Brad

I've gotta get out of here.

Reese and Boof were staring at him as though he had suddenly grown horns.

Jake wouldn't look at him.

"The Marauders? Are you fuckin serious?" Reese's face was pale.

"They're fuckin riding around looking for *you*. You could have fuckin *told* us!"

"You didn't just kick their dog then?" Jake asked quietly.

Brad shuffled his feet.

"It was… I just wanted some weed. I don't fucking know anyone, and this carpark just reeked of it, so… so I found their setup, scruffed what I could and got out of there." He wiped at his face with rough hands. "I didn't know whose fuckin house it was. I just wanted a smoke."

"They saw you, didn't they." Boof was shaking his head. "You weren't quick enough."

"Lucky they didn't shoot you on the spot," Reese said.

"I almost got away except…" Brad cleared his throat. "When I was bailing. They all fuckin rode right past me on the next street, going to the place. One of them looked right at me."

He spat. His bottom lip was shaking.

"And now they're all out looking for you." Reese put a hand to his forehead, as though he was taking his own temperature. "If they see you with us…"

"They'll think we were in on it," Jake finished, his voice flat.

"No, they won't." Brad thought of the girl on the couch. *Will she remember? Does it even matter?* "I was by myself."

"But you're not anymore. If they see you with us… they know *all* of us. They know I live at the bakehouse. They'll think I let you hide there." Jake grimaced. "I *did* fuckin let you hide there."

"This is bullshit," Reese muttered.

"How much did you pinch?" Boof asked. "It must have been a bit, if they're putting up an ounce."

Maybe ten grand.

But he wasn't about to tell them about the yellow envelope. Dylan hadn't mentioned any cash. *At* least *ten grand.*

He hefted the backpack around so that it hung in the crook of his arm, eyed them for a moment, then pulled open the zipper.

"Way more than an ounce. Look."

The others craned their necks.

"Jesus *please* us," breathed Reese. "That's gotta be a dozen bags, right?"

And that's not the least of it. The envelope was heavy in his back pocket.

"A pound, I reckon," Brad shook his head. "I literally just wanted a smoke, but… there was so much just sitting there… I guess I got greedy/"

"Better divvy it up then," Boof said with a sly sneer.

"What?" Brad took a step back, holding the backpack away defensively.

"Come on."

"For Christ's sake Boof," Jake muttered.

"Fuck off Cupcake. I've never *seen* that much weed before. *And* if we're gonna get our *arses* kicked for it, we might as well get some…"

"Don't be a dick, Boofhead," Reese growled.

"Here." Brad took one of the bags out of the backpack and held it out to Jake. "Take it."

Boof and Reese watched, rapt.

"Go on. Take it."

After a moment, Jake shook his head.

"I don't want it, man,"

"Just take it and forget I was even here."

"Nup. No thanks."

Brad lowered the ounce bag, his eyes sad. "Why not?"

"I don't want your stolen bikie weed at my house, mate."

Brad's shoulders slumped. There was no fight in him.

"I didn't mean to get you in the shit. Any of you. I just… I just fuckin freaked out. And I couldn't go home because Dylan and…"

"You're fucked mate," Boof shook his head. "Even if we don't tell the Marauders shit, they're gonna find you."

"Yeah," Reese added glumly. "They're good at that sort of stuff."

"Dylan knows where he lives already," Jake's arms were crossed. "He knows where we all live."

"What do I do then?" Brad raised his arms in appeal. "Go and ask for forgiveness? Dump it on their doorstep and run?"

None of them looked at him.

I wish Dad was here.

He pushed the useless thought away and tried to blink away the burning in his eyes..

"I don't know anyone." His voice was thick in his throat. "I'm just a stoner, not a bloody… bloody… what do I *do?*"

Reese sighed and rolled his eyes.

"Cupcake? You know them more than any of us."

"Yeah man, Noah likes you, he'll talk to you," Boof insisted. "You could smooth it over."

"You?" Brad blinked at Jake. "You fuckin serious? You *know* them?"

Jake shrugged, uncomfortable. "Everyone knows them."

"And you still let me hide behind the gate?"

"Noah's a good bloke, but Rohan would put you in hospital for looking at him sideways." Jake scowled. "Most of them are decent… if you do the right thing by them. If you don't *kick* their fuckin dog."

"Just say that he's the new kid," Reese said. "He didn't know it was their place, he fucked up. They'll listen to you."

With a heavy sigh, Jake kicked a pebble across the roof… then took a step back in surprise.

"Shit. Look out."

"You sneaky little *pricks!*" Dylan's voice was thick with scornful disbelief. "You were fuckin *hiding* him up here."

The blonde Fonzie thumped down on to the roof in front of them, a gleeful sneer curling his lips. He was bouncing on his toes, his eyes fixed on Brad.

"Go climb the fuckin wall, you reckon." Ben Campbell scrambled down the warehouse roof behind him. Grinning, he nodded at Reese and Boof. "You think nobody else has ever been up here before?"

"What's going *on*, Brad," Dylan said, skipping from one foot to the other. *Like a boxer,* Brad realised. *He thinks he's a boxer.*

"Bit *shy* now, are you? I thought we were mates, skater boy."

"Yeah man. Remember how I shouted you that weed?"

"That wasn't fuckin weed," Dylan said. "Can't believe you flogged gear off the bikies. Dumb fuckin move. Little scum bag. I told you they don't mess around."

"Yeah, that's why they've sent down the big guns," Boof rolled his eyes.

"Oh they're gunning for him mate," Dylan sneered. "They're gonna be gunning for all of you after I talk to em."

"How much did you get?" Ben asked.

"Heaps," Brad shrugged warily. "More than I need. I'll give you both a bit."

"He'll *give* us a bit," Dylan chuckled, cracking his knuckles. "Fuck mate, you wanna do better than that."

"You can take it back to them, get the credit."

"No shit, sherlock," said Dylan. "But they want you too. And maybe your mum."

He laughed his nasty laugh, but nobody joined in.

Brad's blood was running cold.

If I can just get around him... if I can beat them back to the manhole...

The trapdoor into the warehouse was just a few metres past the wall where the roofs met. Brad was scrawny but quick, and he was used to scuttling across fences and car parks. He could make it. He skittered back a few more feet, giving himself space.

"You might wanna move back to Hobart, I reckon." Dylan sneered. "You fucked up. They'll give me a medal for dragging your arse back there, Bradley."

"It's not Bradley." The words tasted bitter in his mouth. "It's Bradford."

There was silence for a moment.

When Ben Campbell started laughing it was loud and unconstrained, contagious. Dylan howled along next to him, doubling over. Reese didn't bother hiding his grin and even Boof had a quiet chuckle. Jake looked at them all in turn, mortified.

"Fuckin *Bradford!* Really." Dylan grinned a goofy grin, running a hand through his hair. "Well then, *Bradford,* I guess you'll be going to one of those fancy hospitals today. Let's fu…"

Go!

Brad darted to one side. Dylan was ready for it and lunged at him like a rugby player… but Brad was already moving in the opposite direction.

Running wide of them all, Brad covered the distance in the blink of an eye. He jumped at the wall, catching himself at waist height and risking a look back.

Dylan was still stumbling to turn around.

Reese and Boof were watching, motionless, with identical surprised expressions.

Brad caught Jake's eye. A moment of regret passed between them.

I'm sorry man, I didn…

A fist cracked into Brad's cheek. A meaty fist. It flew out of his blind spot into the side of his face and the force of it rocked his head back, the smack of it echoed across the roof.

Ben Campbell's roundhouse had been perfect.

The skater lost his grip on the wall and scrambled backwards, somehow managing to keep his feet.

And then he was blindly swinging punches.

His fists flew wide, but still surprised Ben Campbell, who had obviously expected his king hit to end the matter. Ben ducked out of the way, barely dodging Brad's wild swings, fists raised in a boxer's guard.

"*Fuckin dog!*" Brad spat, his face flushed with rage and pain. "Hit me from behind like a *fuckin pussy.*"

Dylan feinted on his other side, but when Brad pivoted he backed off, still bouncing on his toes.

Brad spun - but he was too late. Ben Campbell had closed the distance and was reaching for him, growling.

They seized each other's shoulders. Ben was bigger, but Brad was wiry. As they grappled, stumbling closer and closer to the edge of the roof, Ben's fingers curled around one of the backpack's straps.

"Fuck *off!*" Brad grunted.

"*Give it here!*" Ben snarled, pulling at the backpack.

They scuffled over the iron roof, shoving and grunting until they were near the edge. Pulling at the backpack, Ben threw a left jab that missed Brad's head. Twisting, Brad drove his knee into the meaty part of Ben's thigh.

"*Ow!* You little *shit!* Let *go!*"

"It's *mine,*" Brad threw another punch.

This one connected to Ben Campbell's cheek with a satisfying smack.

Ben Campbell's head rocked and he stumbled for a moment, blinking, then gave a roar and ran headlong at the skater.

Brad didn't have time to move before Ben shoved him, grabbing at the backpack.

The backpack's nylon straps pulled at his shoulders briefly... then ripped apart.

For a slow moment the backpack fell through the air, until it landed on the roof a few feet away.

Brad and Ben Campbell both froze, their eyes fixed on the bag.

But Dylan was striding across the roof towards them.

Towards *him.*

He's gonna push me off the roof.

Alarm raced through Brad's body and he tried to turn, far too late.

"Fuck *off!*"

His voice was shrill but Dylan didn't hesitate, smacking into the skater's chest and *shoving* him hard.

With the air knocked from his body, Brad tumbled backwards, his legs tangling, his arms pin-wheeling for balance.

"Jesus, lookout!" somebody squealed.

Brad's heel clipped something.

Abruptly he was falling. Falling into darkness.

The silo!

His surprised yelp was cut off when he dropped into the sawdust.

It swallowed him whole.

Suddenly, everything was dry dust. He was surrounded by it, submerged in it, deep and directionless.

Up. Gotta get up.

He tried to push, to wriggle, to move, but sawdust was pushing under his eyelids and blocking his nose and spilling into his mouth. His chest thumped painfully.

Oh jesus my eyes I can't fucking BREATHE!

Every gasp pulled more dust into his lungs,

He struggled, wriggled, thrashed, eyes blazing with pain.

He tried to get air into his pounding chest, but everything was dry, sharp, formless dust that provided no purchase, that had no weight, that let in no light, It filled his ears and nose and crept into the back of his throat and coated his heaving, desperate lungs.

UP, gotta get UP help!

But he didn't know which way was up, couldn't open his eyes, couldn't feel anything but soft and smothering dryness.

His head swam. His lungs *burned.*

Fucking help me!

A hand would seize him, a hand would reach him, pull him back to the surface, back to sweet air and light and life, a policeman's hand or maybe his father's hand.

Dad! Help, dad!

He flailed against the softness, desperate for purchase... for air... for *air...*

for just *one more*

breath

Jake

"Brad! *Brad!*"

Jake reached the hatch first, but Boof was right behind him. They leaned into the silo.

"Skater boy? You all right?"

There was no reply. The sawdust looked undisturbed; a few specks drifted above what might have been an indent in its surface.

"Where the fuck did he go?" Jake's stomach churned. *"Brad!"*

He sank. It's deeper than it looks.

A shiver ran through his body.

"Why can't we see him?" Reese's eyes were wide over Boof's shoulder. "Where did he go?"

"He's in the *sawdust!*" Boof was pale, his eyes wide.

"Why isn't the sawdust moving?"

"Maybe it knocked him out?"

"Brad! *Brad!*"

"Brad! Answer, you fuckwit!*"*

They held their breath. Nothing moved.

The silo was dry. Silent. Stagnant.

"The chute. *The chute!*" Jake stepped to the edge of the building to look at it, but Reese was already shaking his head.

"He didn't come out the bottom," he said. His face was grey, his voice shaky. "How deep is that fuckin sawdust?"

Deeper than it looks.

Jake's blood was cold.

"*Oi!*" Boof sounded panicked. "Hey come *back!*"

Jake turned and grunted. Dylan and Ben Campbell were already scrambling on to the warehouse roof, the backpack firmly wrapped around Dylan's fist.

"Where the fuck are you *going?*" Jake yelled. "Come back and *help!*"

"Fuck him!" Dylan sneered. "Shouldn't fuck with the Marauders, should he."

"You're not a *bikie*, you fuckin tool!"

Dylan lifted the backpack like a prize fighter. "I am now, dickhead."

"Let's go for Christ's sake," Ben Campbell muttered. He paced over to the manhole and dropped out of sight.

"He's *gone*, Dylan!" Boof shouted. He was shaking. "You fuckin *killed* him!"

"Bullshit," Dylan turned his back on them. "He fell in while you were sucking his dick."

"We've gotta get *help*. We've gotta get him *out.*" said Reese. "We have to get *help!*"

"Help him then, you fuckin sook."

"We can't *see* him!' Jake shouted. "He's not *moving! Dylan!*"

But Dylan was gone.

"Goddamned *coward!*"

"We've gotta get him out," Reese's lips were pressed together in a thin, almost invisible line. He leaned back into the hatch. "*Braaad!*"

"*Brad* can you hear us?"

They watched the sawdust. Moments ticked past.

None of them spoke. None of them moved.

Nothing moved.

"He needs help." Jake shook himself. His cheeks were wet. "We need to find a rope, or a chain or some…

"We've gotta call the cops." Reese looked like he might vomit as he turned and darted towards the manhole.

"Wait!" Jake called to him.

"You can't call the fuckin *cops*," Boof ran after Reese.

"Wait, don't *go…*" Jake was clutching at his head.

"What? Why?" Reese demanded. "We *have* to call the cops!"

"No!" Boof shouted. "They'll blame *us.*"

That made them all pause.

"Manslaughter, they'll say." There was cold certainty in Boof's eyes. "If we make the call, *we're* fucked."

"He's not *dead.*" Jake's mouth was dry. "We've gotta help him, help him *now!*"

"Dylan did it," Reese said, already halfway down the manhole. His eyes were bright, his face fearful. "We all saw it. *He* pushed him in, on *purpose.*"

"The cops will blame *all* of us. Manslaughter, straight to Risdon. Ten years, maybe twelve. You'll never get a decent job in Tassie, *everyone* will know you."

"I'm not going to prison for some little thief," Reese said, his voice bitter, a tear running unnoticed down his cheek.

"Brad," Jake's head was spinning. "His name's *Brad.*"

"Doesn't matter anymore, does it?" Boof wouldn't meet his eyes.

"Dude. What if it was you in there? Or you, Reese? What if we just left *you* in there? Your parents would lose their fucking minds!"

Reese shivered and looked away. When he spoke, his voice was dull.

"You're right. We have to call it in, don't we."

"We have to get him *out! Now!*" Jake was croaking, desperate. "We can't *leave* him!"

Reese was shaking his head, his eyes squeezed closed.

"I'm getting the fuck out of here. Fuck this. *Fuck* this. He's dead, isn't he."

"They *will* blame us," Jake tried to reason. "If we don't try to *help…*"

"It won't matter," Boof moaned. "We didn't stop him. We just fuckin watched. We've gotta get our stories straight…"

"No stories, no bullshit," Reese said. "I'm calling the cops and I'm gonna tell em what I saw. We all should. None of us did anything wrong."

"Just forget you were ever here," Boof scowled. "We'll all forget and if they don't find him… maybe we can just get on with it, you know? Why would they ever look in there?"

"What the *fuck* are you talking about?" Jake pleaded. "Please, just help me find a goddamned rope, or… *something*…"

"It won't work. Only *one* person can keep a secret." Reese's voice was deadpan. "Not bloody *five* of us."

"*I* can keep a secret," said Boof, indignant. He stepped towards the manhole and Reese lowered himself down.

"Don't go," Jake pleaded. "Help me get him out, *please!*"

"You do what you want, Cupcake." Reese hiccupped, out of sight. "I'm going home."

Maynard

Maynard flicked the lighter again and held the little flame against the candle wick. The late afternoon sun barely touched the dusty windows, but all three candles were burning now, giving the pinup-plastered room a flickering, unearthly atmosphere.

He hadn't noticed how musty the room smelled earlier. It smelled of secrets, a peculiar kind of sourness, fresh but old, warm but sharp. It suited the yellowing smiles of the women on the walls, their bubbling, papery skin. It suited his dry mouth and watery eyes.

That was some good weed.

Tommy was examining the pinups again, standing on his tiptoes, his back to Maynard. Maynard's eyes lingered on his friend's denim-wrapped calves. He was glad that they had left the others behind on the mill roof. The rifle was leaning against the wall next to him, its stiff barrel pointed at the ceiling.

"This one here," Tommy said, tapping one of the posters. "She's the one."

"Yeah." Maynard leaned against the wall. "She looks real good."

"*Real* good." The older boy sighed, a deep, bone-felt sigh. "We need to get some women down here."

"Yeah."

"Like that Little Miss Hollywood from school, Evelyn. Get *her* down here."

"Like she'd wanna fuckin hang out with you."

She would though. Of course she would.

Tommy turned to him, his eyelids heavy with weed and lust. He squeezed at the front of his jeans and leered.

"She would once I showed her *this.*"

Maynard's gaze followed his friend's finely tanned and muscled arm down to where it was curled into a fist around... around...

Sweat sparkled along his forehead. The walls flickered.

"I..." His mouth was dry. He didn't trust himself to speak. He couldn't look away.

Staring. You're staring. *You've been staring way too long.*

But he didn't know how to look away now. He could sense Tommy's frown. His head felt light.

Don't.

"I could..." Maynard's lips were rough, his tongue dry. "If you want, I could..."

A loud *bang* made them both jump.

Footsteps approached.

Panicked, his blood whizzing with adrenaline and lust, Maynard picked up Greg's rifle.

Tommy was staring at him.

We weren't doing anything, we weren't...

Boofhead's dopey face appeared in the doorway and Maynard wilted in relief, but only for a moment.

Boof was pale, his eyes strained, and he kept his voice low.

"We gotta get the fuck outta here."

"What? Why?" Maynard hoped his cheeks weren't as flushed as they felt.

Tommy crossed his arms, frowning at his little brother. Boof had put a hand on the wall to steady himself and was taking slow, measured breaths.

"Fuckin Dylan was here."

Tommy bristled.

"Is he still..."

"He was looking for that skater bloke, the Marauders are after him and Dylan... Dylan pushed him in the silo."

"Into that big fucking silo on the roof?" Maynard's mouth fell open.

"Bullshit." Tommy was staring at his brother intently.

"He's in there *now?*" Maynard's blood was abruptly cold.

"Dylan fucking bailed. Reese has gone to call the cops."

"Is he stuck?" Tommy said. "Why didn't you get him out?"

"He disappeared. It's full of sawdust and he…" Boofhead's bottom lip trembled. "We couldn't see him."

Maynard and Tommy blinked at him, then at each other.

I haven't seen Boofhead cry since we were kids.

Another cold shiver passed through him.

"How long ago?" Tommy asked.

"Ten minutes maybe. We gotta get the fuck away from here."

"We've gotta get him *out,*" Maynard said. "We can't just fuckin leave him in there."

Boof ducked out of the room, shaking his head. Maynard and Tommy quickly followed him to the loading bay door.

"Where are you going?" Tommy demanded.

"We gotta go. Reese is gonna call the *cops.*" Boofhead didn't look back to see if they were following. "If we're still here they'll think *we* did it."

"If we don't *help,* they'll think we did it," Maynard said.

"If they see *that* they'll think *you* did it," Tommy nodded at the rifle in Maynard's hand.

Maynard gaped at him. The rifle was cold and heavy. He felt faint.

"But you saw Dylan do it, didn't…"

"Do you reckon that tosser will own up to it?" Boof stopped and looked at them in turn. "Or do you reckon he'll blame it on us?"

Tommy nodded reluctantly. Maynard's stomach clenched.

"Let's get the fuck out of here."

Jake

He strode though the mill's workshop.

He wasn't panicking. He *wasn't* panicking.

Dead.

There were stacks of timber sitting on the abandoned workbenches, a few tools, some rusted saw blades. Empty steel drums gathered in the corners.

He couldn't see any rope. He wasn't panicking.

Dead.

Jake's head pounded as he looked around for anything that might reach the sawdust. His ears strained for any clue that help might be coming; a siren in the distance, a policeman's hail or perhaps even the familiar buzz of his mother's Toyota Corolla.

But there was nothing. He had rarely felt so alone.

Brad's dead.

"You don't know that," he muttered, then jumped as his voice bounced off the quiet, soot-stained walls.

The others had all bailed.

I should go too.

He needs help. It was his mother's voice. *You need to help him, Jakey.*

He would help.

His steps quickened when he spotted several lengths of chain dangling from a rack on the far wall. He pulled the longest one free, looping it over his shoulder. It was heavy.

He wasn't panicking.

The skater might be unconscious, but if Cupcake Jakery from the Bakery pulled him out sore and sad but alive and breathing then all of this would go away and Jakery could go back to his sausage roles and his book and his Enigma.

He hustled back through the warehouse and up the balcony stairs. Climbing through the manhole was difficult - the chain seemed to be getting heavier by the second - but he struggled his way up and out.

A few unsteady steps brought him to the flat roof where - once upon a time - he had shared a joint with a skater he thought might be his new buddy. He could still taste tar in his throat.

The last joint he ever smoked, Jake thought, his stomach twisting. *Maybe the last one I'll ever smoke too.*

He hurried over to the silo. The hatch was still wide open, an empty, arched hole in the burnt-out iron. He held his breath, set his jaw, and peeked inside.

There was no movement, no sound. The surface of the sawdust was undisturbed, the air as still as a tomb.

It is *a tomb.*

"Brad?" He called. His voice shook in the muted space. *"Brad?"*

The sawdust didn't stir.

I'm not sure I can do this.

What if it was you *in there, Jakey?*

His chest hitched. It was all too easy to imagine his mother's face growing wearier and older as the months went on without a sign or a clue of where her son's body might be, of what might have become of her pride and joy.

And what about Brad's parents?

Jake didn't want to think about that.

He dumped the heavy chain on the roof, then carefully dropped one end of it into the silo. It rattled down a few feet and stopped. The sawdust was further down than he realised so he fed the chain through the hatch, hand over hand like a pallbearer.

It wasn't long enough. Not even close.

By the time the lowest links brushed the top of sawdust he was already reaching the end of the chain. He knelt on the roof for balance and lowered it in as far as he could. The chain stirred the top of the light sawdust, which gave no resistance.

It just swallowed him. It must be deeper than it looks.

How much deeper? God only knew.

It all seemed impossible, like a bad dream, as though a made-up, half-forgotten genie was trapped underneath all that dense, weightless sawdust, not some stoned kid who liked to ride a skateboard and had seemed so full of life not half an hour ago.

Jake shuddered.

Maybe he got out already. Maybe he got out and ran away and we just didn't see.

The chain was getting heavy, its weight making his shoulder burn. He was only sifting through the very top of the dust, giving it the vaguest mix, so he lifted the chain out and dropped it on the roof, arms aching, tears of frustration threatening to spill.

Where's that goddamned ambulance, Reece? Where are the police?

His shoulders slumped. His heart thrummed beneath his ribs and his throat was coarse like sandpaper.

They can't help. He's dead.

He could hear the distant traffic, probably from Invermay Road. He could see over the row of cottages on Churchill Park Drive, could see the brown North Esk River pushing lazily against the mud and reeds. There were ducks squabbling, somewhere, out of sight.

If I hadn't let him hide in the driveway, none of this would have happened.

He didn't know if it was true. How *could* he know if it was true?

Rohan might have beaten him up, but he'd still be alive.

Instead, Jake had brought him down to the mill, to the silo, to his death. Brad had died wearing *his* t-shirt.

I have to get him out of there. I have to save him.

The silo loomed over him. He hated it, this hulking, scorched black monstrosity that reared against the sky, radiating disquiet. He wanted to push it off the wall, to hear its metal chute twisting and squealing as the whole thing crashed into the alleyway below.

There must be a way.

The silo had two hatches, the one on the roof Brad had fallen through – been *pushed* through – and the one above the chute in the laneway. On that hatch's side was an iron lever with a hole through the middle where a rope would have once hung. You could pull the rope on the ground and sawdust would tumble into the chute.

If I can get this chain through the hole on the lever, I could open it.

Sawdust would pour out of the silo and the skater would be able climb out.

Jake's energy came back.

It might work. It has to work.

He didn't have any other ideas.

Standing on the very edge of the roof, ignoring the dizzying drop below, he swung the end of the chain back and forth. The lever was a good couple of metres out and down from where he stood on the roof and the hole was very, very small.

A hard shot… but not impossible by any means.

Taking aim, he flung the end of the chain out over the roof. It clanged into the side of the silo, bouncing off and away from the lever.

"Shit!"

He pulled it up to try again.

Dylan

There was an enormous oak tree on the corner of Herbert Street. Acorns crunched beneath Dylan's heavy boots and Ben Campbell's sneakers. They walked quickly.

Ben's head turned this way and that, as though on a swivel. Dylan marched straight ahead, his chest pushed out, his hips and shoulders rolling.

Marauder, Marauder, Marauder. The mantra repeated in time with Dylan's steps.

I spotted that cop. I got their backpack. They have to give me a patch, maybe even tonight.

"Are you just gonna go up and knock on the door?" said Ben.

"Yeah man," Dylan smirked. "I'm only giving it to Noah himself. Pasco and the rest of them can fuck off."

"What about the skater?"

"What about him?"

"Will you tell them what happened?"

"Why? They won't care."

Ben Campbell eyed him sideways.

"Everyone knows they were looking for him. If he doesn't turn up, the cops will blame the Marauders. They might have to fish him out of that silo."

"As if," Dylan laughed. "He's probably skated half-way back to Hobart already."

"If you say so man... *shit,* look."

They pulled up sharply. The Marauders clubhouse was still half a block away, but there was a silver car parked outside it. The car looked brand new, spotless, purposefully unremarkable... aside from the small antenna protruding from the boot.

Dylan swore.

"That's an unmarked cop car," Ben murmured.

"No shit."

"Why are the cops here?"

"How the fuck should I know, Ben." Dylan shifted from foot to foot.

"Well, what are we gonna do?"

"Just shut the fuck up for a minute!" He shifted his grip on the backpack. "We can't go there now. Not with this."

"How much weed do you reckon is in there?"

"How should I know? I'm not gonna just whip it out here on the..."

"Ssshhh..." Ben Campbell held a finger to his lips.

A motorbike, half a block away. Dylan's eyes lit up.

"They're still out looking for him. Fuck the clubhouse, we've just gotta find Rohan. Come on."

They marched back the way they had come.

"There it is," Dylan held up a hand, listening.

He could hear the motorbike on the other side of the block – it was going up South Street, away from them.

"This way, come on!" Dylan said, eyes wide.

He took off at pace, Ben loping along behind him. Dylan was quick on his feet but Ben Campbell, never the athlete, quickly fell behind.

"Come on Benny!" Dylan hissed back at him.

The Harley's engine was fading into the distance.

Useless prick! He stopped, cursing.

Ben Campbell caught up a moment later, out of breath, and bent over with his hands on his knees.

"Man, what if they just take it all" He panted, trying to catch his breath. "What if they just keep it and tell us to fuck off, you know?"

"They won't, man," Dylan shook his head. "You heard Rohan. They wanted that little prick. I got him. For them. And I spotted that cop this morning too. They *owe* me."

"You know that, and I know that, but do *they* know that?"

"Look after the Marauders and they'll look after you. *Everyone* knows that."

"You reckon they'll let you fight?"

"I reckon I'm gonna be a Marauder. Come on."

He jogged away.

After a long moment, Ben Campbell followed.

"You wanna be a fuckin bikie now? Look, let's just tell mum. She'll know what to do."

"How would she know what to do?" Dylan rolled his eyes.

They passed the end of Little Ray Street.

No motorbikes. Come on Rohan!

"She knows the cops," Ben Campbell reminded him. "She'll tell them that the skater flogged the weed and when we went to get it back, he shit himself and jumped in the silo."

"Why would they believe her? He should have just given me the bloody bag."

He could still hear the motorbike rumbling away. It was going down Feral Street.

"Come on! We can catch him up here!"

Dylan took off again. Ben lumbered after him.

They ran past the enormous federation houses, most of them rundown, all of them with barking dogs in their yards. He ignored the barks and yelps because the motorbike was just around the corner… but it moved away in the opposite direction, towards Invermay Road.

"Shit!" shouted Dylan. "Come on man, we can still cut him off!"

"Where?" Ben Campbell panted.

"Down here," said Dylan, veering through the service gate that led to Burwood Estate's long leafy driveway.

They cut through the shaded gardens, sprinting for the white main gate at the other end of the lane. The lawn was unkempt, its fringes thick with bushes.

The motorbike was roaring past on the other side of Burwood's green hedging, speeding down Elm Street. Dylan watched it zoom past the gate without slowing down.

He swore, out of breath.

"Too slow." Ben Campbell caught up with him. "Man, I need to stop for a sec anyway."

He walked over to a white park bench and plonked himself down on it, catching his breath.

"Shit." Dylan was bent over, hands on his knees, watching the front gate. "He'll come back this way in a minute."

"Yeah." Ben's eyes were closed. "Why don't we just go back to my place and call them."

"So you and your mum get all the credit."

"Christ, Dylan. You don't even know how much weed there is."

"Might as well have a look then."

Dylan sat the backpack on the ground and unzipped it with a smug grin. "What. The. *Fuck.*"

He pawed through the plastic bags and the pale green lumps of tight bud they contained, trying to count the bags, giving up quickly.

"Jesus, look at all that weed." Ben Campbell was sitting upright on the bench now, his eyes wide open. "I can smell it from here."

"They're nice buds too," said Dylan, without any idea of whether they were or not. He pulled out one of the bags and threw it to Ben Campbell. "Really nice buds."

"Of course they are, its fuckin swamp weed." Ben pressed the plastic bag against his face and inhaled deeply. "Smells like Marauder."

"Smells like money," Dylan grinned. "And they'll let me into the fights now, for sure."

"Mate. You might have just killed someone for them. You'll wanna hope they fuckin look after you.

"I didn't kill anyone, you dickhead."

"But Reese and that will say…"

"As if *Reese's* gonna go talking to the Marauders. Jake and Boofhead won't say shit either, they're not stupid. Rohan'll never know."

"Reese will tell his parents, *they'll* call the cops."

"So fucking what. You saw what happened to those cops today. Anyway, it'll be Reese's word against ours and we can sort him out later."

"Christ. Let's find Rohan then."

"Yeah." Dylan shoved the ounces back into the bag. "I'm getting hungry."

Maynard

A couple of cars passed them on Forster Street. A cement truck rumbled along slowly, the cylinder on its tray turning. The Railyards seemed to stretch on forever to their left, the old tyres and abandoned carriages relics of another time.

Maynard tried to hold the rifle against the back of his leg as they walked. The sleight-of-body *might* fool the cars driving past if they didn't look too closely.

Tommy walked with his head tilted, listening to the rumble of a distant motorcycle. When it faded away, he cocked an eyebrow at his younger brother.

"How much weed was in that backpack?"

"More than you've ever seen in your life. Christ knows what Dylan thinks he's gonna do with it all."

"Fuck." Tommy kicked at a rock. "We could've had it."

"What, you would've thrown that poor prick into the silo?"

"No, but I'd throw fuckin Dylan in there after him. Anyway," Tommy nodded at Maynard. "Old Ned Kelly here would have sorted him out."

"Dylan would have pissed himself if he'd seen this." Maynard's bravado sounded hollow, at least to his own ears. His hand was sweaty against the polished timber stock.

Just stash it in the railyards. Just throw it away.

He couldn't. It was Greg's rifle and no matter where he hid it, somebody would find it eventually.

Just get it home.

"We could have set up shop and put old Magnus out of business," Tommy continued.

"Fuck that," Boof scoffed. "Who wants dickheads turning up on their doorstep all day, ringing up every five minutes looking for dope."

Tommy rolled his eyes. "Well, what would *you* do then?"

"I'd go out to Rossarden," Boof said promptly. "Camp in one of those little miner's huts and just smoke bongs all day."

"Dick head," Tommy muttered. "He would've…"

"*Shh!*" Maynard waved a hand at them, all business. "Look!"

Ahead of them, on the corner of South Street, was hunched-over figure. He was standing in the shadows with his head down, as if trying to stay out of sight.

"It's Reese," Boof said, then raised his voice. "*Oi!*"

They saw Reese jump. He turned to them and put a finger to his lips. When they stopped walking, he took a furtive look back around the corner and gestured wildly.

"What's he saying?" Tommy squinted. "Why's he…"

Reese had clasped his hands behind his back. He made sure they were watching, then slowly rocked from foot to foot a few times and pointed at South Street.

"What's he on about?" Boof muttered.

Reese still had his hands behind his back, doing that odd shuffle, that creeping walk that reminded Maynard of…

"Lorraine!" he realised suddenly. "Your mum's coming!"

"What?" Tommy chuckled. "How do you fuckin…"

"Hide!" Boof hissed. "Quick! In here!"

Boof had already climbed the waist-high chain-link fence next to them, blundering over a short hedge into somebody's front yard. Tommy vaulted over both in a single movement. Maynard hurried to follow them, but the rifle in his hand made it awkward to climb.

Panicking, he tried to get himself up without success.

Reese had his back to them now and was talking to somebody.

"Shit," Maynard said. "Take this!"

He handed the rifle over the fence to Tommy, who ducked back out of sight just as a shrill voice called out.

"Maynard? *Maynard!*"

And here she was, sauntering towards him, a touch of urgency in her stride. Reese followed along behind her, looking like he would rather be anywhere else.

She was waiting for us on South Street. Maynard swallowed. *Fucking trapdoor spider.*

"How's it going Lorraine?" He called in a sing-song, too-sweet voice. He cut his eyes at Reese, who came and stood next to him, his face a pallid shade of green.

"Where's Boofhead?"

Maynard and Reese shrugged as one.

"Come on," she scowled. "*Where* is he?"

"With Tommy and Cupcake somewhere," Reese told her. "Not with us.

"*Bull*shit," she scoffed. "Where are they?"

"We don't know," Maynard shrugged.

She eyed him up and down and grunted.

"What about that skateboarder?"

"Who?"

"That dickhead on the skateboard. Lives down the end of the street."

"Don't know him," Reese blurted. He looked like he might faint.

"You'll wanna bloody stay away from him. Does Boof know him? Tommy?"

They shook their heads.

"Good. If you see him, you bloody come and tell me."

"Why's that?" Reese asked.

Lorraine licked her lips, then leaned in closer to them.

"The bikies," she whispered. "They're looking for him. Rohan, Jerome, Tyler, they've all been riding around for the last hour or so, looking for a kid with a skateboard."

"We don't know him," Reese said again.

"What did he do?" Maynard asked.

Lorraine snickered and leaned in close, whispering conspiratorially. "He bloody stole money off of them, didn't he. Nearly ten grand. Must be a fuckin halfwit."

"Ten grand?" Reese said.

"I thought it was just weed," Maynard said slowly.

"You *do* know him!" Lorraine barked. "Don't bloody lie to me, *Maynard*. Where's Tommy?"

"I don't know!"

"Of *course* you fuckin know where he is, Tommy can't take a shit without you sniffing at it. *Where* is he?"

Maynard's mouth worked, but nothing came out.

Reese came to his rescue.

"Tommy didn't have anything to do with it. Neither did Boofhead. Neither did we."

"I don't *care*," she growled. "Them fuckin Marauders are gonna kill that boy if they get a hold of him, and probably whoever's with him too. I want my boys home. *Now*."

"He's not with Boof or Tommy."

"How do *you* know?"

"We saw him. Just before."

Maynard's mouth dropped open. *Reese, don't!*

Reese turned his face away, jaw clenched.

"His name's Brad."

"What are you fuckin *doing*…" Maynard said, his voice low and urgent.

"Shut *up*, Maynard?" Lorraine lifted a finger in his direction, but her dark eyes were fixed on Reese. "When?"

"Just before. Maybe fifteen minutes ago."

Her eyes gleamed. "Did he have a backpack?"

"Yeah. He showed us. It was full of weed."

Maynard groaned and shuffled from foot to foot.

Lorraine ignored him. "And the money? They don't care about the dope, they want their money."

Maynard and Reese looked at each other. Reese was shaking his head.

"No," he said. "There was no money."

Lorraine leaned in, her face hungry. "Where is he now?"

Reese hesitated. "He was walking down Churchill Park Drive just before."

"Little *prick*. Was he by himself?"

Reese hesitated again, his face sombre. Maynard watched him, mouth ajar. He was struck by how much older the other boy suddenly seemed.

"I don't wanna get in trouble, Lorraine." Reese looked her in the eye. "You didn't hear it from me."

"Yeah, all right. It didn't come from you."

"He was with Dylan. And Ben Campbell."

"The Campbells? *They've* got the money?"

"I don't know. I guess. The three of them were together."

"Little bastards. You should both go home." She backed away from them, nodding. "Don't stay out here, those bloody bikies will shoot first and ask questions later. You hear me?"

"Yeah."

"*Go. Home.* Both of you." She turned on her heel and strode back up South Street. They watched her go.

"The fuck are you *doing?*" Maynard whispered.

"Calling it in," Reese said.

There was a rustling over the fence as Tommy and Boof stood up, brushing themselves down. Tommy still held the rifle, but he kept it out of sight.

"You hear all that?" Maynard asked them. There was colour is his cheeks. *Tommy can't even take a shit without you sniffing at it.*

Tommy nodded. "Did you see any cash in that bag?"

He's not looking at me.

"As if, man." Reese was shaking his head. "As if he's gonna come and climb around on a factory roof with ten fuckin grand on him."

"Maybe he didn't know he had it," Boof said.

"If there was ten grand in that bag," Reese replied. "Then Dylan's probably on his way to fuckin Bali. Either way, it's not out problem."

"Bullshit it's not out problem," Boof scowled. "Why the fuck did you tell her all that? You know she'll go and tell Rohan, right? This is gonna go south man."

Reese glared at him.

"Go south? That skater's fuckin *dead.* Let the bloody Marauders deal with it."

Maynard, watching Tommy closely, searched for the right words. He didn't find them and settled on a question instead.

"What do *you* reckon we should do?" He asked, hating himself.

"Ten grand." Tommy murmured, his eyes distant. "We could do a lot with ten grand."

A look of disbelief spread across Reese's face. "You're joking, right?"

Boof scowled. "Don't fuckin pretend you're not interested, man. Ten grand. Ten *grand.*"

"Ten years jail," Reese muttered.

Maynard was still watching Tommy. "You want to try and get it, don't you."

They all watched as Tommy considered, then nodded.

"No way," Reese was shaking. "The cops catch us with the money, they'll say that *we* put him in the silo. I'm not going to the pink palace for a few grand. And if Rohan catches us…"

"It's only those dickheads and us that knows he's in there," Boof mused. "If we get to Dylan before the bikies do, then we can shut him up and take the money. And the weed."

"Shut him up how?" Reese demanded, then gestured at the rifle. "You gonna shoot him?"

"Not *shoot* him," Boof said lightly. "Just scare him a bit, you know, so he hands over the cash. Then it'll be his word against ours."

Tommy was nodding thoughtfully.

"Nup, that's fucking mental, sorry." Reese was shaking his head, moving away. "I'm just gonna go. I don't want anything to do with it. With any of it."

His back was stiff as he stepped off the gutter, looking up and down South Street as though he were attempting to cross a busy highway.

"Don't be a pussy," Boof scoffed.

"Nup. Good luck… but leave my name out of it, thanks."

"You're a fuckin old woman, Reese." Boof snarled, but the other boy was walking away without looking back. "Reese!"

They watched him go.

Stephanie

Every time a motorbike roared past on Invermay Road she peered out of the shop's front window. A blink… and they were gone, leaving thunder in their wake.

Their snarls and rumbles matched her mood.

She wanted to scream. She wanted to rage.

She wanted to push the lolly counter over and watch it smash on the tiled floor, watch the shards of glass mix in with the chocolate drops and raspberries. She wanted to slap David's smug, arrogant smile, to shove the pornos into his crying wife's face. She wanted to burn the pile of racing guides that sat amongst the newspapers, burn them out of her world.

Burn it all.

Ooh she's tough.

All of her nights spent sweeping and stacking shelves, all of the rude customers and leering bosses and shoe polishing and worrying about Shirley and having no life… all for nothing. Her father had no right to take her money, but he'd taken it anyway.

Because he knows there's nothing I can do about it.

She thumped the floor with her broom, taking her frustration out on the dust.

David and Julie were doing stocktake in the grocery aisle and had left her to look after the store. There were few customers to attend to, but plenty of things to clean.

As she sprayed the fridge's glass doors and wiped them down, she thought about Dylan looming over her, his greasy hair gleaming, his greasy muscles flexing. She shuddered.

As she stacked the apples into an uneven pyramid she thought about David looming behind her with his greasy smile, his soft hands and his skinny, old man's hips. She grimaced.

As she restocked the lolly cabinet she thought of the bikie. Rohan, rough and rude *and ready* Rohan. He had put Dylan in his place with just a few words and an arrogant, voracious smirk.

For a moment, he had protected her, had cupped her in his tattooed hands, the way he must hold Lily.

Not anymore. He said they weren't together anymore.

Why did he tell me that?

As she licked sugar from her fingers, she wondered what it might be like to climb on top of that bike, to nestle against his broad back and feel the monstrous bike roaring between her thighs, to press against a leather-clad, woolly chested bikie, her name tattooed on his shoulder, her teeth biting *into* his shoulder…

The box of Big Boss cigars was nearly empty. Popular with the tweens who were imitating almost every adult they knew when they pretended to smoke, the musk-flavoured lollies always sold quickly. There would be more in the storeroom.

"I'm just going out back," she called out to the grocery aisle.

There was no response from Julie *or* David, so Stephanie ducked through the bead curtain into the storeroom.

The first things she noticed in the storeroom were the things that were out of place.

Not the timber shelves that lined the length of the walls from floor to ceiling, not the stacked plastic buckets of *Chuppa Chups*, not the neat row of ledger books or the locked safe box next to them. All of those things were as they should be, as she would expect them to be.

What she didn't expect, what was out of place, was her boss, David.

It wasn't unusual that he was in the storeroom, but it *was* unusual for him to be leaning back against the shelves with his eyes closed.

While David himself wasn't *entirely* out of place, the belted tan pants bunched around his knees most certainly *were*. His naked hips and thighs, the dangling tails of his shirt, all out of place.

Julie, kneeling on the floor in front of him.

Julie was out of place.

Her eyes closed, her hands resting calmly on the tops of her knees, her head bobbing gently back and forth.

And, in her mouth, the *most* out of place thing of all; David.

Stephanie took a step back, the cigars forgotten, her breath trapped in her chest.

Julie didn't hear her, didn't look up.

But *he* did.

David's lips curled upwards. He sighed, a deep, satisfied sigh.

He was looking at Stephanie, looking into her eyes.

And *smiling*.

What a good girl.

Stephanie took another step backwards.

David took a deep breath. He would speak, apparently. He would say something she could never forget, tell her something, ask her something, communicate, convey, offer, invite.

Stephanie ran.

The nearest door opened into the alleyway behind the shop and she burst through it at speed. Gravel crunched beneath her sneakered feet as she ran towards the service station, cutting a sharp left on Elm Street.

Once around the corner, she stopped to catch her breath, bent over her knees.

"Stephanie!" David's voice. He was coming. "Stephanie, *stop!*"

She considered, quickly; Elm Street would take her towards home, but he would catch her before she could reach the next corner; the same with Invermay Road. The dirt road behind the servo was long and straight and there was nowhere to go.

Leaving only one real option. She ran across the intersection and into the shaded, leafy driveway of Burwood Estate.

A few steps took her past the thick green hedge into the overgrown gardens. Quickly, she crouched behind a scruffy boxwood, listening to David approach.

His footsteps paused at the intersection.

"Stephanie!"

She didn't move.

There was a moment of silence. Stephanie crouched even lower so that she could see the gate through the boxwood.

David's pale face appeared.

She held her breath.

He was peering up the driveway, doing a slow scan of the gardens.

She was as still as a garden statue, a rabbit hiding from a hawk.

"Stephanie?" His tone was uncertain now. "Are you in there?"

Go away. Just go. Go!

After a few long moments, she heard him mutter and walk away, his steps quickening up Elm Street. Stephanie tracked his progress until she couldn't hear him anymore.

Gradually her breath came back, and her heart started beating again.

He's gone. He's gone.

Her body shook with relief.

A hand seized her wrist.

She drew in breath to scream but another hand covered her mouth, calloused and strong and stinking of motor oil. She tried to wriggle, to run, but the hands had her, a deadlock on her wrist, a clamp across her lips.

"Shhhh!" A voice hissed into her ear. Not David's voice. "Shut *up,* Steph!"

Her eyes rolled. She stopped kicking.

Dylan

Dylan took his hand from Stephanie's face. He kept the other one tight around her wrist.

"We're not gonna hurt you."

Not if you do what I say.

"Fuckin let me go then," Stephanie said.

"Just don't scream, all right? Promise me you won't scream? We're not gonna hurt you."

She nodded. His grip loosened around her wrist, but he didn't let go.

"Sorry I…" he began.

She tore her arm away and bolted, sprinting across Burwood's neat grass.

Bitch!

She almost made it to the wrought-iron gate before his arms closed around her, lifting her away from the ground. Clamping his hand back over her mouth, he dragged her away from the street, deeper into the gardens.

Her eyes rolled helplessly. Her mouth worked, trying to bite his hand, to no avail.

Ben Campbell was watching them, his face a portrait of surprise, his hands half-raised as though he were a surfer trying to keep his balance.

"For fuck's *sake*," Dylan spat as he wrestled her along. "Don't fuckin run, you stupid *bitch*, we just wanna *talk* to you."

Sweat was running off him, dripping onto her work shirt. She kicked at his legs, but before she could properly connect, he threw her to the ground.

The air was knocked out of her. Grass tickled her sides and twigs jammed rudely into her back.

Dylan caught her flailing hands, then kneeled on top of her, pinning her down.

It's about time.

"What are you *doing* man?" Ben said.

Dylan ignored him.

"What did you fuckin run for? Don't fuckin *run*. I told you I'm not gonna *hurt* you."

Her breath was coming back. Her wheezing was furious.

"Get *off* me! Psycho! I'll call the *police*."

"I've already fucked up two cops today, gorgeous. What's a few more?"

"Yeah? And what about Rohan?"

He sneered… but hesitated.

Nobody messes with Rohan's girlfriend.

"Dylan, what the fuck are you doing?" Ben was backing away. "Don't you think we're in enough shit as it is?"

She grinned up at him. "You heard him, he told me to come see him if you…"

Dylan pushed a rough finger against her lips.

"Quiet, baby."

Her eyes gleamed with hate, her teeth clenched, her cheeks burned bright.

Dylan took a deep, wavering breath.

"I'm a fuckin Marauder now, Stephie. I'm *one* of them." He took his finger away from her lips and drew it down the side of her face. "I got the fuckin bag they were looking for and they're gonna line up to suck my dick. I might give you to Pasco, or maybe to all of them. But not till I'm done with you."

"Get *off* me!" She bucked and writhed.

He *slapped* her, hard.

She was shocked into stillness.

"*Dylan!*" Ben Campbell was pleading. "For fuck's sake, leave it!"

"The thing is, I've wanted to do this for a long time." Dylan whispered. He ran a soft hand over her chest, just above her breasts. "And now, I can do whatever the fuck I want."

He stopped with a look of surprise.

Stephanie was leaning into his touch, *pushing* into it, stretching so that her soft breast was filling his hand.

Holy Jesus.

A disbelieving smile played over his lips.

I knew it. I knew she wanted it.

Her body felt… *incredible.*

She eased her head back, gasping, eyes closed, supple in his hands.

Dylan leaned in closer, his body electrified by the firm softness of her breast, and he could *feel* her breath now, could…

Stephanie *slammed* her forehead into his nose.

Pain exploded with an awful crunch as his nose shattered and his lips mashed against hard teeth.

Blood squirted from his squealing mouth.

Suddenly she was wet and warm beneath him, his blood sticky on her neck.

Bubbling, mewling noises came from behind his hands.

Stephanie shoved him aside and while he tumbled to the ground she sprang to her feet.

My nose, my nose is BROKEN, my teeth...

He climbed to his knees, moaning, hands clutching at his face, tears running down bloody cheeks.

I'll kill her.

The rage was coming, falling over the pain like an escaping animal.

I'll strangle her right here and...

"...so fucking *dumb...*"

He saw the kick coming, but far, far too late.

He only had time to shuffle his knees in the dirt before she drove a champion's strike, straight and hard and merciless, deep into the softness of his balls.

"*OOFuuuuuck!*"

He crumpled around her foot.

The world turned white.

It hurts, goddamn it HURRRTTS.

He rolled onto his side, spitting out blood, gasping for air. It felt like he might never walk again.

Stephanie's footsteps thudded away. She was running.

"Little mole!" It was a heave, a rasp, an impotent howl. He could feel Ben Campbell watching and a wave of fury fought back against the pain. "Fuckin *get* her!"

"What are you fucking *doing*, man?" Ben Campbell made no move to go after her. "We gotta get out of here."

Grunting, Dylan slowly climbed to his feet.

His balls were throbbing, sending waves of bright, hot pain into his lower belly. His face ached and he had to breathe through his mouth. He couldn't bring himself to touch his nose, but there wasn't as much blood to spit this time.

"Useless fuck. You do whatever you want." His face felt soft and loose, like a painfully overripe fruit. "I'm gonna go join the Marauders. Where's the bag."

"Jesus Christ, you're a mess. Is that how you fight? Face first?"

"She fuckin *headbutted* me."

"Maybe you got too fuckin close."

"Fuck you, man! Where's the fucking backpack?"

"You know they're not just gonna make you their fuckin leader." Ben Campbell shook his head in disdain. "Just go and tell them about the skater. This is out of our fuckin league."

"Out of *your* league, maybe."

"Come on, man." Ben Campbell rolled his eyes. "You're not your brother."

Dylan swung his fist.

Maynard

Maynard tried not to look at his best friend as they marched up Ray Street, their footsteps falling in time. Boof followed close behind. They were almost back to Maynard's house, where he would put the rifle away, switch on his Nintendo and pretend that today never happened.

And I'll tell mum about the gun cabinet and Greg can lock it and I'll forget it's in there.

"…so they won't give a shit, she's just some old lady stickybeaking, and once they find that skater they won't know that we were even…

Boof was talking, but Maynard only listened with half an ear. He was watching Tommy from the corner of his eyes, trying to gauge his mood.

He hasn't spoken to me since we saw his mum. Since we were in that room.

Why hasn't he said anything? What did I…

An indignant shriek rang out over the rooftops.

They stopped to listen.

There was another brief wail, followed by furious shouting, all coming from further up the street.

"I know that voice," said Boof. "Come on!"

Boof and Tommy took off towards it.

Maynard hesitated, then followed, the rifle awkward in his hands.

Just go, you don't have to do this.

It's Greg's rifle. If anyone sees you, if anything happens, *you'll get all the blame.*

He kept running.

They followed the shouts to the end of the street, slowing down when they reached Burwood's service gate.

"It's Dylan and Campbell." Tommy whispered, his dark eyes flashing. "Come on, we can sneak through the garden."

"What? Hang on!" said Maynard. "What are we gonna *do*? I want to go *home.*"

But Tommy and Boof were already creeping along the last few meters of timber fence. Once they saw it was clear, Boof darted down the driveway and ducked behind the hedge, out of sight.

The shouting had toned down, but there were still angry voices in the garden.

Maynard hesitated again.

Forget about them, just go home, *just take the bloody gun and* go!

A few steps into the driveway, Tommy turned back and finally met his gaze.

There was something unfamiliar in his expression. Something cold.

He looks different.

No.

He's looking at me *differently.*

"They're in the garden," Tommy said, his voice flat. He nodded down the driveway. "Just follow Boof in behind the hedge, they won't see us."

Maynard nodded, not trusting himself to speak.

I'm sorry. I didn't mean it! I didn't mean *it!*

Tommy frowned at him impatiently.

Swallowing, Maynard hefted the rifle and nodded.

On unsteady legs he followed Boof behind the hedge. The younger brother was waiting for him, his face a serious mask. He nodded at a gap in the branches and Maynard stepped up to it.

Dylan and Ben Campbell were arguing in the garden, pushing each other's chests and shouting over the top of each other.

"Trouble in paradise," Maynard said, glancing back over his shoulder.

"Benny must have cracked him one, look," Boof whispered. "There's blood all down his singlet."

Tommy eased in silently behind them. The thick hedge was a good cover.

Maynard tried to hug the rifle against himself, to somehow make it smaller, to make it disappear.

Don't let either of them take it. Don't let him *hold it, even for a second.*

"Busted nose," Tommy whispered approvingly.

"Fuckhead was asking for it." Maynard muttered.

If anything happens, I'll get the blame.

"Where's the bag?" Boof's head bobbed this way and that. "Can you see it?"

"Nope."

"It must be there," Boof insisted. "Maybe they're trying to stash it. We should jump…"

"Hang on." Tommy was staring at the rifle.

Maynard held it tighter to his chest.

No.

"What if we put up warning shot?" Tommy said, grinning his grin. "Just a crack in the sky. They'll shit themselves."

"Then if they bolt, we can just grab it the cash!" Boof was nodding eagerly. "They'll never know who it was!"

"And if they don't bolt, we'll just take it off them." Tommy's teeth were perfect. "Come on, put one up!

I can't tell if you're joking or not.

"Yeah and bring half of Invermay over for a look."

Tommy rolled his eyes. "Not this again, you fuckin p…."

Maynard gaped at him.

Tommy looked at him blankly, his face unreadable.

What was he about to say?

What was he gonna call me?

"Better do something," Boof said. "Look."

They turned to watch, cheek to cheek.

Dylan was talking and waving his hands dramatically, his tone urgent, his words lost to the distance, while Benny was circling around him, clearly trying to leave.

"They're gonna go!" Boof said without looking around. "Fire it *now,*

Maynard!"

"Don't be a *dickhead!*"

Tommy snatched the rifle from Maynard's hands in one smooth grab.

"It's my turn anyway," he sneered.

"Hey, the *fuck* are you *doing?*" Maynard cried.

"Bloody finally."

Tommy cocked the rifle against his shoulder and, without hesitation, swung around to line up the muzzle with Dylan's back.

He ground fell away beneath Maynard's feet.

"Jesus Christ don't bloody *shoot him...*"

Tommy choked out a laugh and pointed the rifle at the sky, grinning his beautiful, mischievous grin.

"Just fuckin around."

He pulled the trigger.

Maynard winced and Boof ducked with his hands halfway to his ears.

But nothing happened.

Tommy pulled the trigger again. And again.

The trigger didn't move.

The safety. He doesn't know how to turn it off.

Relief flooded through him, but his belly was still twisted, his legs still weak.

Boof looked through the hedge and swore in frustration.

"They're going!"

"*Fuck* it!" Tommy lowered the rifle, scowling at it in confusion. "What happened?"

"C'mon man, give it back." Maynard held out his hands.

Please.

"It didn't fuckin work," Tommy complained.

"It's not even fuckin loaded," Boof said, disgusted.

"Look, dickhead..." Maynard reached for the rifle.

Holding it out of reach, Tommy glared at him, his eyes cold.

As though they were strangers.

Maynard recoiled.

"Might as well be a fuckin toy," Tommy muttered.

He sat the rifle's butt against his hip, running his hand over it, squeezing at the immobile trigger, his thumb flicking the little black switch back and forth and back.

The safety, that's the safety...

"What use is a broken piece of..."

Maynard reached for the barrel on instinct, trying to take it back, trying to take it *all* back.

His hand gripped the smooth iron and Tommy's hand clamped down over his.

Their eyes met over the rifle's barrel...

...then something *roared,* an explosive thunderous earthquake that washed over him, filled his ears and his eyes and distilled him away from everything else and shook the entire universe down to its very last particle of light.

And in the next moment.

Nothing.

Stephanie

A loud and obnoxious crack of backfire sent birds squawking out of Burwood's trees.

Was that a motorbike?

Come and find me.

Stephanie risked a look back over her shoulder as she passed through Burwood's white gates. Dylan hadn't followed her.

Not yet. Just keep going!

But which way? Invermay Road, wonderfully public, stunningly normal, was maybe a hundred metres away. She turned towards it… then stopped in her tracks, her hands darting behind her back.

David was standing in the middle of the intersection. The relief on his face faded as he took in her blood-spattered work shirt, and he quickly moved to block her path to the main road.

She backed off, not willing to let him get too close.

"My god, Stephanie! Are you all right? What happened?"

"Stay the *fuck* away from me David."

It didn't sound like her voice. It sounded older. Colder.

Ooh she's tough.

She *liked* it.

"Steph, don't be *stupid,* you're hurt. Why don't you come back in and get…"

He was interrupted by a diesel-chuckle roar that blocked out all other sounds and made Burwood's hedges shiver.

The roaring engine surged… and abruptly *he* was there, pulling his black bike up next to Stephanie, letting it pound and snarl beside her.

Rohan.

A warm flush bloomed in her belly.

Nobody messes with Rohan's girlfriend.

He revved the bike. It bellowed beneath his hands then abruptly went quiet, its engine ticking over softly, dangerously.

Rohan sat back, his hands loose on the Harley's handlebars.

"Didn't think I'd see you again so soon." Rohan's smirk faded as he looked her over. "You all right?"

"Yeah." She looked at the blood on her work shirt and shrugged. "It's not mine."

"Looks like you broke someone's nose."

"Yeah." She allowed herself a small smile as she nodded at the Burwood gate. "I hope so, anyway."

She held something out to him.

"This is what you're looking for, right?"

Rohan looked at the backpack in her outstretched hands. When he met her eyes again it was with a surprised grin.

"That's my bag. How did you…"

"Dylan had it," she shrugged. "I took it off him."

Ooh she's tough.

The big biker took in the blood on her blouse again… then let out a booming laugh. The tattoos on his arms bounced as his big shoulders shook.

"That little blonde shit who thinks he's a boxer? *You* took it off him?" Another boom of laughter. "That sly little fuck. You broke *his* nose?"

Stephanie smiled as he took the backpack out of her hands and eased it into his saddlebag.

What a good girl.

"I'm impressed. Thanks, gorgeous."

There was a strangled sound nearby. David, who had watched this entire exchange in silence, was backing away. His pale face matched his grey hair.

Nobody messes with Rohan's girlfriend.

She touched his arm.

"Can you get me away from here?"

Rohan followed her gaze to the grocery store owner and his easy grin vanished.

"You right, mate?"

David's lingering, confused glare bounced off Stephanie's tight, smug smile.

"I'm *talking* to you, old man."

David jumped as if goosed, and *now* he was looking at Rohan.

"I don't… I don't want any trouble," his voice wavered. His eyes flicked to Stephanie. There were splotches of colour on his grey cheeks. "Stephanie, I just…"

"You don't fucking talk to her," Rohan growled. "You don't fucking *look* at her. You forget you ever fucking *met* her. Got it?"

David gaped at him.

"You understand, you skinny old fuck?"

David hesitated, nodded, hesitated again.

"Then go mind your own fucking business."

With a dazed shrug, David slowly turned and shuffled back towards his shop, his head down.

No more creeping on me, old man, I guess I just quit.

It should have worried her, should have shaken her, but it didn't. Instead, she felt a breathless, delightful thrill at watching her boss – her *ex-boss* – walk away.

She turned to thank Rohan but forgot what she was about to say.

His eyes were fixed on her. His soft, clear, considering eyes.

He looks so strong.

And dangerous.

She met his gaze.

"It looks like we both won our fights today." He raised an eyebrow, smiling broadly. "You wanna go celebrate?"

That warm flush through her belly again.

"What about Lily?"

"Don't worry about Lily."

He pulled a black helmet from his saddlebag and held it out to her.

It fit her perfectly.

Ooh she's tough.

"You haven't been on a bike before."

She shook her head.

"I'll take it easy. Just hold on to me, all right?"

"All right."

She climbed on behind him and he showed her where to rest her feet. As she settled onto the Harley's leather seat, she glanced back at the Burwood gate.

Dylan was watching from the driveway. His bloody singlet was a match for her own bloody blouse. There was gore drying around his nose and his lips and bright fury in his eyes.

She gave him her sweetest smile and lifted her middle finger.

Ooh she's tough.

Rohan kicked the bike into roaring, glorious life.

Her arms grabbed the bikie's thick chest in reflex. The leather and steel seemed *alive* beneath her, the bike was *alive*.

She was alive!

"You all right?" he shouted.

She nodded. She *was* all right. *Better* than all right.

Grinning, he pulled his sunglasses down, straightened up the bike and drove them towards Invermay Road.

Her blood was tingling with excitement, beating at her veins. The air tasted like fresh motor oil and blood. She turned her face towards the late afternoon sun, feeling the warmth on her bare arms and the wind in her hair.

Dylan

They crouched behind Burwood's white gate and watched the motorbike turn onto Invermay Road.

She gave the bag to Rohan. She gave the bag to fucking *Rohan!*

He wanted to scream. Instead, he spat a sticky black clump onto the Burwood driveway.

"Fucking little *mole!*"

There was a panicked shouting was coming from somewhere in the garden.

Not shouting. Shrieking.

There were two voices, one panicked and the other hysterical.

"Jesus, somebody saw us," Ben Campbell breathed, his face pale. "We need to get out of here. now."

"Yeah, no shit."

Ben walked out though the gate, his head turning as he tried to look in every direction at once. Dylan followed with his head down. The blood on his face was drying, but it was still hard to breathe. He quickened his step to keep up with Ben's determined march.

"Mum can ring Noah, tell him what happened."

"Yeah. *Fuck.*"

"You were the one that got the bag back. They'll still let you fight."

Dylan spat more blood on the ground.

Might be time to disappear for a bit.

"If we can just get back to my place, mum will sort it all out."

"Let's fuckin go th…"

Ben had stopped so suddenly that Dylan nearly walked into his back.

"What are you fuckin…"

"Shut up!" Ben hissed. *"Look!"*

Dylan followed his friend's gaze and his stomach flipped.

Halfway up Ray Street, not a hundred metres away, were three bikies astride their machines. Three towers of black leather and muscle and fat and tatts. They were pulled off to the side of the street, talking to an animated woman in grey trackpants.

Lorraine. What's that old…

Lorraine spotted them.

Dylan saw her eyes go wide, saw her arm sweep up to point a finger at him.

He couldn't hear her words. He didn't need to.

There they are!

"Oh fuck," Ben's voice was high, panicked. "They've seen us!"

He was right. One of the bikes started with growl, and the other two quickly made a grim harmony. Dylan watched Lorraine step back, her finger still outstretched, as the bikes took off.

"Run. *Go!*"

They turned and ran back towards Burwood, their feet pumping for all they were worth.

The three motorbikes drew closer, louder, angrier.

The Marauders were coming.

As he sprinted, Dylan could see the bright green glow of the BP service station up ahead. It was a lifetime away.

"Come *on!*"

They reached the front gate as the bike's roared into Elm Street. There was nowhere to run except towards Invermay Road, lazy with mid-evening traffic.

There was a shout from the BP Service Station.

Warren O'Brien, the hairy little mechanic, was calling out to ask a bearded man filling up the tank of a classic blue HQ Holden if knew the results of the Bombers versus the Eagles, if he knew how many goals Wanganeen had kicked in the fourth quarter and if…

Good old Warren, keep the old prick talking.

Dylan's face and groin throbbed with each heavy step. Bloody mist pumped from his ruined nose as he panted.

The bikes were close, would reach them in seconds…

"Come *on*," Dylan said. "Follow me."

Crouching, he ran across the back of the service station's yard, trying to stay out of sight. Ben followed in a shambling jog, his head down.

Dylan reached the corner of the building and hid behind it, waiting. The motorbikes slow down as they reached Burwood's main gate.

They'll see you. You've only got a few seconds.

"What are you doing?" Ben wheezed as he caught up. "We've gotta get ho…"

"Shut up! Are you ready?"

"Ready for what?"

"The blue Holden. You go the passenger side."

"What?"

"When I say go, just *go,* all right?"

"The *fuck,* Dylan! You can't *drive!*"

The revving started again; they had been spotted.

"Come *on!*"

Dylan took off at a dead run, not waiting to see if Ben followed.

In a few leaping strides he had rounded the pumps and was looking into the open driver's side window.

The keys were dangling from the column.

Fucking jackpot!

Without pausing, he sat down in the driver's seat and quickly oriented himself. Three pedals and a gear stick. A manual.

A wave of doubt flushed over him.

He had only started his brother's car once, but when he pushed in the HQ's clutch and turned the key, the engine grunted and turned over.

As it did, the passenger door was reefed open.

Dylan recoiled, expecting the car's owner or a raging bikie or even little

Warren fucking O'Brien… but it was Ben Campbell who swung into the seat and slammed the door shut.

"Dickhead!" Ben shouted. "You could've *waited!"*

Dylan pressed the accelerator down and the car's engine thrummed.

Now old man and Warren O'Brien were coming – he could see them scrambling out of the servo's little shop.

The three motorbikes pulled onto the tarmac. The HQ's engine screamed again, but the car didn't move.

Come on, you piece of shit!

"Ben!" Warren's shouting was a mix of fury and disbelief. "Ben Campbell! What are you fuckin playing at…"

"The fuckin *handbrake's* on!" Ben yelled.

Dylan pulled the handbrake and eased it off, then raised the clutch a little like Luke had told him, pressing the accelerator at the same time.

The car stalled.

Swearing, Dylan pushed the clutch in and twisted the key again, glancing over his shoulder.

Warren had stopped in his tracks as the Marauders rode up.

"Put it in gear, you've gotta put it in gear!" Ben Campbell was quickly winding up his window as one of the bikies pulled in beside them.

The biker's fist struck the passenger-side window, and again, trying to break the glass..

Clutch in.

The car rocked as the bikie punched the window again.

Another bike pulled up on the driver's side.

Into first. The gearstick moved easily enough.

A window smashed, spraying the two boys with hard blue droplets of glass.

Dylan let the clutch out again, more slowly this time, and the car lurched across the service station's driveway.

Furious curses followed them onto Invermay Road. Engines rattled behind them.

Dylan eased onto the accelerator and the HQ purred. Ben flopped into his seat, breathing hard.

"I fuckin *told* you, no worries." Dylan laughed, but it was a shrill, frightened laugh.

"They're still fuckin chasing us!"

"Not for long." He pushed the accelerator and the HQ's engine strained painfully.

The car began to shake.

"Change *gears* man, you've gotta go up to second," Ben moaned. "Warren knows my fuckin *parents!*"

"Then he'll keep his mouth shut, won't he."

Dylan pulled the gearstick down, but it wouldn't slot in where it was supposed to and the car shuddered with a rude, grinding squeal.

"Just go back to my place! They won't come in there! Warren's probably already calling the cops!"

"Too late I reckon," Dylan said dully.

There were blue and red lights flashing ahead of them.

Three Harley's grunting behind them.

Caught, I'm caught.

"Come *on* man," Ben's voice was cold. "Get us *out* of here, Dylan!"

Dylan pushed the accelerator down. The engine growled, but the car didn't go any faster.

"Put it in *gear, man!*"

"I'm fuckin *trying!*"

The engine made that awful scraping sound again.

Ahead of them, the police car had almost reached the intersection of Forster Street and Invermay Road.

Behind them, the bikies had eased off.

"Oh, we're so screwed," Ben moaned. "Mum's gonna kill us both."

Dylan yanked the stick and let out the clutch. The HQ hiccupped into gear and took off with a sudden power, cruising towards the intersection.

"Left! Forster Street. Go *Left!*"

"Fuck *that!*"

"Turn *left,* you *fuckin...*"

Ben Campbell reached over and grabbed the wheel, twisting it towards himself.

The HQ swept around the corner in a wide arc, just as the police drove through the intersection in the opposite direction. For one surreal moment, Dylan thought the car might flip over onto its side, but the HQ straightened up and lurched down Forster Street.

"What the *fuck* did you do that for?" Dylan shouted as they accelerate past the bowls club. "We've gotta get away from them you dickhead!"

"Just take me back *home!*" Ben shouted. "*Now, Dylan! I'm fuckin out.*"

The HQ was hitting sixty in second gear and still had head room. The long chain link fence bordering Invermay Park passed in a blur.

Dylan put all of his weight on the accelerator.

"We're *not* going back there!"

"Come *on* man, mum'll sort it out, she can hide us, she'll know…"

"*Bullshit!*" Dylan screamed at him. "*I'll* fuckin sort it out!"

"Slow down."

"*Fuck* you, man."

"Slow *down!*" Ben squealed, pushing back in his seat.

"*What's your fuc…*"

Dylan turned away from him.

Just in time to see the telegraph pole speeding towards them.

It slammed into the front of the car, unyielding and implacable.

The HQ crumpled around them as thunder twisted the entire world.

Shock pounded into Dylan's gut.

The steering wheel pounded into his chest.

Glass and steel exploded inwards.

Breath squeezed out of his lungs.

Light flickered out of his eyes.

Jake

The laneway between the mill and the woolstore was taking on a cooler shade of blue as the sun swung lower in the sky. It was quiet enough for Jake's grating bluestone footsteps to reverberate between the two buildings.

Please Christ let this work.

The police weren't coming.

There was no ambulance on the way.

It had been too long. Reese would have made it home ages ago and if he had called triple zero, help would have arrived by now.

It had taken dozens of attempts to throw the end of the goddamned chain through the goddamned hole in the hatch's goddamned lever, but eventually a couple of links had dropped into it and the rest of the chain followed. Now the end of the chain swung above Jake's head, within easy reach.

Jake gave it a couple of test yanks. The chain seemed to be firmly attached to the latch above, so he took hold of it with both hands, set his feet and *pulled*.

The latch didn't budge.

He tried a few short, sharp pulls instead and on the last yank, the lever shifted. Only a few millimetres… but it shifted.

That's it! Open up!

He gave the chain another heave, then another, lifting himself off the ground in his efforts. His blood thumped and his arms ached, but the next pull saw him stumble back as the lever finally gave way. The silo's lower hatch opened with a low, rusty yawn.

Got it!

Jake let go of the chain, watching and holding his breath.

The silo gave an airy, pattering sigh. Bright sawdust dribbled onto the first few feet of the chute, shockingly white against the silo's charred iron… but that was all.

Why isn't it pouring out?

The hatch was wide open, but the sawdust inside the silo was packed tight. It reminded Jake of the bottled pancake powder his mother would buy for special breakfasts - without a solid shake or stir, no more would fall out.

Jake grabbed the chain again and yanked on it as hard as he could. The lever slid easily now.

The hatch closed, then opened again, the winking of an iron eye.

More sawdust crumbled out. Not enough.

I need to stir the dust, make it move, make him *move…*

He bent over and scrabbled in the alleyway until he found a good-sized rock. Hefting its weight and eyeing the imposing black silo, he sighed.

Sorry, Brad.

He aimed for the open hatch and threw the rock as hard as he could.

The silo rang like a bell, a sharp tong that wobbled through the air.

No more dust fell.

He was already looking for another rock when a distant rumble made him pause. A rumble he'd heard too many times today and could probably go his entire life without ever hearing again.

A motorbike was coming.

He groaned.

No! Not now!

Maybe it was Noah, coming to help.

Or to make sure Brad's dead.

His indecision lasted only a moment.

Hide. Hide!

He sprinted for the mill's loading bay and ducked inside.

From the workshop, Jake could track the grunting bike's progress over the vacant block and into the dimly lit alleyway where he had been standing moments earlier.

The motorbike pulled up, its engine revving needlessly hard and loud. Somebody was showing off.

The roar of the Harley made the mill's cracked windows rattle in their frames. The walls shook and groaned. Jake shrunk away from the sound.

When the noise abruptly tapered away, it left a strange silence in its wake.

I'm screwed, I'm so screwed.

Jake tip-toed through the workshop, holding his breath. He hadn't ever realised just how loud walking across a floor could be, how many pops and creaks and groans would vibrate away from your foot and up into the building's walls. Every step sounded like a bridge collapsing.

He'll hear me, he'll hear me...

But there was no voice calling from outside.

There were no footsteps either.

Then, a giggle.

A *girl's* giggle.

Jake held his breath, listening.

The girl said something.

There was a low rumble. A man replying.

Then silence again.

Still holding his breath, Jake extended a slow, ballerina step into the small room that was wallpapered with naked women. There were candles burning on one of the shelves and the room reeked of must and musk.

He tiptoed to the window, hovering as lightly as a balloon, staying carefully out of sight. Sweat dripped from his temples.

There were no more voices from outside, no sounds of movement.

One look, just for a second. Move slow. Be invisible.

He wiped his eyes with a rust-stained palm, then slowly, ever so slowly, leaned over and peeked through the window.

A motorbike was parked just outside, and a bikie was standing next to it, the Marauders insignia spread across his back.

He knew that bike, knew that bikie.

Rohan.

Rohan and a girl, judging by the arm wrapped around his neck.

They were sitting on his bike, making out.

Romeo Rohan.

The couple shifted, coming up for air, and Jake saw the girl's face.

He could have laughed out loud.

Stephanie. Her eyes were lidded, and she kissed the Marauder eagerly.

She had watched Jake steal a porno only a couple of hours ago and now here he was, crouched in a room full of old pin-ups, watching her make out with a bikie prize fighter.

I'm not a pervert, Stephanie. It's just a small fucking world.

He sighed, turning carefully away from the window.

This wasn't the help he'd been hoping for.

Stephanie

Her legs were shaking, uncontrollable spasms flicked along her thighs.

It felt odd and electric and delightful and powerful, much like the sparkling at the base of her spine.

But she couldn't quite focus on either sensation.

Not while his huge, gentle hand was on her cheek. Not while his other hand rested on her hips, or while his thick thighs held her knees apart.

She leaned back, gasping for breath, her lips wet. He grinned at her, green eyes amused. Flakes of sawdust drifted through the air around them.

While Stephanie had never spent too much time daydreaming about what her first kiss might be like, she had never imagined it to be quite like this; perched on a gleaming Harley Davidson near a burnt-out mill, her shirt covered in somebody else's blood, making out with a bikie - *a bikie!* - that she had barely even spoken to.

This is dangerous. He is dangerous.

His stubble was rough. There were tattoos snaking along his forearms and up his neck.

She wanted to see more of them.

Just keep going.

She pulled at him, hungry for another kiss. He obliged, his strong hand drifting to the small of her back.

Nobody messes with Rohan's girlfriend.

As their tongues danced, he pulled her closer and closer until he was pushing against her, *grinding* her. Her legs shook again.

He broke off the kiss, smiling, his eyes reading her face.

"Nervous?"

She hesitated and he smirked.

I've never been kissed before, she wanted to say. *Not like that.*

Instead, she leaned into him, her hands tiny on his giant shoulders.

He squeezed her butt through her work jeans and this time she *did* gasp in surprise. He was swaying his hips and she felt something down there, something pushing against her *down there*, something hard and…

She broke the kiss. Now his breath was heavy too.

"I… I…" her voice was hoarse and when he brushed the pad of his thumb against her lips, she had to swallow.

His hand tickled over her collar bone, along the buttons of her shirt, stroking her breast softly, confidently.

Her thighs shook again, her hips too.

He was swaying slowly, pulling her against him, pushing against *her*, squeezing her butt, *grinding into her.*

She threw her head back, eyes half-lidded, as he ran his tongue over the base of her neck. His hands were insistent.

What if he doesn't stop?

The thought was a splash of shocking cold across her thoughts, but the heat in her body overcame it.

Could I stop him?

The alleyway walls felt close, suffocating, The rusted silo loomed above.

Do I want *to stop him?*

There was an odd kind of hunger pulsing through her body, a new, delicious heat; she wanted more of his lips, more his taste, more of *him.* She might never get her fill of him.

What a good girl.

One of his hands was firm on her ass, holding her in place while he swayed more and more urgently. His other hand had pulled her shirt out of her jeans and was stroking the skin of her belly, along her ribs and across the soft satin cup of her bra…

Another splash of cold.

"Stop," she gasped. "Wait!"

She pulled back, her breath coming quickly. Her body was hot, cold, confused.

His eyes were dopey, her lips slightly ajar, his hands hungry.

So dumb.

She wanted to run. She wanted to claw at his back.

"I... I never..."

"Are you okay?" Now *he* pulled back, his smile faltering.

"This is..." She didn't want to say it.

He's probably been with dozens of girls. Hundreds.

She could feel the flush in her cheeks as the moment dragged on. The only sound was the pattering of sawdust as it streamed onto the alleyway floor from a nearby chute.

He lifted her chin, looking into her eyes.

His voice was gentle.

"You're a virgin."

She looked down and nodded, not trusting herself to speak.

Ooh she's tough!

He chewed his lip, then whispered.

"It's okay. Here."

He took her by the wrist, gently but with unmistakable strength, and put her hand *there*, on the hardness in his jeans.

Blood pounded in her cheeks. Fire flickered against her groin.

She could feel his stiffness, his rigid iron flesh, filling her hand.

His cock. It's his cock.

This *is what he cares about.*

Her hand felt along his length, wrapped around it, squeezing its weight.

Now *he* gasped. Her legs spasmed again.

So dumb.

"Do you..." she could barely make the words. "Can I..."

Without waiting for an answer, she pushed him back and slid off the Harley to stand on her weak legs.

Her hand never left him, and she squeezed when they kissed again.

He groaned in her mouth.

She lowered herself to the ground, kneeling on the rough gravel, rubbing her fingertips along his jeans, searching.

There was a sprinkling sound nearby, like flour being poured from a sack, but she didn't look away from his eyes.

Rohan was looking down at her with an expression of mild surprise on his flushed face. Then he smiled, that easy smile that was almost a smirk, as he guided her fingers to his zipper and leaned back, waiting.

A waterfall of white dust was shivering onto the ground nearby but she ignored it, biting her lip and slowly drawing down his zipper down.

Her shaking hand slipped inside his jeans.

She felt him sigh as she gripped his hard flesh through the thin cotton of his underwear and as she pulled the cotton aside…

Something thumped heavily on to the ground next to her.

Her hands kept moving, feeling, *squeezing,* for the few moments it took her to realise what she was seeing.

It was a boy.

He lay motionless on the ground next to her in an odd sprawl, beneath a growing pile of sawdust.

It was a *dead* boy.

Stephanie *screamed*, her hands flying to her cheeks, the heat draining from her gut, Rohan and his cock forgotten as she screamed a guttural, terrified shriek.

"Fuck!" Rohan pulled her to her feet. *"Get up!"*

She couldn't look away.

There was sawdust stuck to the boy's eyes, packed into his mouth.

She *screamed* again… then her cheek was stinging, her head rocking back.

The sharp pain pushed her into coldness.

He slapped me did he slap me?

because that kid is dead he's DEAD!

Rohan's hands were on her face, holding her still. Her eyes rolled wildly. "Stop. *Stop.*"

His voice was low and urgent.

"It's *all right*. You're *okay*."

Her chest hitched and she wanted to swoon, but he was holding her up. He raised a finger in front of her face and she focused on it, shoulders shivering.

"It's all right. It's *all right*. No more screaming. All right?"

She watched his finger, blinked at it. Swallowed. Her eyes were hot. Her cheek stung.

"*All right?*"

She nodded. Nodded again.

What a good girl.

Sawdust drifted onto the gravel next to them, the waterfall slowing to a trickle.

"Do you know him?" Rohan was looking down at the body, catching his own breath.

She forced herself to look, turned her head and *forced* herself to look.

The boy's eyes were white. Dry dust was caked in his hair and trickling from his lips.

She turned away.

"I've seen him before. Riding a skateboard. Near the shop."

"A skateboard?"

Stephanie leaned against him. A silent sob shook her shoulders.

"I've gotta show Dad," Rohan declared. He turned her, guiding her away. "Come on."

He threw a leg over his bike and waited.

Numb, she climbed onto the back of the seat.

He took her hands and wrapped them around his waist.

"It's all right," he said again. "Nobody knows we were here. Hold on."

Her arms had no strength, but she managed to grip him while he kicked the motorbike to life.

They rolled down the alley, away from the silo, away from the sawdust and the body it had seasoned.

When they reached the edge of the vacant lot, Rohan revved the bike and a moment later his wheels hit the stiff black bitumen, gaining purchase and speed.

That boy was dead.

Stephanie took one last, tearful glance at the silo… and her breath caught again.

Somebody was there.

Somebody was kneeling over the body.

Somebody she recognised.

Then Rohan gunned the bike again and they sailed along Churchill Park Drive, dropping sawdust in their wake.

Jake

It wasn't the first dead body Jake had ever seen – that honour went to his great-grandfather, nearly ten years passed. His great-grandfather had reposed in a dignified hardwood coffin, its handles polished to a sliver shine, its flowers bobbing carefully in the wake of a line of mourners.

There were no flowers here, no dignified silver.

Twisted awkwardly on the gravel, Brad's body was framed by weeds and burnt beer cans and discarded condoms.

The boy seemed to be made of sawdust; it leaked from his ears and his pockets and his mouth, clung to every inch of his clothes. It gave his eyes a blank, dry stare.

Rohan's motorbike trailed away in the distance.

Jake's chest hitched again.

I'm sorry man. I'm so fuckin sorry. I shouldn't have brought you here. I shouldn't have let you hide behind the gate. I shouldn't have... I should have...

It was hopeless. He couldn't turn back time.

He couldn't bring Brad back to life.

Nobody had called for help. Jake cursed Reese, Boof, all of them. They had left him here alone. They had scurried back to their cosy little houses, probably to have dinner, while Jake was left kneeling over the body of a kid he'd only met a few hours earlier wondering what the fuck he should do.

Rohan will call it in. And Steph. She'll definitely call the police.

But would they?

Rohan and the Marauders had made no secret of searching for Brad this afternoon. It might be better for them if the body was never found.

I have to do it. I have to tell somebody.

Jake had done his best to get the skater out.

He had been far, *far* too slow.

He would go home and call the police.

Maybe that would help him sleep at night. Maybe not.

But there was nothing else he could do. It was time to go.

His breath hitched again and tears stung his eyes.

I'm so, so fuckin sorry man.

He knelt over Brad's body one last time, sending out something like a wordless prayer or a plea for forgiveness.

Through his keening, he saw something out of place.

He sniffed, rubbing at his eyes, and looked again.

There was something bright and yellow and clean amidst the all the white sawdust, something that reached through his guilt and despair and snapped him back to attention.

There was an envelope poking out from Brad's back pocket.

Dylan

Smack!

Every breath tasted like copper. His lungs rattled with blood. His head was ringing. Water was dripping, regular and insistent.

Smack!

The sound hurt.

And it sparked some kind of light, some blur that radiated agony.

Dylan woke slowly, fading back into his body… only to find pain.

He was hurt. Badly hurt. His chest and his face and his right leg seared in bright white agony.

"… the *fuck* up, you little shit! Dylan! *Dylan!*"

The shouting was close to his face but muffled by the ringing in his ears.

Smack!

The time the slap rocked his head back and opened his eyes.

The blur became a streetlight on Churchill Park Drive. Specks of blood and sweat clouded under the streetlight's glow.

His face *throbbed*.

"Where's the *money?*"

Dylan tried to sit up, but his legs wouldn't respond. His hands reached for something to push off and found the HQ's steering wheel just inches from his waist. It was hard to focus on it, to understand the crumpled mess of car around him.

Everything was out of place.

The dashboard was twisted and busted, the windscreen a crystalline frame, the destroyed engine a landscape of steaming steel mountains.

"Dylan!"

Smack!

"Stop fucking hitting me!" Dylan moaned. "I can't move my *legs*."

"No *shit*."

He looked then, opened his eyes and *looked*, then shrunk back with a sob.

His legs were trapped under the dashboard, pinned and pinched and crushed. His jeans were dyed crimson and scarlet. It wasn't water dripping onto the bitumen; it was him.

"Where's the fucking money?"

"Help me!" Dylan looked with wide, agonised eyes.

What he saw made him sob again.

Rohan was leaning over the smashed windscreen, glaring down at him.

Not Rohan, anyone but fucking ROHAN...

"Where is it, Dylan?"

Smack!

"Bag..."

"What?"

"The bag!" he shrieked and it hurt and he sobbed. "That bitch fuckin took it."

Rohan leaned back, looking over his shoulder.

Gasping, Dylan followed his gaze, then let out a despairing moan.

Stephanie was standing under the glow of the streetlight, looking through him with a neutral expression. Next to her, Noah was pawing through the black backpack with a deep frown. There were others standing behind them, tattooed men grim in black leather, their silver bikes parked orderly in the gloom.

It hurt to breathe.

"I was... bringing it back... to *you!*"

"The *fuck* you were. How did you get it?"

A dog barked in the distance.

"You... *told* me to find him," Dylan wheezed. "You *told* me... to find that skater. And I *did*... I took it *off* him and... I was bringing it *back* but she...

she…"

Noah unzipped the front pocket of the backpack and groped through it roughly. Finally, he looked up at Rohan and shook his head.

"It's not here. Only the weed."

Dylan whimpered as Rohan swooped back in through the windscreen, spittle bouncing from his lips.

"Where's the fuckin money?"

"What?" Dylan blinked. Blood was running out him in ropes. Everything hurt.

"Where's the ten grand, you fuckin *fuckwit!"*

"It was just them buds." Dylan whispered, confused. He tried to shift again, but his leg was trapped in a vice and his strength was gone. "You gotta call an ambulance, you gotta…"

"There was *money* in that bag, a heap of *money,* now *where the fuck is it?"*

"There wasn't… no money." Dylan coughed, wet and weak.

"Bullshit! Who's fuckin got it?" Rohan's roar echoed up Churchill Park Drive.

More dogs were barking now.

"Skater," there was no small amount of wonder in Dylan's rasping. "That sly… little *shit."*

"Sly?" Rohan shouted. "That skater's fucking *dead,* mate!"

Dylan blinked again. He was exhausted.

"He… died?"

"You put him in the fuckin silo, didn't you? And you didn't even get the fucking *cash.* You killed that kid for a few bags of weed, Jesus *fucking* Christ."

Rohan walked away without looking back.

"No… *wait… help me! Rohan!"* Dylan tried to reach after the bikie, but he couldn't move.

He twisted anyway, then shrieked as leg sank deeper into a white wave of agony.

"Steph. Steph! You gotta *help* me!"

Stephanie was staring past him.

"Steph… I'm sorry. I didn't *mean* it… Stephie *please!"*

She didn't even look at him.

Confused, he followed her gaze… and screamed an airless, barely audible scream.

Ben Campbell was in the seat next to him, propped up by the engine parts that had punctured through his skinny chest. His dead eyes were wide open and gleaming under the white streetlight. His face was ruined, twisted unnaturally, his body mangled, his skin bloodless, colourless, his arms smeared with grease, a perverse oil painting, serenely violent.

"Benny!"

Dylan ignored the tearing at his leg as he tried to reach his friend.

"Benny!"

There was no reply, only the squealing of tyres in the night air.

Two more vehicles were pulling up. One was Pasco's old ute.

The other was an ancient, rumbling Plymouth.

Dylan let out a pitiful, disbelieving whine.

No, no, no!

Doors opened and closed.

No, no, no, no, no!

Judy Campbell stood under the streetlight, her fists on her stout hips, her thinning bottle-blonde hair blowing gently around her shoulders.

Allan Campbell stepped out from behind her, casting a mechanic's eye over the wreck of the HQ.

Get away... gotta get away...

But there was nowhere to go.

"I'm sorry, Judy," Noah was saying. "It was nothing to do with us, right?"

Run. Run. Run.

"What are you talking about?" Judy scowled at the leader of the Marauders, but when she turned to her husband and saw his face, she seemed to shrink a little.

"Allan?"

Allan Campbell was crying, a silent, shoulder-shaking cry.

"Allan?"

He put his hands over his face and turned away from her.

Eyes wide, Judy Campbell turned to the wrecked HQ. She saw Dylan and swore.

Rohan and Stephanie stepped aside to let her past.

She approached the wreck, her shoulders square, her lips tight.

Silently, they all watched her.

They all watched her fall to her knees.

They all heard her shriek her son's name.

Dylan jerked in his seat, trying to free himself, trying to move as Judy Campbell screamed into the bitumen.

Pain rocked him. The world was liquid, sticky and burning and cold and his breathing was wet and warm and choking and airless. He warbled, helpless.

There were dogs barking, every dog in Invermay it sounded like.

Allan Campbell's lips twisted into a snarling rictus, mad fury bright in his dark eyes.

Judy Campbell's screaming cracked and faded. Her face was lowered, her shoulders slumped and heaving.

Behind them, by the side of the road, Rohan was whispering to his father, his voice low and urgent.

Help me Steph?

Dylan tried to make the words, but there was too much blood in his mouth.

He tried to twist, tried to plead as Allan Campbell marched toward him, openly weeping, his teeth bared, his murderous fists stained black.

Help...help!

A small white hand touched Allan's chest and stopped him in his tracks. His eyes didn't leave Dylan's face.

Judy Campbell turned to face him, her hair hanging wild around her eyes.

Dylan panted faster as she approached, his eyes rolling in mindless panic

She touched the wrecked steel, a delicate stroke of the fingertips, and stopped next to the smashed windscreen.

"Judy..." he tried to say, but there was no air to push the words out. *"Judy... accident..."*

"You," she said, shaking her head. *"You."*

"…accident!"

There was tinkling sound.

A long shard of broken glass appeared in her pale hand.

"You."

She pointed the glass at Dylan as the dogs of Invermay howled, smelling blood, *his* blood.

"You were his fuckin *friend,* you stupid… *little… FUCK!"*

She was as quick as a snake. Her glass fang punctured his cheek.

Bright fire burned across his face.

There was no air for him to squeal with because the glass was plunging into his throat.

"…as stupid as you *look…"*

Another slash, harder, deeper. He felt parts of his neck break, felt things spill out of him that should never spill, felt a wet inferno in his throat and his mouth and his everything.

"…stupid…

She was screaming now, thrusting her fist into him, plunging the glass into his chest over and over.

"…STUPID…STUPID!!"

She tore at him, ripped at him, dragged the jagged glass through his ruined flesh.

Dylan couldn't feel it.

He couldn't see his colours spilling up her arm and across the dashboard, couldn't feel the cold glass scraping his spine, couldn't hear her the dogs howling in their backyards or Judy Campbell's guttural banshee screaming.

All he knew was darkness.

Jake

Shut up you noisy bastards!

The fucking dogs were going to get him caught.

Jake had been making good time ducking from yard to yard before he spotted the commotion near the bottom of South Street.

Marauders.

There had been an accident. They were gathered around it.

Jake spotted Noah right away, but Rohan and Pasco and even Stephanie were there too, standing around a car he didn't recognise.

None of his business. If it kept them distracted while he snuck home, then all the better.

As quiet as a shadow, he climbed into another yard, staying well out of sight. The envelope was bulging in his pocket.

It's so light. How can so much money be so light?

Another guilty flush tingled his skin. Jake hadn't stopped to count the green and yellow bank notes - that would come later.

For now, he just had to get to somewhere safe.

He had to get home.

They'll never know.

Exuberance mixed with a grim dread, making his mind blank and his sneaking focused.

His blood ran cold. His heart might burst. He wanted to scream and dance and caper and cry.

The police or the Marauders, none of them will ever know.

He didn't think about the sawdust in Brad's open eyes, or the way the gravel had sunk into the boy's pale wrists.

Instead, he ducked over the next fence.

Just gotta get up South Street without being seen.

I'm sorry, Brad.

He cut across Little Ray, jogging towards Boof's house, then veered into the overgrown lane back that led back to Monash reserve - the way he and Brad had taken earlier.

I'm so fucking sorry.

As he dashed across the park, he remembered the skater vomiting.

The envelope bounced in his pocket.

Home was so close he could *feel* it.

Stephanie

Rohan kept asking if she was okay, and she *was* okay.

She had just watched a boy being killed, a boy she had known all her life, but she felt… *calm.*

Rohan's arm was around her and that was okay too, but she would have been fine if it wasn't.

She was okay.

Judy Campbell was most definitely *not* okay.

The tiny blonde woman was crouched under the streetlight next to the wrecked car, sobbing, keening, calling for her son.

Allan Campbell stood silently next his wife.

Stephanie leaned into Rohan.

"Can we get out of here now?"

"Not yet," Noah answered, his voice brooking no disagreement. "Where's this skater prick? He must still have the money."

"Some kids saw them going to the old mill on Churchill Park Drive," Pasco said, his voice low. "Pretty boy and the Campbell kid over there, with the little cunt who took the bag."

"We found him." Rohan told them. "I can show you."

"Let's go then," Noah shook his head. "What a fuckin mess."

Stephanie turned to follow Rohan to his bike, but Noah spoke again.

"No. You come with me and Pasco, girl."

Stephanie froze.

The leader of the Marauders was watching her, unblinking.

Ooh she's tough.

She glanced at Rohan, who frowned at his father before nodding sharply. Her stomach sank as he turned away without a word, climbing onto his motorbike.

"Come on girl, into the ute." Noah's voice was firm.

She gave Rohan another glance. He was sitting astride his bike, waiting, watching.

He met her eye and gave her the slightest nod.

Nobody messes with Rohan's girlfriend.

The ute's cabin was small but surprisingly clean with a single padded bench seat. She tried to make herself small.

Pasco eased into the driver's seat next to her, his huge frame blocking the door. When big Noah sat on her other side, the whole ute rocked on its suspension.

There wasn't enough room, so Stephanie had no choice but to put one leg either side of the gear stick that was sticking out of the ute floor. The gearstick had a clear, round glass handle that contained the preserved body of a redback spider.

She tried not to squirm when Pasco reached between her thighs to put the ute in gear, moving the spider closer to her body.

He waited for Rohan to swerve past them, then followed the motorbike down Churchill Park Drive, away from the scene of the crash.

Stephanie sat between the two big bikers, watching the cracked bitumen pass beneath them. There were three other Marauders following the ute and the grim procession made its way towards the burnt-out mill.

Robin Hood: Prince of Thieves would have started by now.

Noah rubbed at his forehead, then sighed.

"Bit fuckin intense. Ben was a good kid."

He examined Stephanie with a frown.

"You all right?"

"I'm all right."

He nodded, but his serious expression didn't change.

"How much of all that did you see?"

She looked him in the eye.

"None of it."

He didn't quite smile, but his face relaxed a little.

"Good."

He patted her knee gently with a giant, tattooed hand, once, twice... then left his hand resting on the top of her thigh.

She looked at it, looked up at him, but he was staring out through the windscreen at the approaching mill.

His hand didn't move.

What a good girl.

The ute bumped over the gutter, following Rohan's motorbike onto the vacant lot next to the mill. Pasco shifted the gears with a chubby hand that was covered in scars.

The silo was a patch of black against the night sky.

Rohan was already climbing off his bike when they pulled into the alleyway. The ute's headlights reflected off the pile of white sawdust that cushioned the skater's prone body.

"Jesus fucking Christ," Noah muttered, opening the ute door and climbing out.

Stephanie hurried after him.

Rohan was crouching over the body, scowling.

"Somebody else has been here," he said to Noah. "Look."

He nodded at the edge of the sawdust, at the clearly visible footprints.

Stephanie's stomach clenched as she thought about the figure she had seen crouching over the skater's body.

Twice in one day. She almost laughed.

"*Fuck!*" Noah spat. "The money's gone too?"

Rohan looked at Pasco.

"Help me turn him over."

Pasco came to kneel next to the sawdust, and the two bikes turned the skater onto his back. Soft sawdust fell off him onto the gravel. Clumps of white dust stuck to his chin, his hair, his shoelaces.

Pasco was patting the body down. All he found was a wrinkled tobacco pouch, which he promptly shoved into his own pocket.

"It's not here."

Rohan growled. "Whoever found him took it."

Frowning, Noah knelt next to his son, his huge bulk moving easily. He reached out a rugged hand and brushed some of the dust of the skater's t-shirt.

Faith No More. A black and white dog snarled up at him.

Noah rubbed at his temples.

"This just fucking gets better and better."

"What do we do with him?" Pasco asked quietly. "We can't leave him here, half of bloody Invermay knows we were out looking…"

Pasco stopped, head cocked.

Rohan started as well, standing up straight and looking down the alleyway. Noah swore.

Stephanie looked from one to the other, wondering what was happening. Then she heard it too.

Police sirens.

"Fuck!" Rohan muttered. "That's three cars, at least."

"They're going to the crash," Pasco stood up beside him. "We need to get the fuck out of here."

As one, they turned to look at Noah.

The sirens were getting louder, piercing through the quiet night air.

"Rohan?" Stephanie whispered.

"Dad?" Rohan said. "Dad. What do we do?"

Noah scowled, climbing to his feet. He spoke with a snarl.

"Put him in the back of the ute."

Jake

Jake hoisted himself over the fence and landed in the alleyway behind the old stables.

As soon as his feet hit the familiar ground of his own back yard, a wave of relief shivered through his body.

Home. Safe and sound.

He was exhausted.

He stood there for a moment, steadying himself. He had sprinted from the end of Monash Reserve to his back fence, avoiding the streetlights along the way. He had heard the police sirens, but they stopped near the bottom of South Street, where the mangled car was.

Nobody saw me. Nobody will ever know.

He was home.

It was time for a hot meal and a bath, time to put on a movie and eat *Doritos* and forget about the day. He might even put on his *Enigma* CD.

And later - *much* later - he would count the hundred-dollar bills in his pocket.

Giddy, he walked out of the alley and along the fence, staying in the shadows.

He was home.

Even with his senses on high alert he didn't notice the Old Tom lurking near the fence, and when he almost stepped on the black cat's tail it darted away with an annoyed yowl.

Jake swore, his heart in his throat.

Cats scattered in all directions, pelting through the weeds, and the Old Tom disappeared into the night.

A deep voice floated through the darkness.

"Jake."

The voice was low, urgent.

"Is that you, boy?"

Jake froze.

There were shadows over near the bakehouse, large shadows.

One of them was moving towards him.

"Christ, I'm glad to see you mate," said the shadow as it became Noah.

Jake tried to think of something to say, but nothing came out.

"You got your keys on you?"

"Yep. Yep."

Jake patted his pocket, his stomach queasy. His keys were under the bulging envelope.

Give him the money. It's theirs. Brad stole it from them.

Do they know I helped him get away?

"I need to get into the bakery. Is that all right?"

Noah was looking over his shoulder at where the other shadows waited. There was a blue ute parked under the awning, along with a row of motorbikes.

He's not here for lamingtons.

Jake hesitated.

"Is that all right?"

Jake licked his lips.

He doesn't know. It's none of my business. Nothing to do with me.

"Sure. Yep."

He carefully pulled out his keys, pushing the envelope deeper into his pocket, conscious of Noah's eyes. His shaking hand felt awkward, disconnected. His heartbeat thrummed in his ears.

He held the key out to Noah.

"This one. It's this one."

"Come on," Noah said. "You need to help us."

"I… I…"

"I'm not gonna ask again, mate." The leader of the Marauders spoke through gritted teeth.

Jake's hair stood on end. He led the bikie over to the bakehouse door.

Other grim shadows crowded around them. Jake recognised some of them.

Rohan. And Pasco. And…

"Stephanie?"

"Hi Jake." She put her hands on Rohan's arm, leaning into the big biker.

"Hi… hi."

Jake shook his head to clear it.

What the fuck is going on?

He opened the bakehouse door - slide, unlatch, unlock – then flicked on the light with his palm. The fluorescents under the awning flashed on, illuminating an old blue ute with three other bikies standing next to it.

"Lights *off!*" Noah hissed. "Fuckin turn em *off!*"

Jake swiped his palm back the other way and the light snapped off, leaving a negative of the bikies burned into his retina.

"Christ's sake," Noah muttered. "Get inside."

Jake held the screen door open as they all filed into the bakehouse; Stephanie and Rohan looking around curiously, Pasco measuring Jake up as he passed, Noah rubbing his hands and getting down to business.

"Will anyone come in tonight?"

"No," said Jake. "They finish cooking early on Saturdays."

"Good. Good."

Noah walked over to the furnace and pried open the heavy iron door.

The huge fireplace was three feet wide and about ten feet deep, lined with scorched black bricks that had endured almost a century's worth of flames. Its floor was heaped with grey and white ash, spread across coals that still glowed orange from the day's baking. The chimney above was lost to darkness.

"There's wood down that hallway," Noah said to Pasco. "Milk some diesel from the ute. We want it to burn hot, and fast."

"Why are you lighting the oven?" Jake said.

"We got some shit to get rid of," Noah scowled. "You're gonna help, and you're gonna keep your fuckin mouth shut."

Pasco dropped a stack of kindling into the furnace and followed it with a hand full of Redhead firelighters. A flame crackled to life and quickly spread across the hot coals. Pasco tossed in a few larger sticks, pushing them in with a long iron poker, then went outside.

Noah was watching Jake.

"I've known you for a while, kid. I know you'll do the right thing. You've helped me out a few times, you know a bit of my business. I trusted you with that. But this is big business now. This is some serious shit, all right?"

Jake swallowed. It felt like there was sand in his mouth.

"There are cops down the bottom of South Street," he whispered. "Stacks of them. Two or three cars at least."

"Don't worry about the cops," Noah said. "They've got their hands full."

The fire was reaching out over the kindling, licking at the larger pieces, crackling, stretching.

"Nothing to do with us," Rohan said.

He was leaning against one of the long benches and Stephanie was sitting on the bench next to him. The huge bikie had his arm around her.

The bakehouse door banged open.

Two bikies marched in, carrying something between them, something wrapped in a sheet. Pasco hustled between them, a jerrycan dangling from his fist.

The smell of diesel stung Jake's nostrils.

"Holy shit," he whispered.

No, it can't be...

When the bikies stopped in front of the furnace, a corner of the sheet fell away.

The skater's white eyes were open and motionless. The fire made irregular shadows dance over his pale skin. His mouth hung open and dry dust coated his tongue.

Stephanie lay her head against Rohan's shoulder.

Jake could no longer control the shaking in his belly, in his knees and hands. There was ice in his veins. There was a dull throb in his solar plexus and his throat was aching. He sucked in a deep breath, hoping it didn't sound too much like a sob.

Pasco hoisted the jerrycan towards the furnace, splashing diesel onto the flames in short bursts until the furnace roared.

"This stupid little cunt stole our money and our weed," Rohan said.

"Kid had balls. What a fuckin waste." Noah nodded at the furnace. "Put him in."

The bikies came as close as they could to the open furnace, turning their faces away from the heat. They swung Brad's body back and forth, like two uncles throwing a cheeky nephew into a swimming pool.

Once, twice… and on the third swing, they threw him in.

The skater landed amongst the flames with a thud.

Jake couldn't hold the sob this time. He tried to control his breathing, but it was still a series of shuddering gasps. He looked away, squeezed his eyes closed.

"Get some more wood in there," Noah barked at Pasco. "More diesel."

Pasco went outside.

When Noah spoke again, his voice was quiet.

"You knew him, didn't you Jake."

Jake's eyes were squeezed shut.

"Look at him. Now"

Jake looked.

Brad was surrounded by a halo of dancing fire.

Brad *glowed.*

The sawdust burned brightly where it clung to his clothes and hair. Flames rose from his eyes and mouth as though he was some furious demon.

"That's your t-shirt, isn't it Jake?"

Noah's voice was calm, almost soft.

"What?" Jake could barely form the word.

"You heard me."

Flames were flicking out of the iron door, burning hot and fast, but Jake could still see the black and white dog howling amongst them.

He would have recognised that dog anywhere.

A log rolled in the furnace, sending up a swirl of orange embers.

"I…" he trailed off, his face numb. He rubbed his palms against his eyes and they came away wet. "Lots of people have that shirt."

"You were wearing it last night. Now he's wearing it."

"Jesus Christ," somebody muttered at the back of the room.

Stephanie, Jake thought. *What are you doing here?*

It didn't matter.

"You gave him your t-shirt? Was that after you sucked his… wait." Rohan was standing up straight now, staring at Jake. "You helped him hide, didn't you! You told me you didn't fucking know him, and he was right *here!*"

"No! I don't *know* him!"

"You don't know him," Noah nodded. He began to pace back and forth. "You didn't hide him. You've never seen him before."

"Never! You know I would…"

The screen door squealed, a sound Jake knew even in his sleep.

Pasco came back into the bakehouse.

When Jake saw what the bikie was holding, his knees buckled.

It was a skateboard.

Noah was wearing an expression Jake had never seen before.

An expression he didn't like at all.

"It wasn't anything to do with me." Jake tried to back away. *"Noah."*

"Where's the money?" Rohan snarled. "Where's our *fucking* money? You'd better fuckin *talk,* boy."

Caught. I'm caught.

Jake wanted to cry. Shame and embarrassment He felt so tired. He tried to find words, but none came.

His numb fingers dug into the front pocket of his jeans.

"Here." He pulled the envelope free. The cash inside felt heavy enough now. "I found this after Dylan… Dylan…"

Rohan swept over and snatched the envelope from Jake's outstretched hand. He opened it, glanced inside, and nodded.

"Looks like it's all here."

He held the envelope out to Stephanie, who took it without speaking.

"I didn't know it was *yours!*" Jake pleaded. "I would have given it *back*, you *know* I would!"

"Bullshit." Noah's voice is flat "More bullshit."

The fire was roaring now, surging, filling the furnace. The body within was completely charred, barely visible. The iron door was glowing along its edge; Jake had never seen it do that before.

Sweat ran down him in rivulets, freezing his spine.

Hot. Too hot.

"What do you reckon, Rohan?" Noah said. He sounded disgusted, almost embarrassed.

Rohan shrugged.

"I dunno, Dad. I don't know him from shit." He rubbed Stephanie's arm. "What about you, gorgeous?"

Jake's mouth hung open.

They're asking her *what they should do. Steph from the shop.*

Noah turned to look at her, an eyebrow raised, waiting for an answer.

The fire sounded like an avalanche, a constant rushing roar.

"He's a *thief*," she said finally. "A thief and a liar."

"Oh," said Jake, deflating. "Oh, you fuckin *bitch*."

"The *fuck* did you say?" growled Rohan, stepping towards him.

"No!" barked Noah. "We haven't got time."

He looked Jake up and down, almost regretfully, then glanced at the two waiting bikies.

"Put him in too."

"*What?* No!" Jake almost laughed. The idea was ridiculous. "Noah, mate, I can... hey let me *go!*"

The bikies had him by the shoulders. He struggled, but Pasco kicked his feet from under him and the huge men pulled him back.

Back towards the furnace.

"Noah *wait...*"

They're just scaring me, teaching me a lesson, just...

"I don't want to watch this," Stephanie said, in a voice that suggested she *could* very well watch it if she chose.

"Wait outside," Rohan told her. "We'll be done here in a minute."

Jake thrashed. The arms wrapped around him didn't budge so he *wailed* and a fist drove into his stomach, forcing the air out of him.

"Noah... *please!*" It was a panicked wheeze. "*...gave* you money... brought... it *back!*"

"Bullshit."

The grizzled Marauder turned away.

Jake felt his bladder go and he squealed in disbelief, kicking at the bikers.

"Oh *fuck* Noah you've *gotta* believe me, mate, *please, dooon't...*"

They thrust him at the furnace feet first and he *screamed* now because the fire was *too* hot, *deathly* hot and they weren't playing or trying to scare him, they were trying to *put him in it* and he didn't want to die, he didn't want to go in the fire with Brad but they were shoving him and kicking at him and his head rammed into the glowing iron frame and he screamed as he fell amongst the glowing logs because it was *too hot* and it *burned* and his mother wouldn't find him and he *screamed* and the furnace door was *closing* and everything *burned* it was *too fucking hot and everything burned* it all *burned* and *he* burned and *burned and burned and burned.*

Stephanie

The screen door squealed as it swung closed behind her.

Stephanie took a deep, shaking breath. Cool night air filled her lungs and kissed her sweat-damp neck.

It had been hot in there.

Hot and... *exhilarating.*

The bakery looked dark from the outside, with only the faintest flickering window glow betraying any presence.

Jake's choking screams lasted only a few seconds.

He's dead. Dylan's dead. Ben Campbell. All of them.

"Get more wood in there, don't fuck around with it!" Even muffled by the bakehouse walls, Noah's voice was commanding. "Of *course* it's fuckin hot! Just chuck it in if you can't get close enough..."

Stephanie turned away and tiptoed across the yard, her heart in her throat. Cats scattered from her path, but she paid them no mind.

There was something in her hands, something she wanted to look at.

A yellow envelope.

Its weight was intriguing.

She thumbed its flap open, just far enough to see what was inside.

Money. Lots of money.

Fifty-dollar bills, hundred-dollar bills, all bundled into a neat stack.

People had died – people had been *killed* – for this money.

And Rohan trusted *her* to hold it.

She shivered.

What a good girl.

She ran a finger along the edge of the bundle. The light on the envelope flickered and seemed to move.

"Rohan, I…" She turned back to the bakery, a slow grin spreading across her face. "I've never seen so much…"

The words died on her lips.

The bakehouse roof was on fire.

Flames had sprouted around the base of the chimney, directly above the furnace. Flames were spreading across the tin roof, even as she watched. Flames that were bright and tall and full of life against the empty night.

They were dangerous.

They were *beautiful.*

Thrusting the envelope into her pocket, Stephanie ran back over to the bakehouse and looked through the screen door.

Rohan had taken his shirt off and was stoking the furnace. The hands that had touched her so gently an hour ago were now wrapped around a long iron poker. He was swearing and sweating, thrusting at the coals, jousting the flames, his tattooed muscles gleaming.

He was beautiful.

He was *dangerous.*

Noah was watching his son burn the bodies. The enormous hand that had rested so comfortably on her thigh was curled into a fist on his hip.

So dumb. All of them, so fucking dumb.

They haven't even noticed that the roof is on fire.

None of them saw her through the screen door.

Just keep going.

Her hand reached up, seemingly of its own accord, and unhooked the heavy timber roller door. Jake's keys still hung from the lock. They tinkled as she rolled the heavy door shut.

There was a loud rumbling sound inside the bakery, followed by a crash of timber and iron and a chorus of startled shouts.

Quick.

She slid the heavy iron latch into place, just as somebody banged on the other side of the door.

"Stephanie!"

Just keep going.

She turned the key in the enormous deadlock. It settled into place with a loud click.

"Girl? Open the door!"

More banging. More voices.

"Steph, what are you *doing?"*

"Open the fuckin door, bitch!"

She backed away.

The heavy timber door was bouncing under their fists, but it was solid, well made, unbreakable.

The fire had had danced across the roof to reach the awning. She watched it spread along the timber frame. All of the windows were glowing now. The old building was catching quickly.

"Let us OUT, for fuck's sake let us OUT!"

"STEPHANIE OPEN THE FUCKIN DOOR!"

They were all thumping on the timber now. Five men's voices, high-pitched and screaming for her to open the door, to *fuckin* open it, to *fuckin open it now!*

Stephanie turned away and calmly walked up the dark driveway.

What a good girl.

Behind her, the bakery's walls whooshed alight like a bonfire.

She didn't look back.

Just keep going.

It only took a few steps to cross Bryan Street and a few more to turn down Doolan.

She walked away from the red and blue police lights that still flashed at the end of South Street, away from Judy Campbell's darkly sombre house, away from the fully alight bakery burning a three-storey beacon into the night sky.

There were more sirens in the distance now.

It was a night for sirens.

Just keep going.

Nobody noticed her walk up the dark street.

Nobody noticed the blood-stained blouse or the bulge of her pocket.

Nobody noticed her quietly unlock the front door of her house.

Nobody noticed the door clicking softly closed behind her.

Acknowledgments

I would like to thank my entire family for supporting my late-night writing sessions, sudden disappearances, and odd rambles around Launceston. Thank you, Mum and Nan, for your insights about the bakehouse and the history of Invermay. My first readers, Janell and Saul, I'm so grateful for your interest and gentle feedback. Many amongst my friends and networks have expressed curiosity and enthusiasm for this book; you're all brilliant.

I would like to thank Arts Tasmania and the Australian Society of Authors for supporting my work and my wonderful mentor, Kate Ryan, for her invaluable encouragement and guidance.

This book wouldn't exist without the patience and confidence of my gorgeous, talented partner-in-crime Saria, or without the cheer leading of our two brilliant boys.

All my love x.

This work was short-listed for the University of Tasmania Prize in 2022 as part of the Tasmanian Literary Awards. It was also included in the 2023 Arts Tasmania Award Mentorship administered by the Australian Society of Authors and Arts Tasmania.

About the Author

Zane Pinner is a writer and artist from Tasmania, Australia. He likes playing guitar, swimming in the ocean and watching his family grow. He has worked in the screen industry for over twenty years and is currently a producer at the Australian Broadcasting Corporation.

yaybooks.com.au